THE ROUND SPEAR

BOOK ONE OF THE MYRIAR SERIES

Frion Farrell

Best Wishes,

Frion Farrell

Tinobar Books (New Edition)

(Copyright Frion Farrell 2017)

First Edition 2013 (Wordbranch Publishing) – New edition Tinobar Books 2022)

Other books in this series:

The Stone of Mesa (Wordbranch: 2014; New edition, Tinobar Books 2022)

The Auric Flame (Platform One 2017)   New edition, Tinobar Books 2022

DEDICATION

For the Coppersmith's Daughter

My Wonderful Mum and Friend

GLOSSARY

Alleator- music maker of Ordovicia, the first city of mankind.

Amron Cloch – the Song Stone of the Lute, one of the five seeds of the Myriar.

Arwres – the key stone of the Inscriptor, one of the five seeds of the Myriar.

Chalycion- key stone of the Creta, one of the five seeds of the Myriar.

Chimera - part lion, part goat, part serpent

Creta- Seed of the Myriar- artist

Devouril- Once Mourangils, followers of Belluvour

Fossilia – tiny, butterfly-like beings that facilitate movement between space and time.

Frindy- shortened version of Pont y Ffrindiau, Bridge of Friends

Galinir – female Devouril

Irresythe- giant winged creature

Iridice– the key stone of the Reeder, seed of the Myriar

Inscriptor-Seed of the Myriar – translates ancient and modern language

Kejambuck - eel-like director of the dark energy that is the Undercreature

Lute- Seed of the Myriar- hears the melody of all things, manipulates sound

Mesa - mankind's origin and Moura's sister-planet

Mensira- mind control used for evil

Magluck Bawah – the Undercreature- malevolent energy

Mourangil- one of the bejewelled race, indigenous to the planet

Ordovicia – the first human habitation on the planet

Perfidium- obsidian stone that has been refashioned to disguise a powerful weapon

Pont y ffrindiau – means Bridge of friends- Welsh university town

Reeder- Seed of the Myriar- telepath

Reuben – inhabits a cavern in a hidden dimension

Stozcist – Seed of the Myriar. Can manipulate stone.

Tanes- a group of elementals in Dublin

Tenements- the name of the Rugby team populated by the Tanes

Teifi- river in Wales.

Tinobar- a magical healing place

Tolbranach – mythical sea creature inhabiting the Caher

mountains in Ireland

Prologue

"It is almost time," Tremachus informed the formless being once known on earth as Candillium.

"Time?" came the reply, "yes, I remember time. Eons have passed since I last mulled in the quagmire of earthly life. To cloak myself in heavy bones and flesh again, ah Tremachus!"

"There is always choice."

"Choice?" the voice lingered, "perhaps. Toomaaris does not call me, yet in my freedom have I felt his great spirit wearying. There on earth he has stayed and worked ceaselessly towards the Myriar, and I am still its centrepiece. Ordovicia has passed even beyond the memory of man but Toomaaris still walks the earth, holding his triumph and guilt in the balance of his heart. Will he know me?"

"Only when and if you become known to yourself."

"To return to ignorance and folly from the great realms of space? To become less than I ever was and perhaps never know?"

"Then Belluvour will indeed complete the destruction he began before you bound him. In this time of man, the bonds are weak; he prepares the surface for his dark purpose. Should you pass through the portals, the echoes will sound in the Secret Vaults and the Myriar should certainly fail. If, however, you become again as once you were, then will be heard only the harmless footfall of a human child. The Seeds will be given time to gather and the human race may, after all, evolve as Moura intended."

"Well then Tremachus," came the whispered response, "I have made my choice."

The Round Spear

Chapter One

Josef let his eyes roam the massive expanse of monumental stone that rose from the ancient city of Caral. Even now, he felt a sense of awe at the six pyramids that had been unearthed from the arid desert, just two hours from Lima. A breeze, from the foothills of the Andean mountains, floated wisps of dust and sand across the now deserted site. The shadow of a condor, soaring above, dipped in and out of the sunken plazas, magically shrinking and enlarging as the great bird moved across the sky. In his fifties, Josef had been more than glad to accept the job of caretaker and guide for this hidden sacred city; its secrets, until the last few decades, buried deep within the earth.

An engine growled, a signal to turn back towards his cabin where Domingo's jeep laboured across the rubble. How many times had he told the boy to leave it further down the slope!

Buenos tardes Kier," he called, reaching them. The him closely on the tour and then, as now, he could see she had fallen under the spell of the ancient city. Ignoring the strands of long dark hair that blew across her face, her eyes were fixed on what remained of lives that had been lived over four thousand years previously. English woman waved towards him as she stepped out of the vehicle, an alpaca fleece draped over her shoulders. She wore a white vest and a pair of blue cotton shorts that revealed the well-defined muscles of her long legs

Buenos tardes Kier," he called, reaching them. The him closely on the tour and then, as now, he could see she had fallen under the spell of the ancient city. Ignoring the strands of long dark hair that blew across her face, her eyes were fixed on what remained of lives that had been lived over four thousand years previously. English woman waved towards him as she stepped out of the vehicle, an alpaca fleece draped over her shoulders. She wore a white vest and a pair of blue cotton shorts that revealed the well-defined muscles of her long legs. On her wrist was a collection of woven bracelets, bought, no doubt, from the street children, he thought absently, and not of the same quality as those of his own village. He had noticed her immediately, one week ago, when she had descended from the tour bus. She was beautiful no doubt, in a European way, but there was something else that set her apart. A simplicity that was deeply complex, a conundrum he had yet to solve. She had questioned

Josef stepped beside her to join in the perusal of the uncovered contours of the huge site; one hundred and fifty acres in total. Excavations had revealed the remains of a peaceful civilisation that traded inwards towards the Amazon rain forest, and outwards towards the Pacific Ocean. He followed Kier's gaze as if fixed on the Altar of the Sacred Fire, a circle of stones in the main amphitheatre.

"You should see it as the sun goes down," he told her.

She turned and smiled at him. "Hola Josef," she said cheerfully. "I'm sorry, even in a week I'd forgotten how amazing this place is."

The caretaker pushed his grey hair underneath the red and white striped chullo that flapped over his ears. He laughed as he guided her to his cabin. Positioned behind large screens of tent fabric, it was designed to keep out both the sand and the curious. Inside he had done as he had agreed and placed several boxes of crafted products made by hand.

Josef felt unusually nervous, stroking the smooth brown skin of his face as he watched Kier rummage through the boxes. On the tour, she had asked him about an unusual tapestry he had made. She had come to Peru to purchase objects for English shops but had not yet found what she had been looking for. Josef agreed that he would hand pick goods from the best local craft-workers and bring them to Caral the following week. He turned to hide the sigh of relief as the English woman smiled in appreciation at the finely painted bowls and plates. She examined the alpaca rugs and an array of jewellery, including a box of semi-precious stones.

Domingo remained outside smoking; catching the older man's eye, he grinned widely. His parents owned the hotel in Lima where Kier was staying. Their son often acted as trusted taxi driver for the guests, in a city where trust could be hard to find. Moving over to the doorway Josef threw the young man a bottle of water and then listened as he gave him news of his family. After a short spell Kier joined them.

"You're right Josef, these are better than anything else I've seen." She smiled, "how much?"

He fixed his face with his best bargaining expression, warming happily to the task. Several times he bowed his head within the vivid red of his geometrically patterned poncho as he rejected her offers.

"2,000 sols, final," he stated.

"Done." Kier replied after a moment, holding out her hand. Josef took it, smiling warmly. She dug in a leather bag and brought out the notes.

"Fair price," laughed Domingo, "but he would have dropped another two hundred sols."

Kier shrugged her shoulders, "like you said, fair price."

"Now let me see." Kier bent down and started to rearrange the objects. "They'll be shipped tomorrow to Manchester in Northern England. If I sort them now, they can go straight to the business for which they are most suited" She held up a box of semi-precious gems, "these will sell well in Pulton." Josef had never heard of Pulton, but he smiled politely.

Kier grinned, "it's a shop called 'Seven Rivers' on the North-West coast.

"Why Seven Rivers?"

"Pulton is on the edge of a bay, like a harbour," she explained, seeing his puzzled expression. "It's tidal, and if you look across from the shop you can see the mountains of Cumbria, the Lake District."

Josef nodded confidently," Si, I know this place."

"Five rivers flow into the bay that can be seen. But I once read in a very old book, that deep underground, there are another two. So, I called it 'Seven Rivers.'

"The shop, it is your shop?" asked Josef, surprised.

"Yes, I own the shop."

"And the others?"

She nodded, her full mouth breaking into an understanding grin. It was not unusual that her youth and sex led people to misjudge her business success.

"I would have charged 3,000 sols if I had known," he replied, a wry grin on his face.

They turned sharply towards the door as a string of curses came from outside. Emerging from the hut, they found Domingo delivering an angry kick to the jeep.

"The tyre is ruined," he told Kier.

Josef shook his head, suppressing annoyance that the boy had ignored the designated parking areas.

"I carry no other," the exasperated youth continued. "The earliest I can get someone to bring out another, is tomorrow morning."

The caretaker saw a brief flutter of uncertainty in Kier's face. He knew she would have heard many tales of tourists being tricked and attacked in the area around Lima. He smiled reassuringly and she seemed to decide that no harm was intended.

"It can't be helped," she told Domingo. Can we get a taxi back to the hotel?

Josef 's mouth tightened with disdain at Domingo failing to bring a spare on such a rough trip. He knew that there would be little chance of bringing any one out to the site to pick them up tonight.

"You will stay with me," he told them.

The stranded visitors followed him to the display centre where, in the office cupboard, he found two pallets and blankets that were sometimes used by the archaeologists. In the cabin, there was plenty of room as he spread them out on the floor, pulling his own bed from under a long table. A bottle of Pisco and a bowl full of causa were retrieved from a cabinet. At Kier's curious glance, he laughed.

"Yellow potato, lettuce, cheese, eggs and olives," he told her. "See, there is plenty."

Domingo, meanwhile, had brought a cool box from the jeep.

"My mother," he explained with a lopsided grin. He produced tacos filled with salad, beans, meat and various fruits. There were bottles of water and juice, even wine.

"A feast." Kier grinned.

Later, after they had eaten, Kier took the Pisco sour that Josef had made and followed him to the door of the hut.

"This is seriously good," she told him, holding up her glass as she stepped outside.

"My special recipe for you," he bowed, "and if you would come and see…" he pointed towards the fabric sheet surrounding the cabin. Kier put down her drink and followed him to the far corner of the screen. The caretaker smiled at her gasp of pleasure as he drew back the stiff fabric to reveal the red-gold of the setting sun streaming across the ancient site.

The huge circular amphitheatre was a glowing dish; like an offering to a sky that had seen the city's first flourish, and now presided over its exposed remains. Her eyes lingered on the last of the golden rays that illuminated a circle of small stones around a slab of rock within the sunken plaza.

"The Sacred Fire Altar," Josef explained, "it was the centre of worship here."

"Of what?" Her gaze seemed to take in the way that the structure was deliberately created to frame this last tribute of the day. "What did they worship?"

He pointed to the pyramids that surrounded the city.

"They are considered temples for the sun, the moon and the stars. For myself I think the people also worshipped the stone itself."

In response to Kier's querulous expression, he shrugged his shoulders.

"To create all this, for us to have so much still standing? They really knew stone. I believe these rocks were revered. The stars and the stone are like two arms that cradle the city."

He turned to Kier who nodded and smiled in agreement. The haunting sunset was now replaced by a tableau of startlingly bright stars in the desert sky, illuminating the ponderous pyramids below. They stayed quietly watching until they heard the rumpled snoring of Domingo within the cabin. Laughing, they turned back to the cabin, aware that the night was progressing. Josef made sure that his guest was comfortable before turning off the lamps and bedding down by the cabin door.

It was long after midnight when, amid the quiet breathing of the two young people, Josef heard the sound of stones scattering. The area was full of sandy paths to guide the tourists to the main points of interest, and to protect the dig. Over the years, he had attuned himself to the night sounds in the city of Caral; he was sure someone had scattered the small stoned edging on one of the paths. Quietly, he eased himself out of bed and allowed his vision to adjust to the darkness. By his poncho lay a black fleece coat left by one of the tourists; he pulled it on and carefully unlatched the door.

Cloud had gathered, shrouding the stars. Soundlessly, his feet found the sandy pathway leading to the main amphitheatre where he could hear sounds of movement. Tourists, he decided, yet something in the muted sound and secretive movements of the small group, told him that this was altogether different from the thrill seekers and joy riders that he had dealt with previously. Thieves? The most valuable artefacts were locked away, there was little to steal where they had gathered and it was too dark to dig properly. Just as this thought crossed his mind, strobes of torchlight appeared around the Sacred Fire Altar. Instinctively Josef flattened his body on the ground. He waited for a few moments but no beam of light passed over him.

Slowly, he crawled towards the outer area of the amphitheatre and tucked himself lengthways underneath the low circular wall. The smell of the organic dry shrica fibres, woven within the walls, filled his nostrils. Peering over the edge, he saw a wide-shouldered bear of a man wedge a torch between two rocks so that it shone directly over the altar. Next to him was a slim young girl, her dark hair hanging loosely to her shoulders. The third figure stood a little apart, slightly behind the others. He turned his head, vulture-like, towards where Josef was hiding. The caretaker froze. He felt his chest ache with held breath until the eyes, torch-lit innards of cruelty, shifted their malevolent gaze to arc around the amphitheatre. This man looked Eastern European, hair black and slick, an arresting angularity of his jaw and cheek bones. An expensive dark suit covered a tall lean body like the sleek coat of a panther. Trembling, Josef felt his heart chill. He judged this man to have come forth from the shadows and wherever he walked, he would take shadow with him.

"Swift," the man of shadows said quietly. It was as if the voice rose from the sand; a sinister sound that lingered in the arid desert. Obediently the girl moved towards him; he pointed to the hollow in the centre of the altar.

"You're sure this is the place?" he demanded, biting anticipation now raw within his voice.

The girl nodded and moved forward. Josef had to cover his mouth to prevent a gasp of astonishment as she stepped into the slight hollow and disappeared. He knew that the space could not hold even her slight body.

A stone dislodged by his foot, echoed in the silent valley. A few seconds later, the big man turned and walked towards the outer rim of the circle. Hurriedly, Josef pressed himself firmly against the wall, trusting to the ledge above to hide him. He prayed silently as his taut muscles screamed with the effort of holding himself completely still. A demanding hiss from the dark figure that remained by the altar, halted the heavy footsteps.

"Brassock, where's the pouch?"

"It's here," the rough voice replied, virtually above Josef's head. He allowed the air to escape through his pursed lips as he heard the man called Brassock head back towards the other. Relaxing his muscles, the caretaker peered at the two men, increasingly sinister in the disconnected glow of torchlight. He saw the malignant figure take a leather pouch from his companion. He reached inside to produce a piece of glass; reassured, he placed it back within the pouch.

"The stone must stay with the baryte until we're ready to use it. That way it can't affect us."

"What can a stone do?" Josef saw violence engraved on the coarse features of the heavyset figure. The threatening tone of his companion wiped the mocking sneer from his face.

"It would have one of us slitting the other's throat before we got to the airport." There was no doubt, his tone informed, that he would not be the one harmed. Brassock turned outward with a grunt, scanning the pyramids.

"I don't like it here," he muttered, "where is she?"

"Be quiet," commanded the other as the stone began to shake.

Josef blinked at the sight of the girl's body as it tumbled from the circular space. Her eyes fixed wide with horror as she flung an object into the circular space. Weeping, she sank to the ground, murmuring a frantic prayer to St Rose of Lima. He inched himself forwards to the opening of the amphitheatre where she had thrown a round, dark stone. A moment later, the heavy man had covered the distance and scooped the stone into the pouch with the sleeve of his leather jacket.

The girl began to scream in earnest. "Take it away, it is terrible," she was shrieking hysterically now, picking herself up to run.

The shadow-man's hand lashed out, a flicking snake-tongue across her face that silenced the exhausted girl. He reached out his other hand and grasped the pouch that Brassock offered. Carefully, his eyes gleaming with triumph, he lifted the two stones from the pouch.

"The Perfidium," he whispered hoarsely, mesmerised by the round stone.

A sense of evil washed over the ruins of the ancient temple. The torchlight still angled towards the altar but it was enough for Josef to see the silent tears that dropped from the girl's face to the dry earth below. Placing the two stones back in the pouch, the malevolent figure handed it back to the large man and turned his gaze towards the girl.

Shame washed over Josef, he should help her; he should be shouting at this gringo and demand that he replace what had been taken. Still, he did not move. The heavy man stood next to the slight, crumpled form, a question on his face. The other man shook his head.

"Take her back to the others," he instructed.

Brassock moved towards the girl but stopped abruptly, dropping the pouch, as lightening flared across the site. Flame burst upon the altar, knocking out the torch. The air sizzled as a booming drum-beat of thunder rang out. Josef clung to the wall as wind whipped the dust into swirling clouds within the sunken plaza. He saw the girl run towards the exit from the amphitheatre to be followed by the hulking bodyguard. Quickly, Josef scrambled to the north side of the wall as the unhurried step of expensive shoes made their way across to where the pair had exited the circle. The girl was light and quick and seemed to have managed a good distance. Even so, he soon heard the thuggish sounds that halted her escape and tore at him more than the biting wind as he lifted his eyes above the ledge.

The man of shadows waited, barely visible amid the swathes of sand, his back now to the altar, on the opposite side of the circle. As Josef dropped his glance, he spotted the pouch containing the two stones. It was less than a metre away from where he was now positioned. Despite the cold, the caretaker removed the black fleece, tucking it beneath his arm as he crawled over the wall towards the altar. As he reached for the pouch, he heard voices along the path on the far side, where the weeping girl was being dragged back to her tormentor. Carefully he emptied the two stones from the pouch. A white flash tore through the sky and he saw that one was a circle of smooth obsidian. Checking that the remaining intruder was still facing the outside of the circle, he scrambled nervously on the dusty ground to find two pieces of rock of similar size. He placed these within pouch. |He held his breath as the bodyguard came in to view, roughly pulling the girl towards the forbidding figure who waited with predatory stillness.

Carefully Josef replaced the pouch where he had found it. Wrapping the stones in the black fleece, he retreated silently from the altar. He had barely lodged himself behind the low wall when the big man appeared inches away, his breath coming in short gasps as he retrieved the pouch. Alarmed, Josef saw the girl drop to the ground in front of the waiting man, on the other side of the circle. He peered anxiously, through clouds of sand, for any sign of movement. The man of shadows turned and took the pouch, signalling to the other to carry the girl. Tears pricked Josef's eyes as the bodyguard roughly lifted the small body over his shoulder. At that point, a soft murmur emitted from her lips and he stifled a cry of relief. No thanks to him, he thought, she was still alive.

Barely daring to breathe, the caretaker remained as still as the stones around him, until he was sure he was alone in the amphitheatre. He watched them disappear among the paths at the opposite part of the huge site from where the cabin was situated. Finally, he heard an engine rumble to life. Josef straightened his limbs, preparing to navigate his way back in the darkness. As he stepped quietly among the shapes of the ancient city he felt as if the heart of Caral whispered to him that the man and the stones should be kept as far apart as possible.

The rain came in a deluge of stabbing cold shards that made him race towards the hut. Kier was awake, sleep heavy in her eyes but already wearing her fleece. She sprang up in alarm as he entered.

"Iluvia solo, rain only," Josef forced himself to say as brightly as he could. He knew the amphitheatre was far enough away for little sound to carry to the cabin; unlike him, their ears were not attuned to the night sounds of the site. Silently, he gave thanks that they had not been disturbed; that the shadow man had no reason to discover them sleeping nearby. He pushed the fleece underneath the table on top of one of the boxes and lit the lamps. Kier went to make him a hot drink.

"I was getting worried," she said gently as Josef, still wet, slumped into a chair.

He smiled wearily, knowing it had not reached his eyes. Thanking her for the drink, he found himself restless with the return of daylight. The brief storm had abated. His mind flitted back and forth as he swallowed the hot coffee. Standing, he grabbed his poncho and prepared to leave.

"Excuse me," Josef told her distractedly, ignoring her concern, "my morning duties."

It astonished him that there was so little sign of the night's events, just a few scuffed stones around the altar. He examined the concave depression; there was just no place for the girl to have gone but inside the altar. Had his eyes deceived him? Thoughts of her brought shame flooding back, she was surely a local child; he determined he would take advice from his police friend in Lima. At least he had saved the stone, whatever their significance. Going over and over the events, he traced the path of the intruders to the other side of the site. Losing track of time, he was unaware of the arrival of Domingo's spare tyre. Arriving back at the cabin he found Kier and Domingo packed and ready to leave.

"I'm sorry," he told them, "I had work to do."

Over |Kier's shoulder he saw the fleece bundled up on his chair.

"No problem," Kier smiled, offering her hand, "thank you for your hospitality."

"Goodbye and good fortune," he said seriously, seeing concern touch her eyes once more. He forced himself to smile brightly as he shook her hand.

"Adios," she replied, unconvinced, before climbing into the car.

"Drive carefully Domingo," he called as he watched them negotiate the track, following the vehicle until it was out of sight. Turning back to the cabin, he very carefully unfolded the fleece. Nothing. He quickly scanned the floor and furniture, searching under the table where the boxes had been stored. Becoming frantic and confused he made himself sit in the chair, slowing his breath, allowing memory to explain. He raised his chin in alarm.

"Domingo" he said out loud. The young man must have picked up the coat and thought the stones entangled within were part of the goods that Kier had purchased. Josef gritted his teeth at the sound of the first tour bus arriving. Never had he felt less like showing visitors around the site. It was his last shift for a week. That night he would go to |Lima and talk to the police, and then to Kier.

*

Josef wandered through the day in a haze of exhaustion and indecision. The archaeologists came and went again; still he said nothing about the stones. Who, after all, would believe what he had seen? The last bus had barely left the site when he found himself slumped in the chair, nursing his lined face in one hand, his eyelids drooping.

The step on to the wooden floor was distinct in its arrogance. Josef opened his eyes to see a figure towering above him, peering through eyes that seared his spirit. The man of shadows was now dressed in a light suit, immaculate and deadly. Behind him the caretaker sensed another: Brassock from the bulk in his peripheral vision. Trembling, he did not turn his eyes to confirm his supposition; he could not, they were held in the dark gaze of the man standing in front of his chair.

"Where are my stones?" The quiet predatory voice bored a hole in Josef's sense of himself. He grasped to maintain his courage as he saw at once that there was no point in denying he had been responsible for changing the contents of the pouch. Even as he forcibly clamped his mouth shut, he felt his voice begin to tell the story of how the stones had been accidentally taken. The result was a strange gurgling noise that he barely recognized as issuing form his own body. The compulsion was almost unbearable as he pressed his lips together, biting hard until they bled. The man who had brought with him the shadow of evil, leaned closer.

"Tell me, "he demanded.

Anguished, Josef felt the words torn from him.

"Pulton," he spat, blood flowing on to his chin. The interrogator leaned forwards and placed his palm against his victim's face. Pain coursed through Josef's entire body, his lungs were aflame. "Seven Rivers," he gasped. The agony continued for a few moments and then mercifully ended. Released from the cruel hold that had imprisoned his mind, the caretaker fell backwards against the chair.

Of all things, he last expected to hear laughter. He looked up into the cold eyes that met his with cruel disdain and sadistic amusement. Behind him came the rumbling sound of nervous laughter from the bodyguard.

"You've saved us the trouble of carrying them home," his aggressor told him, showing perfect teeth in a mirthless grim. It took the caretaker some moments to understand, his hand made the sign of the cross.

"Cristo salvar a su, Christ save her."

The cold eyes lost any hint of amusement as they lifted to his companion. The man of shadows gave a brief dismissive nod and turned, without looking back, to leave the cabin. Before Josef could react to his fatal sentence, before he even registered the hard knuckles of the massive fist to his right, the remorseless blow was delivered and Josef's days in Caral were ended.

Chapter Two

The sun was already breaking through the city haze and its warmth tingled on the back of her neck. The inevitable hum of traffic was a distant murmur against the slap of the wooden paddle as it sliced through the still water of the Manchester Ship Canal. On this stretch of water, not far from Victoria Bridge, the canal had yet to become the swollen artery that had been the lifeblood of Manchester's industrial heritage. Here, it was a drowsy capillary that quietly carried the kayak towards the city centre. Her mother once told Kier that she was named for a river. A good name, she thought, for someone always on the move, twisting and turning, gathering the debris of all that she touched.

The red brick of a refurbished mill, now a prestigious hotel, shimmered in watery reflection. Kier remembered working the rooms; heaped piles of musty sheets and air-robbed corridors that never seemed to end. When she left home after Martha's death - when her world turned to dry fibre, never to be reignited – her parents were unable to comprehend why their star student should choose to work as a chambermaid. Kier could not explain her need to abandon all the 'should dos' that had dutifully structured her life; even knowing that it added to the grief-stricken disarray of her parents' marriage. Her sister's death had split open the cracks in a relationship that had floundered since her infancy. Now her parents were literally continents apart.

Sunlight turned to dank cold as Kier manoeuvred the kayak under a stone bridge. Once again, she felt the weight of pummelling guilt that sent her spinning into a mind-numbing schedule of work and night school. She still fruitlessly sought the object – if it was really an object at all? A dream that had manifested to reality the day her sister had died.

Breathing deeply, she pulled the paddle hard through the water for a few final yards to reach a concrete slope. It took her a matter of minutes to stow away the lightweight vessel in the nearby shed. Moments later she had climbed the metal ladder that brought her to a tree-lined courtyard where a scattering of sparrows hopped between summer leaves. Adam's bike was chained up as she had guessed, more than likely he had stayed all night again. Her mood lightened as she pushed back strands of damp hair and punched in the key code for the dark-glassed building. Once inside, she made her way to the ground floor locker room to change her wet suit for shirt and jeans. Kier's office was three flights up, she took the stairs two at a time. There was a blue sign by the door that said 'Morton Enterprises;' next to this was a contact plate against which she pressed her ID card.

The space was light and airy and covered the whole of the top floor. She smiled as the smell of toast wafted into the visitor area from a small flat to her right. Kier made her way to the coffee machine in between a pair of large sinkable sofas, designed to tame any impatient client. She turned as the door to the flat opened and she was greeted by her personal assistant and friend.

"Good morning, mermaid of the ship canal?" Adam came out of the flat carrying a large mug in one hand and a piece of toast in the other. His Edinburgh accent hummed.

"And to what do I attribute this unexpected sight on this fine Saturday morning?"

Kier moved forwards and kissed his cheek as he grimaced.

"I missed you," she replied, her eyes twinkling. Standing back, she folded her arms and made her inspection.

"Adam Kirkbride, you're as white as a ghost! When was the last time you saw the outside of this building?"

Adam's jet-black hair made a stark contrast against his pale skin. Purple -rimmed glasses were perched over a pointed nose and his shoulder-length hair was uncombed, giving him a slightly mad-professor look. About the same height as Kier and a little older at twenty-eight, he wore a black T-shirt and baggy blue jeans over a thin frame. He put down his mug and plate and shuffled his bare feet uneasily.

"Why this overly kind concern? Somehow I think I can rule out the prevention of rickets."

"A little fresh air wouldn't hurt you. You look like a vampire," she patted his cheek.

"Ah, so cruel is woman. And where would you be dragging your faithful servant to this time?" He put his mug underneath the spout of the machine and pressed a button that caused it to hiss and spit as it produced a concentrated black liquid that Adam liked to call coffee.

"Servant by choice Adam, not my inclination."

He frowned at her, picking up the plate. "Hmm… do you want toast? I've lost my appetite."

Kier raised her eyebrows. Adam sighed and turned back to the flat. She poured more water into the coffee maker before making her way behind the large screen that showed a seascape painting of a blue Indonesian sea and a long empty beach that divided the workspace from the visitors' area. At her workstation, she switched on her computer and flicked through the files until she found the one she wanted. By the time this was done, Adam had returned carrying a cup of white coffee and laid it on the coaster by her right hand.

"Cheers," she smiled up at him. He had combed his hair and put on trainers. He leaned over Kier to peer at the screen.

"You said you got all the reports about the acquisitions you sent from Lima?" he checked.

Kier nodded, scrolling down the screen, remembering the city where extremes of poverty and wealth was included in the price of a bus ticket.

"Some great pieces, now if you were thinking of going back...?"

Kier lifted one side of her mouth in a wry grin, "I'm not," she told him, turning the screen towards her friend.

Adam looked over and shook his head.

"You're not making me go to Pulton?" He sounded affronted but Kier simply turned the computer back towards her and continued to flick through the files.

"There's been a break-in," she told him, still staring at the screen.

"When?" Adam asked, his tone business-like.

"Early hours of this morning. Gina phoned, she's a bit shaken."

"What did they take?"

"Well that's the odd thing...look here." She brought an inventory of objects up on the screen as Adam leaned over the computer. Her index finger pointed to a list of rocks, each one having a picture by its side, Kier pointed to a smooth black rock about the size of a paperweight. "An obsidian piece and some unshaped baryte, worth practically nothing. They came in through the café and trashed the adjoining door. Made a hell of a mess, broke some shelves and glass casing but took nothing else."

"I hate to say I told you so Kier."

"Come on Adam, the Seven Rivers has made more than enough to justify its existence in the last two years."

"I said Pulton was a big risk Kier, even with your magic touch, I don't think this will be the first senseless act of criminality that we'll need to deal with in this shop."

She swivelled her chair around and look directly into Adam's green eyes.

"When was the last time you visited Pulton?"

"In 1998. I was a sensitive teenager and to this day I attest I saw dead people forming an orderly queue outside Tesco. "

"That's not fair," Kier told him, the corners of her mouth twitching.

"It wasn't me that voted it the third worst place in Britain to spend a holiday."

"There's been at least two recent articles saying it's now one of the best places to buy a house," she countered.

"Who for, those of suicidal intent?"

Kier shook her head. Pressing her lips together, she stood up, stretching her back. Adam sat in her place and continued scrolling through the shop details. She gathered her thoughts to the rhythm of the keyboard tapping.

The room was lined on either side by tinted glass walls that allowed the light in without baking the occupants. They gave a view overlooking the canal on one side and inwards towards the heart of the city on the other. The tall sleek constructions of the Spinningfields and the old limestone architecture of the Central Reference Library were both visible from where she now stood. To her right, she could see beyond the canal to the elegant spire of Salford Cathedral. A little to the left was a distinctive tower of a 1960s block of flats. Concrete balconies and faded yellow paint a reminder that in parts, Lowry's Manchester still existed. Kier moved back toward the desk.

"You'll need to pack enough for a week," she said casually.

Adam looked horrified. He glanced towards his own workstation and placed a finger on the bridge of his glasses in a characteristic gesture of anxiety.

"You're joking, I've a hundred things to do here."

"I need you with me."

Adam fell silent and stood up, ready to continue the argument.

Kier smiled sweetly, "And if you rein in that cruel tongue of yours, I'll let you bring the lap top." She ignored his complaints and started printing out the papers she needed to bring with them.

One hour later they were boarding a train at Piccadilly Station, Kier chatting easily, her assistant rooted in sullen silence. Pulton was two hours away and unable to stay long away from his computer, Adam unpacked the laptop and tackled his emails, which were many, even on a Saturday. A glance down below the railway bridge showed the motorway was grid-locked. Kier felt relieved that both she and Adam preferred not to drive where it could be avoided. The motion of the train lulled her to sleep so that she saw little of the familiar journey whilst her companion remained submerged behind the laptop, tapping away with the speed of long practice.

The sky was a clear blue as they arrived in Pulton. Kier stood back a little as she watched Adam begin to revise his opinion of the apparently blighted resort. The station, though small, was modern. The paving was a warm pink and several tubs of blooming flowers were dotted along the path. A few steps away, in the middle of a mini-roundabout, stood a striking sculpture of two avocets on top of a boulder. Their black and white bodies stood beak to beak in prefect symmetry.

Kier caught a glimpse of the sea beckoning at the end of a street that emptied on to the scaled- down dual carriageway now in front of them. A few moments later, she had crossed the road and stopped to wait for her companion, her small cotton rucksack hanging lightly over one shoulder. Adam wheeled a suitcase and negotiated the road as if it were a muddy field; one toe venturing forward and then being drawn back again, as a steady volume of holiday makers filled the carriageway.

Laughing at her own schoolgirl excitement, Kier headed out along the path towards the sea. Adam followed, feet and wheels awkwardly trying to keep pace with the gazelle-like creature in front. The jetty ran high above the sands and she remembered summer evenings when the sun melted into the seas, casting the mountains behind in a blanket of blue slate. Today the sun was high in the sky in what had, three years ago, been a depressingly run-down seaside resort on the North-West coast. Looking around, Kier could feel the hope of prosperity again with uniquely refurbished properties and plans for development along the prom.

It had been pure accident, a delayed train, that had landed her at this same spot three years ago. The town had been crying out for investors. The boarded-up buildings, ramshackle hotels and scent of deprivation had not prevented her instant love affair with the place. Bejewelled by views over the imposing Lakeland Hills this northern bay had called to her in a way that she could not ignore. The air tingled with salt and fish as a pair of swans whistled overhead. When she turned around, expecting a sarcastic comment from her friend, she was surprised by a serious look in his eyes.

"What?" she challenged him.

"You are very beautiful," he said simply. No smirk, no laconic addendum. Kier's brow crinkled as she stared back at him, equally serious.

"I've never seen you like this, Kier. Yes, it's a bonny place, but you make it beautiful."

She patted his cheek."

"I'm touched Adam, but you scare me when you're nice."

The edge of his lip curved and the mischief came back into his eyes.

"Ah well, I wouldn't worry. I don't intend to make a habit of it."

She folded her arm in his and pointed to the middle of the town.

"Come on, I'll show you our Pulton investment."

Laughing, he caught her mood as they made their way down the prom to the Seven Rivers café and gift shop.

*

"It's a magic line." Kier squatted on jean-covered legs, her long dark hair almost touching the floor.

The four-year-old adjusted his small round glasses and peered at the floor, unable to see any line, magic or otherwise.

"If you cross the magi line then mummy can't see you any more Kyle.

Pointing with her finger, she ran it along the wooden floor where the café ended and the gift shop began. Blue, serious eyes, left Kier's face to glance back at the table where a young woman struggled with the strap of a car seat. Inside it, Kyle's younger sister objected loudly.

"Come on Kyle, we have to go now." The young mother clipped the belt shut and reached out her hand to her son. The small boy looked eagerly at the shining objects in the gift shop and then back at Kier's calmly smiling face.

"Have to go now," he told her solemnly.

"Ok Kyle, see you soon." Kier waved as his mum took firm hold of his hand. As they left, Gina, a vivid redhead in her thirties, came through the door.

Kier stood up, her hands resting in the back pockets of her jeans. She glanced at Adam who was busy on the computer behind the gift shop counter. They had spent lunch time discussing the break-in with Gina, whose lively personality and solid background in retail, had made her an obvious choice to manage the café.

Each business that Kier owned was unique and this meant that Gina had little awareness of the size of the company of which she had become a part. Neither Adam nor Kier, by tacit agreement, discussed the business portfolio in detail unless they were alone. The redhead was therefore surprised to meet a personal assistant. She noticed that he was smart, very smart. Everything had been arranged quickly to make sure the manageress was ok and to return Seven Rivers to its original state.

The gift shop area was closed. It was decided that they would open the café however; Gina's face glowed as it became obvious that the place had become even more popular in her employer's absence. Pulton was packed with visitors arriving for a series of events, culminating in the Light and Water display the following Saturday evening. It was an unusually hot spell of summer weather and Kier had spent enough time in the resort to appreciate that every shop owner would need to make the most of the period of tourist activity.

In a former life, the building had been a three-storied hotel, later converted to flats. Eventually the building had lapsed into disrepair and Kier had bought it, loving the massive Victorian rooms and wide sea-front windows. The main body of the café was taken up with brightly painted tables and chairs, mostly filled with families. Along one side was a series of wooden booths, each one containing a picture painted by a local artist.

Kier made her way behind the counter and was soon producing a tinny, gurgling sound as she happily created a full, foaming and chocolate-topped cappuccino for Gina. Beside Adam, she placed what she referred to as some black sticky stuff. He raised an eyebrow in a gesture of thanks. Gina's green eyes twinkled as she reached for the drink.

"Mmm. You haven't lost your touch. You not having one?"

Kier glanced around the room and then out towards the sea front.

"I'm going to head out for a bit," she decided.

Gina nodded and Adam looked up curiously as she was leaving before immediately re-focusing on his work.

Chapter Three

Out in the bay a small group of fishing boats huddled together, sails leaning from side to side in the breeze, their hulls exposed in watery residue. It was late afternoon and the watchful glimmer of retreating waters flashed in the distance, a reminder that in a few hours, this tidal inhabitant, would return to reclaim its perilous abode. Inevitably Kier's feet took her against the flow of human traffic that was now congregating around the temporary fairground. An old-style Punch and Judy stall emitted the strangely familiar and oddly disturbing sounds that had been heard in the town's Victorian heyday. Half a mile further on, she could hear the piping notes of birds foraging in the wake of the retreating sea. She stopped to take off her trainers and slid her feet into the recently imported sand that softened the coastline.

She walked the stretch of beach that nestled between two curved arms of carefully placed rocks that had been formed to prevent the sea washing away the new sand. Away from the town centre, it provided a peaceful haven to enjoy the sea -front. Kier perched herself on one of the rocks at the furthest point from the town. A flock of dunlins formed a fragile daisy-chain against the mountainous backdrop that semi-circled this unmade bed of the sea. She slid down so that her back rested against the rocks and rolled up her jeans. She let her eyes close and revelled in the feel of warm sun. It was the first time since returning from Peru, that she felt the comforting embrace of being home.

A strange sensation roused her. It was not an unfamiliar visitor but one she thought had ceased with Martha's death. Until, that is, she had bought bracelets from the thin, dark-haired young woman at El Silencio in Peru. Like then, it began with the fluttering wing-beat of her heart as she became doused in the hum of being, sparked by a current of connection to another that seemed to have weight beyond the current dimension. As if she were hauled out of time to mark something deeply significant.

All drowsiness fell away. Kier examined the almost deserted beach. Nothing. A flicker of light brought her attention to a male figure, some distance away, steering easily through pockets of quicksand. The locals could tell an endless number of tragic stories about the dangers of crossing the bay on foot. None of them would venture it without a designated guide. Fascinated, she continued to watch as he drew nearer. There was something about his fluid movement, a familiarity; a recognition that knotted her stomach and conflicted with the certain knowledge that she had never seen him before. As he moved closer, the still strong sun reflected flecks of moisture amidst waves of dark hair. She estimated his age at early thirties; he wore a white vest, blue jeans and sturdy boots. It must have taken twenty minutes for him to reach the shore but it seemed a faction of that time. He stepped on to dry sand near enough for her to notice a firm set to his jaw. No, she had never seen this enigmatic vibrant man, yet the sense of familiarity remained. She found herself unwilling to remove her gaze from him. He, on the other hand, seemed focused only on reaching the prom where, with ease, he vaulted the barrier on to the pavement.

Kier sat for a few moments, noticing the tingling of her limbs, the inevitable sequel to these episodes. Still trembling slightly, she reached for her trainers and pulled them on, hoisting herself upright. Directly across the road was her intended destination. The bookshop occupied the bottom of a three-storey building with a higgledy-piggledy assortment of stacked shelves that spilled out on to the pavement. Painted on the corner-facing wall in copper plate writing, was simply 'Bookshop.'

Once inside the narrow corridor she smiled at the small rooms lined with books, each one containing its own particular type of hard or paper-backed treasure. In a time of electronic downloads and internet buying, the bookshop thrived. People lingered amongst its nooks and crannies just for the pleasure of being there. Sometimes she heard customers comment that a particular book seemed to have fallen into their hands, only to find it had a special relevance for their individual situation.

The scent of the sea intermingled with an infusion of wood pulp and greeted her like an old friend. Inevitably she made her way towards the reference room at the bottom right of the narrow corridor. It never ceased to fascinate, this threshold into another time and place. The exquisitely carved door looked heavy and solid but opened lightly at her touch. A stained-glass window, whose filtered light always gave the impression of sunset, sat high on the wall opposite. Oddly, she had never found a glimpse of this window from outside the building.

In the reference room, she had found a strange world of literature. It drew her in, captured hours of her day, so that she had learnt to ration her visits when she came to Pulton. As always, and it had never occurred to her to question why, the room was empty. The large bare table, with its two tall armchairs, all intricately engraved in a kind of wood she had never identified, beckoned to her. Stepping towards them, she saw she had been wrong, she was not alone.

Tucked away in the corner was a chair she had never previously noticed. The broad wooden arms seemed shaped perfectly to support the muscular limbs that rested upon them. The pale wood had been expertly carved to caress the neck and seemed as pliant as a pillow for the mop of dark hair that rested in its embrace. It was as if the chair had wrapped itself around the deeply sleeping figure.

Undoubtedly, it was the man she had seen emerge from the bay. The red and gold of the window stroked his skin with soft light and outlined the shadows beneath his eyes. He was clean-shaven and his mouth relaxed in a half-smile as he breathed softly and steadily. Kier turned away, embarrassed by her intimate perusal.

Even with her eyes elsewhere, she was still scanning the distinctive contours of his face in repose. Her lips twitched a self-mocking smile and she closed her eyes to wipe the image from her mind. She scanned the shelves and reached for a book that was lying on its side on the bottom shelf. The pages were soft, with a waxy sheen and filled with meticulous italic lettering. There was no title and no named author but by its look of random entries, she thought it might have been a diary or a notebook. Sitting with her back to the stranger, she quietly eased herself into one of chairs. Laying out the book in front of her, it fell open to reveal a few lines written in the centre of the page.

"Always there is what we know and what we have learned to unknow. Our memories haunt the breeze and ride the sinuous currents of the ocean. Our footsteps imprint the sands and shape the surface to diversity. In the end, it only takes a strand of thought, followed, to wash away the detritus of human pre-occupation and begin the journey home."

The rest of the book was filled with short descriptions that seemed to document visits to a place called Mengebara. One passage told of a long journey downriver and captured the grief of the person who had left home behind. She noticed that the words were written like musical notes; changing length, height and distance in the text. Kier found herself returning to the lines she had first found, mulling them over.

After a while she closed the book carefully and glanced towards the corner chair. It was empty, she had been too absorbed to notice her silent companion leaving. Unusually, her appetite for the strange literature that she found in the reference room vanished. Instead Kier found herself exploring the labyrinthine passages and small rooms, making a dozen apologies as she twisted past customers, aimlessly browsing through rows of paperbacks. Finally, she squeezed past a number of customers waiting to pay in the narrow entrance. As she did so Kier wondered irritably how the place managed to be so popular and yet have so little regard for basic commercial organisation.

*

The promenade at the North End of Pulton was virtually empty as the light began to fade. Gabbie Owen watched as Mrs Porpett, long and lean, walked her sleek hound along the pavement opposite the bookshop. A signal that it was seven o'clock and closing time. Gabbie, a young woman of seventeen years, wiped some of the dust from her red t-shirt and adjusted the pin that held her blonde hair. She began wheeling in the shelves of books up a wooden ramp and deposited them in the largest of the rooms. Once she had closed the outside door she wandered down the corridor and unlocked and entrance to the left of the passage that led to the cellar.

Gabbie carefully descended the series of stone steps, her eyes drifting to the middle of the wall opposite to a window full of crystals; except that it wasn't a window at all. It was an odd thing, built into the whitewashed stone that gave a continuous glow so that the room was never dark. She turned at the bottom of the step; behind her, a lapis piece within the strange mural glowed a deep resonating blue. Gabbie glanced up at the whisper of movement, shrugging her shoulders as she saw nothing had changed. Finally, she spotted a small box of paperbacks perched on a chair. Picking them up, she made her way carefully back up the steps. Using the box, she pushed open the door but unable to look down, tripped and lurched forwards. To her surprise, instead of the sound of paperbacks scattering on the floor, she straightened up to find them safe in the hands of a total stranger grinning down at her. Before she could react, a rich Welsh baritone rand down the corridor.

"Gabrielle, I need those books in here now."

Nobody but Evan Gwyn called her Gabrielle, to everyone else she was Gabbie. The newcomer winked and her large blue eyes smiled up at him. She wondered how she could have missed this customer when she had checked the rooms.

Evan's firm tread followed his voice a moment later, his large and striking figure appearing in the hallway. He was in his fifties with hair an untidy mop of thick grey waves, skin toughened from a life spent outdoors and grey eyes hidden behind heavily-lined lids. The Welshman was dressed in one of his usual flamboyantly embroidered waistcoats; this one a vivid orange that covered a midriff that once had been lean and muscular but now folded around him like a soft belt.

Gabbie's mouth tightened a little, ready for the inevitable sarcasm that was his natural response to being kept waiting. She had been the only employee that had managed to manoeuvre around her employer's tempestuous moods. All the others, and there had been many, had found themselves unsuited to the man or the place. Gabbie, on the other hand, had been unimpressed by his deliberate rudeness, ignoring what she perceived as the surface of a rich and green, if slightly volcanic, mountain. It was now a year since she had joined him, the youngest and least studious of all his assistants and neither had mentioned her leaving.

Whatever Evan intended to say was lost in an exclamation of surprise as he noticed the stranger. With a lightness of foot, she could hardly believe for a big man, he quickly closed the space between himself and the newcomer.

"Echin," he exclaimed joyously, enveloping the stranger in a bear hug.

Gabbie stood back amazed. She had not yet seen her employer fully smile, now he was standing, arms stretched out upon the other man's shoulders, with a foolish grin on his face. The scowl that hovered permanently around his strong features appeared to have vanished.

Echin smiled and it seemed to Gabbie that the shabby surroundings felt as if someone had given them a coat of paint. The Welshman put an arm around his young employee.

"Ah, Gabrielle, let me introduce you to my good friend Echinod Deem. Echin, this is Gabrielle Owen, my chief assistant."

He waved his arm expansively around them both and Gabbie, still speechless, was unable to point out that actually, she was his only assistant. Something in the amused expression of the stranger told her that he probably knew anyway. Eventually she managed to make her vocal chords connect to her brain again.

"Er…can I get you both a cup of tea?"

"No, my little blodyn, we will help ourselves to something a little stronger."

He looked around at the empty hallway," I'll finish closing up, you get off home and enjoy a wonderful evening."

Gabbie looked with amazement at the irascible Welshman. The grey eyes were alight with good humour; he seemed suddenly to have lost ten years. The way she had clearly already passed from his mind, however, made her realise he was inescapably her crusty employer. She moved lightly towards the front door, picking up her bag and jacket from behind the desk.

"Bye then," she called out to the retreating backs of the two men as they headed towards the kitchen. Both men turned and she found herself looking up into the striking blue eyes of the stranger and avoiding those of her employer as much as possible. The man called Echin wished her a good night in a thoughtful kind of way so that she felt he actually meant it. Smiling softly, Gabbie made her way to the promenade just as the sun was preparing its spectacular final bow over the bay.

*

Inside the hallway, the man who had so fascinated Kier and Gabbie, followed his friend back through the narrow corridor. The large cluttered kitchen had not changed significantly in a hundred years. The whitewashed stone walls reflected the last of the sunlight as it filtered through small square windows. Evan signalled his old friend towards a solid oak table as he reached into a cupboard and produced a bottle of fifty-year-old cognac. With great care, he poured two glasses and sat opposite his newly arrived companion. The grey eyes twinkled with pleasure as he lifted the glass and sipped the red-brown liquid. Evan then carefully put down the glass and looked directly at the other man. His eyes lost a little of their sparkle and his mouth tightened to a thin line.

"You're late," he told him, "by ten years! You said a short while, not a fifth of my life!"

Chapter Four

The rooms above the cafe had been restored in order to rent out as a flat. Somehow, Kier had never got around to putting it on the rental market, retaining the two large stories for her own use. A modern kitchen had been installed and the two rooms on the third floor had been fully refurbished. The large windows were usually left open slightly when she stayed, so that a subtle breath of the sea was always present.

"Well?" she asked her companion who stood beside her holding a glass of red wine. His thin mouth curved to a smile as he looked at her, the dark shadows under his eyes not completely obscured by his glasses.

"Well ok, I'll grant you the place has come on since I was here last," Adam reluctantly replied.

"And..." she coaxed, hand on hips, her head tipped to one side.

He sighed and turned away from the window.

"It may just have been a good investment." He smiled to himself as he turned away and made for an old chesterfield sofa, swinging his glass around the room, "apart from grandma's parlour, that is."

The main room was virtually unchanged, even down to the original furnishing. Kier had merely lifted the carpet and revitalised the wooden floor. She sat opposite Adam and lifted her glass from the small table in between, "it's cosy."

Adam patted the empty sofa, "and most likely transplanted here from the nursing home up the road. There's probably a whole layer of deliberately dropped medication in these chairs, earn us a fortune up the lane."

Kier shook her head in despair and her tone became more serious.

"So, when are you going to go into partnership with me?" Adam put his glass down and the lost look in his green eyes reminded her of the first time they had met.

"No thank you." His forefinger came up to the bridge of his nose lifting his glasses. He stood up and walked towards the kitchen

"Why not?" she asked his back.

"Same reason as last time," he called out "I like things the way they are."

"Adam, I wouldn't have this business without you, you've earned it."

He turned towards her, both hands in his pockets; there was an expression in his eyes she was unable to read and she knew he wouldn't want her to try.

"You saved my life Kier, that's partnership enough." He looked into her intense brown eyes for a moment longer and then turned away.

"I'm making toast," he said fiddling in the cupboards. His friend and employer smiled ruefully.

"You live on toast," she said, "bread's in the cupboard just to the right."

A look of pure mischief lit Adam's clever face as he manoeuvred toast and lap top back into the armchair.

"Gina tells me she thinks you might have someone special in tow, she said that you disappear for hours at a time and never mention where you've been!" Kier's eyebrows rose a little.

"Does she really?"

Before she could comment on Gina's indiscretion her mobile flashing interrupted them and Gally's strong face came up on the display.

"Hi," she said smiling as she answered the phone.

"Hey little sis, where are you?" came the tinny reply.

"Pulton, How about you?"

"At the university."

Kier frowned, "at this time?"

"Yeah. Working on a project," her brother explained, "look I'm coming up to the Dales tomorrow for a few days, do you fancy coming over to see me?"

"Whereabouts? I've no car," she told him.

"I'll be staying at the Mountain Inn near Whistmorden Scar, it's about five miles out of Gladdendale. I did some research from there a few years ago."

"I don't know Gally, there's no public transport to Gladdendale from here. How about you stay with us?"

"Nah, I've booked in now Kier. Look, leave it open, I'll be there for a week or so, if you do decide to hire a car why don't you stop the night?"

Kier paused to think and caught Adam's eye as his brows formed a question mark.

"Maybe. I'll have to decide what to do with Scraggy here."

Adam gave her a pained look shaking his head. Kier laughed as her brother echoed her own thoughts.

"Adam? He'd hate it, seriously you should bring him."

She laughed, her eyes alight as they fell on Adam.

"Ok sweets, I'll think on it. Sleep tight."

"Night," Gally replied before she pressed the 'end call' button. She looked speculatively at her companion. He sat upright placing his empty plate on the coffee table and looked over the top of his laptop.

"Not a chance, sack me. Anyway, it's time I got back to the office.'' She came over and her lip curled as she measured his determination.

"Fine. But I'm going to stay on for a few days."

"Right," he said waiting for her to say something else but she merely walked on into the kitchen to make a drink. Adam followed her with his eyes, still waiting for a further comment but none came. He plugged his earpiece into his laptop and tapped away at the keyboard.

"Just one thing," Kier said placing a hot chocolate on the coffee table in front of her companion and perching on the arm of the chair. Sighing he looked up at her holding his earpiece out from his ear.

"I want to see if you can find out more about the pieces that were taken."

Adam's expression was perplexed.

"Their history and so on," she continued

"It's with the police Kier, we don't need to get involved."

She looked out over the rim of her coffee mug. Reflected in the windowpane the two friends looked close enough to be a couple.

"It's too bizarre not to be important and you're the best person to sift out the information."

"So, I do get to go back to the office this week?"

"If you want to," she smiled.

Adam yawned and closed his laptop.

"Early night then," he said. Standing up he moved to the door. Kier blew him a kiss knowing that his mind would be already searching for the stolen pieces.

*

Gabbie had found herself unusually reluctant to leave the bookshop and briefly toyed with the idea of going back with some excuse. Once out on the prom she realised there was something about the man named Echinod Deem that made her want to stay despite the anticipation of an extra hour to herself. The early bus was almost empty and she hopped on lightly as it set off northwards up the coast. Gabbie released her hair from its clip and adjusted her make up using the daintily decorated mirror that was practically the only thing her mother had left her.

It was Saturday night and her Dad would bring home fish and chips on his way back from the Railway club. They only had this weekend together and then he'd be doing a run to Italy next week as a HGV driver. Only for this year, he had promised, would he work so far away and only because Gabbie was now old enough to look after herself. The money was three times better than the local jobs that had dotted her school years but she hated going home to the small empty house when he was away.

Her Dad wasn't expecting her to be home until later so she texted Klim to meet her at the park. Gabbie sighed, his eighteenth birthday, but with his mother in a home and his Father dead he'd told her he just wanted to forget it. He said the main thing he would celebrate was that his uncle's guardianship was ended and he would no longer have anything to do with a man he hated. Gabbie had tried to tell him that family was family and they should try to get along even though she'd never met the man. Klim had sat silently, his mouth in a tight line until she changed the subject.

A few miles north of Pulton was a small expanse of grassland ringed by carefully planted trees and bushes. The area nestled at the edge of a hastily built estate bordering farmland and below a thick woodland of conifer and beech trees. Gabbie walked towards a group of youths gathered together at a gateway where the woodland emerged onto the tamed surface of the park.

Luke was smoking a cigarette as he leaned against the staggered gate that straddled the entrance. He wore a blue hoody over his jeans but his head was uncovered as he watched a stranger emerge on the woodland path and come towards them. Luke, small for his sixteen years, his fair hair cropped short, signalled hello to Gabbie but kept his eyes on the stranger. As she reached the gate she looked up to see the newcomer standing, waiting patiently to pass.

The little group easily divided but Luke deliberately obstructed the way. On closer examination, she thought the man was older than he looked. He wore a dark sweatshirt and light blue jeans and was a little smaller than average. His build was stocky without carrying any extra weight and Gabbie, now standing next to Luke, thought he was cute. Besides the woollen hat, she thought, he definitely needed to lose the hat. To her surprise the face under the close-fitting cap turned directly towards her and his hand crossed over his head bringing with it the offending wool, which slipped into his jeans pocket.

Close-cropped blond hair framed a sculpted face with amused and unafraid blue eyes that looked at each of the small group in turn. Luke took in the fact that what he thought was padded jacket was in fact all shoulder. A frown creased Gabbie's forehead as she noticed the aggression in Luke's face, he looked stoned. She looked around at the others, Klim was not part of the small group. Her frown deepened and was then suddenly replaced by laughter as she put her arm through that of Luke's. Surprised and pleased the youth turned towards her and she began turning away from the gate and pointing to edge of the field.

"There's Danny, bet she's been waiting ages. Come on Luke."

She tugged on his arm. Luke gave a belligerent glance towards the man waiting patiently to pass through the gate and then let his attention be drawn to the slim dark-haired girl at the edge of the field. The stranger's gaze followed the small group as they left and noticed the unsteady gait of the boy called Luke.

Gabbie let out a small exclamation and gestured her friends to keep going whilst she came back to retrieve the coin he had seen her drop moments earlier. Her long hair parted as she stood back up and she found herself looking directly into the light blue eyes of the blond newcomer and realised that there was something familiar about him. She wondered what he was doing on their field. A well-known coastal footpath was nearby and walkers quite often asked for directions but this man had the confidence of a local. Gabbie put the coin in her pocket, smiled at the stranger who nodded and smiled in return and walked back to her friends. Faer slowly put his hat back on and grinned softly as he made his way along the coast to Pulton.

*

Kier shivered slightly as the breeze from the open window snuck underneath the oversized t-shirt that she used for nightwear. It was her habit to sit in the wooden rocking chair by the window in darkness, letting its gentle motion dissipate the tension that was never far from the surface, but was deeply hidden from those around her, even Adam. The nightmares were coming more often, an awareness of a brooding enemy that remained faceless and from whom she was constantly hiding. Adam had asked her why she always preferred to fly below the radar and she pretended to look puzzled, dismissing him with some jibe or other. She knew exactly what he meant of course, she rarely fronted her own success, the instinct to hide was so strong and also inexplicable.

She looked out on the still promenade, eerily bright beneath a row of streetlamps, that provided the border between the town and the inky blackness beyond. Her mind flitted back to the man who had emerged from the treacherous sands and had seemed somehow to be so vitally a part of the landscape. Where on earth could he have disappeared to? Kier laughed at herself, she had been a teenager the last time she had become remotely fixated by a man and the blue-eyed stranger had shown no awareness of her. She shook her head, her few partnerships had not lasted long and she had more than once described herself as suffering from romantic gene deficiency.

Midnight chimed on an antique carriage clock as she listened to the rhythmic breaking of water on the beach. Yawning she put down her drink on a small table and stretched upwards allowing herself to drift towards sleep only to find she was wide awake a moment later, eyes wide in concentration.

Long legs climbed easily over the boulders on to the prom. A narrow torso elongated into an oval face with a ponytail of Green-black hair that shone in the lamplight. He was dark skinned and wore a loose black shirt over light trousers and a small rucksack hung over his shoulder. He lifted his face towards the buildings opposite and Kier snapped back into the chair but not before his luminous eyes had caught her own and held them for a moment with only the slightest curiosity before his gaze continued across the rest of the buildings.

There was a change in the breeze and something within Kier stirred as she watched the tall figure turn and head northwards along the prom. Her spine tingled and she remembered one of the phrases she had read in the reference room of the bookshop:

"He spired high above us and upon him we hung our garments of the past and our ribbons for the future."

Perhaps it was the hour and the darkness that made Kier feel as if her world had suddenly turned in on itself. She picked up her dressing gown from the back of the chair and wrapped it around her before climbing the stairs to her bedroom.

Chapter Five

Without the variety of shop frontage to direct the eye, the reverse perspective, from the narrow alleyway behind, showed a long row of old terraced buildings. The corner bookshop, recently white washed, glowed in the moonlight. The steps down to the back door of the bookshop had been repaired and a curving metal rail added for safety. Stretching upwards there were three floors but the tall figure made his way towards the cellar door that opened easily to the touch of long fingers. Once inside he made his way to the back of the narrow room towards a mosaic of glittering minerals that illuminated the small place and emitted a soft green light as he grew nearer. In the way of his kind he allowed his long limbs to merge with the crystalline mural, his human body disappearing into a shard of tourmaline where a thousand interwoven whispers suffused his being.

A little while later, in the early hours of the new day, Faer warmed his hands by the stove in the bookshop kitchen. The grey wool hat was a perfect mould over his angular scalp and covered both forehead and ears. Wisps of steam rose from his clothes and a smile touched his lips as he heard the bump of flesh against the wooden frame of the kitchen doorway.

"Tor!" Faer's face lit in a huge grin as he walked over to embrace the unusually tall and thin figure that had finally managed to become disentangled from the doorway.

"In the flesh," Tormaigh replied standing back and lifting his arms in a gesture that said a significant effort had been made.

"So I see!" laughed Faer. "I saw that you had arrived and were embedded. "

The tall figure removed his rucksack and strings of dark hair fell across a pale face. A smile creased blue tinged lips and ignited the glimmering green rock pools that were his eyes.

"It's been a long time since I have done this," he said. Faer nodded and his hand reached out to his brother's shoulder.

"Come and eat, you look famished. Well," he added smiling, "you always look famished in that form, but let's fill these human stomachs and stop them growling!"

Hot food had been prepared and left on the table. Unlike Echin and Faer, Tormaigh spent little time in human company and perhaps as a result there was always a quirky awkwardness to his human form. Faer removed his hat and the two sat across from each other, helping themselves from the large tureen to a thick soup accompanied by brown rolls of grain bread. Tormaigh sipped half-heartedly despite his body's hunger. He looked over at his companion's earnest sea blue eyes and held them for a moment.

"Do you think Candillium is here?"

"If she is she does not know it yet," a voice answered from the door.

Echinod Deem stood in the doorway. Of the three he wore his human form with most grace and ease, moonstone shone from his right ear lobe and his blue eyes were luminous. The two figures at the table rose and all three were soon enveloped in an embrace.

"What news do you have of her?" Tormaigh asked, disentangling his long limbs awkwardly. Echin's eyes were bleak.

"I don't know for certain that she has returned. The choice is hers but she knows the times that are upon us. Having left she cannot come back by the doorways for Belluvour's power has grown so that such an imprint would be heard even in the secret vaults. It has to be through human birth if

Tremachus has allowed it. And that means that her identity is locked away, even from her."

Tormaigh's mouth was an exaggerated line.

"Are you sure?" he asked Echin, who nodded in reply.

A green glitter flashed in Tormaigh's cheekbone as his emotion heightened.

"Remember that in Ordovicia she was human when we knew her last," Echin reminded him gently.

Tormaigh shook his head, "but the times and the human race have changed. Now she could pass beside us from birth to death and we may never know."

Echin nodded, "and yet their awareness is raised once more. Technology mimics the world they have left behind. They speak their awareness in literature, films, music and many other ways. They know the times that are upon them."

"They are not ready." Tormaigh bowed his head, "they are still destroying each other and Moura with ignorance and folly. I hear it on the current walls and in the weeping of the shattered earth."

Faer sighed, "minds shrouded on one side by desperate want and on the other by overfed ease, and by wretched violence on both."

"And yet they have managed to nurture the seeds of the Myriar in preparation for Candillium's return," Echin said with a weak smile.

"Have you found them?" Faer asked, his tone lightening.

"One, I know, another I suspect, "Echin replied. "They will gather inevitably around each other. They will be drawn to Candillium and she to them. None can yet be aware of the dangers they face."

"What if she has not come?" asked Tormaigh

Echin's firm jaw line lifted, "Tremachus will have brought her here in time if she has agreed to come. And even in the realms in which she has travelled Candillium will not forget us."

Faer looked at his companion's face and softened his expression.

"Even you cannot be sure of that my friend."

Echin stood and his eyes seemed to be watching another place.

"As you say."

Tormaigh stiffened his already long torso as the front door opened and closed. Echin grinned and opened the kitchen door as Evan arrived, his mop of grey hair covered by a hooded sweatshirt, his eyes weary. Echin moved aside to let his friend enter the kitchen. Putting one arm around the other man's broad shoulders he swept the other in a gesture of introduction.

"Evan, meet Faer and Tormaigh," he pointed to each in turn. "Your host, gentlemen, Evan Gwynn."

The two guests stood up and shook hands with Evan and then Tormaigh retreated to the table allowing Faer to express their thanks for the meal and hospitality.

"Not at all," replied the big man expansively as each of them pulled a chair to the table. Evan reached for the jug of water and poured himself a glass and slowly drank it. Echin leaned his elbows on the table, his fingers interlaced as he leaned forward. Tormaigh tried the same gesture but his long fingers stood up like sentinels and he folded his arms instead.

"Did you find any trace of it?" Echin asked the Welshman

Evan's face grimaced. "Indeed, I did," he told his three guests who leaned forward with interest.

"It is a stone that I could not change, black hearted and dreadful. It was certainly here, I found its dark trace a little down the prom, but it is no longer nearby. What is this thing? I sense it has great power."

"For evil only," Tormaigh said sharply. Evan turned to his friend.

"So where did it come from?" he asked.

It was Echin who replied, his human eyes sad.

"We know it as the Perfidium, created by Belluvour in Obason, where he resided in the days before the binding. It is an obsidian blade impregnated with the blood of the Ordovicians he murdered and the spear has stained your history down through the centuries. Where man has marked his passing with the worst atrocities then you will know that the Perfidium was in the hands of those who committed them.

"We captured the spear in the middle of the last century and sought to place it beyond human touch in Peru. After a struggle, it was possible to transmute its physical shape into a round stone and unharness the force within it, making dormant the evil within."

Echin's expression was grim as he continued, "it was found and somehow removed from its place of safety twenty-one days ago."

"By who?" asked Evan.

"We have yet to discover," Tormaigh replied with a hard edge to his voice.

Evan's brow creased as he tried to understand.

"But you said its power was unharnessed," he repeated.

"That's right," said Faer continuing, "but human deeds can reshape it. It has to re-charge its destructive nature to return to its original form. The quickest way to achieve this would be its use to corrupt the young."

Tormaigh interrupted the exchange.

'Someone is trying to get through to you on the machine upstairs," he told the Welshman. Evan surprised, stood up listening.

"You have the ears of a bat!" he told Tormaigh. "I'm expecting a call from my daughter, she travels to Carmarthen early today." Quickly he left the kitchen and when his boots sounded at the top of the stairs Tormaigh turned towards Echin.

"Do you still defend him? The Perfidium was taken with the aid of a Stozcist and now we know it is here in Pulton."

Echin turned his eyes towards his brother and they contained an ineffable sadness.

"Do you still accuse him seeing no lie in his imprint and the sacrifice he still makes at my request? Do you expect me to thank Evan for his years of work by doubting his loyalty?" Tormaigh was unmoved.

"Only a Devouril could have found the dark stone where we laid it. Only a Stozcist could reach through the crysaline to release the Perfidium once more."

"Or a Mourangil," pointed out Faer.

"Perhaps we have another Stozcist," Echin suggested.

Faer looked up thoughtfully, "If so this would be the first time to our knowledge that two human Stozcists are alive on Moura."

Echin nodded,

"Evan and those before him did not discover their gift until they reached the age of thirty. Perhaps Candillium's return has ignited the power in a person earlier than it would otherwise have emerged."

Faer looked up thoughtfully, "I cannot feel her presence but I hope you are right."

Tormaigh distorted his long face in what was meant to be a thoughtful frown but somehow just made him look unbalanced.

"You need to spend more time in human form," Echin commented, "You're out of practice."

"I am a Mourangil," Tormaigh shrugged his shoulders and the movement was so awkward that Faer laughed. Tormaigh smiled in response but then his liquid eyes focused gently on Echin.

"Our service is to Moura, to be part of the integral embrace of our planet. You sacrifice much for them but I see your great heart breaking with care for this race over more years than they can understand. "

Echin's expression was solemn.

"They are in peril Tor. Nephragm is here."

The other two Mourangils were silent then Faer sighed, "then this time we must find him. Doubtless it was he who found the spear and opened the pathway for some perverted soul to bring it here. If the Stozcist is under his influence, then…."

"Then Candillium and the Myriar may be lost before even she is found," Echin finished.

Tormaigh bowed his head but ended up knocking it upon the table. He straightened himself up just as the kitchen door opened.

"The young," the Welshman said shaking his head in mock annoyance but beaming with pride, "my grandchildren grow in size and cheek!" Evan's smile slid from his face as he looked around the kitchen.

"You all seem so forlorn!" he commented, his welsh lilt making the word tragic, the expression of excitement falling from his face. It was, to Echin's surprise, Tormaigh that answered.

"No, my friend, we are not forlorn, only narrowed by absence and tainted by long usage." He smiled, "tell us of your family."

Evan felt the room lighten and his eyes sparkled once more as he began in his best bardic voice to give his three guests an account of recent years in the life of his family. He did not mention, though it was evident in the telling, that he had sacrificed their nearness, visiting merely once a year, keeping to Echin's instructions.

Tormaigh listened intently as was always his way, his individual affection subsuming long disillusionment. In many ways, Echin thought, Tor was the most human of the three of them. Then Echin listened with great reverence to a man who had hidden himself away in a dusty bookshop for the last ten years. He had never used his gift for personal gain nor wavered from the instructions he had been asked to follow, and yet in his heart Echinod Deem was aware that his friend's trials had only just begun.

Chapter Six

Kier came downstairs to the sound of a keyboard tapping and she shook her head at Adam as the carriage clock struck six am.

"Adam, how long have you been working?" Her assistant did not register the question, still absorbed in his laptop.

"Your instinct was good," he told her, fingers continuing their rhythm without pause. 'There's something odd about those two pieces. For a start, the record of the robbery has been altered in the police file."

"How do you know?" she enquired nudging alongside him on the sofa. Adam pushed his glasses back above his nose. The screen in front of him had turned empty as Kier sat down.

"Best not to ask." he told her. She opened her mouth to reply but thought better of it. However, Adam obtained it, the information would be accurate, his days on the streets had taught him to be safe and she trusted that his enquiries would be discreet.

"Coffee?" she asked him getting up and heading towards the kitchen. He nodded and the keyboard restarted its customary tapping.

"Can you tell me in what way it was altered?" she asked him, her voice rising above the sound of opening cupboards and filling cups. Adam waited until she was back in the room before replying.

"It records two pieces of quartz, neither in your original inventory. No mention of the obsidian or baryte." Kier came back into the room placing two mugs on the coffee table.

"But why and how?" she asked, looking puzzled.

"The how I can't tell you as the audit trails have been wiped and there's no trace to follow and the why is still a mystery. But..." he changed screens and swung it around to show an excel chart with several items, "the other thing is I didn't buy them, you did!"

"What?" she answered, her brow furrowing.

"According to this file they came with a box of assorted minerals and stones you picked up in Peru."

Kier examined the chart that listed meticulously her purchases in Peru. Pursing her lips, she thought back to Josef and the box of crystals she had put together from the exquisitely crafted goods he had gathered for her. They were all crystalline and there was no obsidian of any colour. The rest of the stones, as far as she could remember, were listed with the obsidian and baryte on Adam's file.

"They may have been added to a box I did buy, I never saw these pieces apart from in the inventory catalogue." The catalogue was compiled when the goods were received in the Manchester warehouse, each piece being photographed and sent to Adam for distribution.

"I remember the photographer said that there was a note inside the box saying 'Pulton.' Actually, being George, he just sent me a picture of the note."

He clicked on the bottom of his screen and a picture of the box of gemstones that kier had purchased filled the screen. There in the middle, looking out of place in their bleakness, were the two added pieces. A simple slip of paper was inside the box with one word "PULTON" written in capitals.

"It's pretty much your style and what you would do." Adam looked at her quizzically. Kier frowned.

"I added that note, but I didn't include the obsidian or baryte." Adam put the laptop on the sofa beside him.

"Smuggled then, we'd best get in touch with the police." He was reaching for his mobile.

"Hang on Adam," Kier put her hand on his, "whoever's responsible for altering the recording of the robbery has to have a police connection. I think we should keep digging for now and then approach someone higher up." Adam paused a moment to think it through and then stood up.

"Fine. I'm going to make some..."

"Toast," she finished for him.

"Toast." He repeated.

"Do you want some or are you going to run for an indecent number of miles?" Kier was already putting on her trainers and smiled.

"Even more indecent than usual, I have a lot to think about."

In Pulton she often ran along the coastline but Kier decided to head inland towards the canal and Roust, billed in tourist language as an historical city of cultural interest. There were very few people about, a couple of cyclists early on but then she was alone, glad the morning was a little cooler than yesterday.

The sense of liberation was intoxicating and she gave herself up to the exercise in those first few miles, her mind wandering once again to the stranger she had seen on the beach, where he could have gone when he crossed the road. A kingfisher sometimes adorned the quietist part of the canal and this morning she was thrilled to see its iridescent blue flash along the embankment. Eventually she headed down to the road and to the city itself. Kier was fully into her stride now, her muscles stretched with fluid rhythm and her skin tingled with sweat. A cobbled path took her down to an impressive castle and up again to the Old Priory.

The view at the top of the hill was spectacular and she took a short breathing space as she pulled her water bottle from the side of her belt. The Lune River ran though the city and down to the sea and its course to the open water was visible from her grassy vantage point. The small city emanated history, it poured from the old buildings such as the Maritime museum on the quay, and even from the river itself so near journeys end.

Stretching her legs, she started to run downhill and came to an abrupt halt. There was a house on the quayside tucked behind the main row, a narrow path led to the gate of the three-storied building. As she went to pass she felt a jolt that began in her stomach and then tingled all the way up her spine.

A man came out of the front door and they made eye contact. He had an angular striking face that most would call handsome but Kier found chilling. His short carefully styled hair was coal black and his skin a Mediterranean brown. His dark eyes held hers for a disturbing length of time and Kier was repelled by the malice in his leering expression but it was he who broke contact first. She dropped to tie a shoelace and watched him go out of vision from the narrow alleyway. Shocked, her hands shook as she squatted down over the opposite knee.

A few moments later a black Mercedes pulled out from a gap between the buildings further along the quay. She saw the cut of an expensive suit and a pristine white shirt as he turned the car. Kier stood up to find herself assaulted by a malignant gaze as the driver locked his eyes with hers for a second time. Disembodied in the driving mirror they were black tunnels that sent spikes of fear leaving her unable to move even as the car disappeared.

Mechanically she stretched up once more and her limbs began to gather their smooth stride. Vaguely she was aware that a truck had pulled out from a warehouse further up the quay. As it came closer she found her legs changing direction, her body jerking off the pavement into the path of the vehicle.

"Move!" A voice screamed from somewhere and she was catapulted in strong arms across the road as the truck swerved, its tyres squealing, dust splaying from the tarmac. Before she could regain her feet, the heavy vehicle had stopped and the driver, pale and shaken, was heading towards her. She unravelled herself from the body that had used itself to cushion her fall, aware only of a tangle of long blond hair.

'Thank you." Kier finally found her voice and she squeezed her rescuer's hand, "sorry," she added turning to the driver of the truck. Then she jerked her limbs into a spurt and ran without looking back. Adrenalin still pumping, she raced across the bridge and back towards the canal, hardly aware that the city had now fully awoken as she dodged other runners and cyclists.

On another occasion, she might have revelled in the short space of time it had taken her to run back to the flat. Flying up the stairs she continued on to her room and slid down behind the door. Her head tilted upwards as she gasped for air, her lungs burnt and she was too breathless to think. Slowly the gulping breaths eased into her normal pattern and she tried to process what had happened. If it hadn't been for the blond-haired man she would have been killed, of that there could be no doubt. Ashamed she berated herself for running away, was she a coward? Why had she acted in a way that felt totally alien to her?

Tears pricked her eyes as she gathered herself up from the floor and staggered into the shower. The cold water stung fresh grazes on her elbows, the only part of her not cushioned by the body of the brave man who had saved her. Why had she not done more to thank him! And the poor truck driver, she could have ended his career! Her momentary glance had seen the stark horror in his wide-eyed and what he knew was to be a futile attempt to avoid hitting her.

She let the water calm her, her hair feeling heavy as she raised it into a soapy mound on top of her head. Afterwards, as she plaited the long strands with practised hands she gave way to a sensation of languor and fell into an exhausted sleep.

Gina's knock woke her and Kier was startled to see it was lunchtime. Her mind shied away from the collection of morbid thoughts that emerged in her consciousness where black eyes followed her every move. She pushed back strands of hair from her face and opened the door. Gina's words however took her straight back to those dark thoughts.

"There's some guy wants to see you, about this morning. Nice," Gina winked. Kier's reaction was to step backwards and her face must have blanched for the other woman moved forward to touch her arm. Kier pulled back involuntarily as her friend touched the graze on her elbow.

"Are you ok?" Gina asked with a look of concern.

Kier nodded, "what does he look like?" she asked, her voice sounded shaky even to her own ears.

"Kind of a built arty type. Long fair hair, a bit above average height." The joking tone had been replaced by a sense of anxiety. Kier sighed with relief and she smiled reassuringly at her friend. She asked Gina to send the visitor up in ten minutes.

"I'll come down to the living room," she told her, suddenly conscious of her state of undress, "where's Adam?"

The other woman shook her head, "he left about half an hour ago, not seen him since."

Gina turned back down the stairs without further questions and Kier headed back towards the bathroom. She bent to pick up her jogging gear from the floor realising that the belt she always wore around her midriff was missing. Cold water helped, its splash brought her fully awake. The eyes that looked back at her in the mirror seemed vulnerable and made her irritated with herself. The wide-eyed mockery of her own image made her reach for some make up to cover the pallor of her face and change the long nightie of a t-shirt to a red blouse and cropped leggings. This guy, she decided, had probably already decided she was incapable.

The knock on the flat door coincided with her descent to the living room. The stranger's acorn brown eyes smiled a charismatic greeting as she opened the door.

"Hi, my name's Siskin," he said in an American accent, "we met this morning, briefly." Kier nodded, and opened the door.

"Kier," she smiled back. Looking uncomfortable she added, "I'm sorry, I should have stayed. I felt I just needed to get away."

"You left this behind," he replied handing her a canvas bag that contained, as she expected, the belt that had obviously slipped off when she hit the pavement. Inside the belt, she knew, were small pockets one of which held business cards for the Seven Rivers and some money.

Kier nodded and signalled him into the room, indicating the armchair. She sat on the sofa noting how the light played favourably upon the angles of his face.

"Thank you, you saved my life," she said seriously. "I can't explain why I ran straight out in front of the truck," she said simply, "you risked your own life to pull me away."

Siskin smiled, shaking his head.

"I was just glad I could be there."

Kier returned his smile with relief but her brown eyes remained large with consternation.

"I didn't even stop to say thank you," she said softly.

"You did say thank you," he replied, "you were in shock, that's all. Then you did your best impression of an Olympic sprinter."

He smiled his admiration, "you were out of sight by the time I picked up the belt." He hesitated a moment and then went on.

"I think I saw a Mercedes just beforehand."

Already pale, Kier's face was now a white mask.

"Yes, I saw it," she told him haltingly.

"Did you see the driver?" he asked, his expression attentive.

"Only for a moment," she replied evasively "why?" When she looked up he was scrutinising her and she was sure that her answer had told him more than she had intended. It was his turn to be evasive.

"Just thought something had distracted your thoughts for you to run out the way you did."

Before he could continue Kier recalled the truck driver.

"Was he alright, the poor man who nearly hit me?"

"Relieved more than anything, decided you must be high on something."

"But you didn't think that?" She looked into his soft brown eyes but there was no hesitation in his reply.

"No, I didn't." Kier looked at him carefully and somewhere inside her she suddenly felt as if she glimpsed an intangible memory that she had always laboured to recognise. There was something important he wasn't telling her, she was certain.

"I'm getting that you're from America, at a guess New York from the accent?" she asked.

He laughed, "good guess, I've was brought up in New York but my mom's from Cumbria and I do a lot of work over here."

"What kind of work?" she queried and then before he could answer added, "What were you doing on the quay?"

"I was running, like you," he told her. "I live up the coast in Bankside. My birth name is Eamon Keogh. I'm a songwriter and I work out most of my lyrics when I run."

"It must be twenty miles round trip," she replied." That's a lot of lyrics."

He shrugged his shoulders and smiled.

"I write a lot of songs."

Vaguely Kier recalled seeing his name in the press and the lean and muscular frame was consistent with a committed runner. He was studying her and Kier said nothing, waiting. Siskin's expression was serious as he reached into his pocket and took out a photograph of a young girl with blonde curling hair. She was laughing delightedly at the photographer and holding a small pink teddy bear.

"Have you by any chance seen her?" he asked.

Surprised Kier reached over and examined the photo carefully. She shook her head.

"I'm sorry, no," she told him. "Who is she?"

Siskin sighed.

"A friend's daughter. She went missing some weeks ago."

In response to the puzzled expression on her face he continued, "I am a runner and a songwriter. But I also work for an organisation called 'Red Light.' its purpose is to stop human trafficking. A number of missing children have been tracked to Roust and then seemed to disappear into mid-air. The man in the Mercedes is called Alex Jackson, I think he's involved. I should tell you I have no proof."

Kier shivered, "then why do you think he's involved?" she asked. The visitor placed the photograph carefully back in his wallet.

"Red Light has tracked his movements over the last five years. He's visited Peru on a number of occasions. Jackson has been known to have had contact with operators involved in the sale of human organs and children."

Kier gasped as he mentioned Peru and the man called Eamon Keogh sharpened his glance. Quickly she went on, "why would anyone do something so evil? "Even as she spoke she remembered her chilling response to the man in the Mercedes.

Siskin stood up, his eyes flint.

"Money mainly. And a total disregard for human life other than their own." He paused and held her eyes for a moment, his expression grim. "And with Jackson I suspect even darker motives, he's known to dabble in occult artefacts."

From his back pocket, he took out a business card with a mobile number written on it and nothing else.

"Just in case you come across anything that you think relevant," he explained.

Kier nodded, raising herself from the couch and accompanying him to the door.

"Thank you again," she said, holding out her hand.

"Please. There's no need to thank me," he told her as he took it.

"Take care of yourself," he said seriously and he turned to descend the staircase. Kier watched him go with regret, her hand trembling slightly on the side of the door.

She was still stood there a few moments later when Adam entered the flat and ascended the stairs with a loaf of bread, a quizzical expression on his face.

"So, what's Eamon Keogh doing in our humble abode?" he asked her as he followed her back inside the living room, "I take it you had a good run to bring home such a distinguished prize."

"Adam your incorrigible." she laughed, "how did you know his name?"

"One day I'll introduce you to the joys of the written word," he replied, "they sometimes come with pictures."

He dived out of the way as she picked up a cushion and threw it at him, ducking into the kitchen. As he made coffee she felt duty bound to give him an account of the morning's events. She explained how she had foolishly run into the path of a HGV and was saved by a passing jogger who turned out to be the songwriter.

"Impressive," he told her. "Good choice of hero, Eamon Keogh was American Special Forces before he became a songwriter."

"Really?" another shock, she thought. "He looks so gentle."

He shrugged, "smart and tough. And he likes you," he added shrewdly. Kier ignored the comment.

"There was something else Adam," and the tremble in her voice made him switch off the coffee maker to hear her more clearly.

"Do you think you could see if you can find anything on a local man named Alex Jackson?"

"Why?" he asked, tight lipped.

"He was nearby. I didn't like the feel of him and Siskin thinks he's got something to do with missing children."

She repeated what her visitor had told her and Adam listened, his green eyes darkening.

"Is this really something you want to get involved with?" he asked her seriously.

Kier's response was a nod of her head, her eyes meeting his as he fidgeted with the bridge of his glasses and nodded in return.

Adam turned back to the kitchen and Kier returned to the sofa. A few minutes later he put a mug of coffee beside her.

"I know I said Pulton was the place for suicidal intent," he told her, "thank you for verifying that fact but I need a little more notice if I'm to wind up your affairs."

She smiled, too weary to notice that Adam seemed to share her own loss of appetite as the toast remained unmade. Kier curled her long legs beneath her, grateful for the close friendship she shared with the quirky individual absently sipping his coffee, attributing his unusually quiet demeanour as admonishment for her stupidity.

Her mind drifted to the homeless shelter four years ago. New Year's Eve and the smell of hot bread as she spread thick butter on to each slice. It was how she filled the public holidays when Gally was not there. Her naïve idea of volunteer work had already been banished to a sentimental memory by that time.

The shelter was a sixth form block that converted to a stable of makeshift beds over the Christmas period. Marta, a black African woman with a cherubic face and a voice like a bellows, wheezed her way round the kitchen opening shoe boxes filled with tins, most of them given by kids from the school. She remembered the compassionate but completely wary eyes of Tony the shelter manager, a mental health nurse in his forties. He held the keys to the cupboards and carefully weighed his resources and responsibilities. Kier was both. She deflected his skilled questioning with an ease that surprised her at the time but Marta was less subtle.

"What you doin' here girl on New Year's Eve? You like me? Family all gone?" Kier's insides had lurched; Gally was with a group of students abroad and her hope that her parents, at least one, would return to England, had died. Marta had a handful of individually wrapped pieces of Christmas cake and shoved a packet in front of Kier, nodding her head towards a bed in the far corner. Kier picked up the cake and made her way through the various human bundles. The central heating fermented the smell of the street. Grey blankets were hung to mark individual space as men and women slept in every stitch they owned. This shelter was a last chance of refuge over Christmas for those who had nowhere else to go. Most of them slept, some scavenged, continually waiting for the times when Tony took out his keys to the store cupboard, watching everything that came in and out.

Many had been brought down by drugs or drink. Others chattered to themselves, exhibiting the movements and traits associated with severe and enduring mental illness. Tragic stories were commonplace in an understated underclass. As she reached the other side of the room the bundle of clothes stirred and Adam's green eyes, overlarge in his emaciated face, looked at her for the first time. Physical, biting, intolerable misery screamed silently at her in that one look. Against everything she had been told and taught she sat on the bed and cradled the wasted form in her arms. In moments Marta and Tony were beside the bed.

"He's ill, really ill." Kier's voice was trembling, Adam had become unconscious in her arms. Tony was examining him with experienced hands.

"His breath is shallow and his pulse rapid, I think he's bleeding somewhere," he said tersely. "He's very young, no more than early twenties. He must have slipped in off the street while I was doing the rounds of the shops. No smell of alcohol."

Tony turned his head away from Adam and spoke urgently, "call an ambulance Marta."

There was a doctor who came twice in the two weeks. Most of the clients had no access to health care, long ago forgetting who might have been their registered GP. Tony clearly felt that he couldn't wait until the Doctor visited again in two days' time.

Adam would have died of internal bleeding had he not been operated on that night when his spleen was removed and his punctured lung repaired. It was clear that he had been the victim of a savage beating but Adam said nothing but his name. He carried no identification nor money. Kier sat by his bedside listening to his disturbed memories knowing that somehow their lives had become inextricably linked. It was assumed that the incident was robbery and probably drug-related, she knew better.

It was strange to Kier that he so often referred to that terrible night as fortunate. He described it as his re-birth. She had never told him what she had overheard in the long hours as she sat in the hospital side room praying for him to recover, the disjointed story of a beating he had endured by someone he loved. Suddenly she realised Adam was speaking again.

"You're shattered Kier. Put your feet up and take it easy this afternoon, watch a film and forget."

She smiled and let him fuss her a little, he put on a DVD of the film 'Casablanca' that she loved and then tapped away at his keyboard most of the afternoon.

Kier drifted in and out of sleep wishing her brother was nearer remembering suddenly how near he was.

"Adam I'm heading to the Dales tomorrow," she told him as she roused herself.

He looked across but continued to tap on the computer. "I'll get a hire car sorted. Do you want me to come with you?" She smiled at his noble sacrifice but her tone was serious.

"Actually, I know I promised you could go back home but I'd be really grateful if you stay here." The rhythmic tapping hardly changed pace as he looked over his glasses and nodded.

Chapter Seven

The last of the daylight had slipped beyond the horizon more than two hours ago, and the sea was lost in darkness, but every breath Luke took gave him an awareness of its nearness. A distinctive salty tang mingled with damp leaves and the rich earth of nearby farms. The remains of a climbing frame stood isolated in the centre of the small park, the metal chains from the swings hanging motionless and limp.

Leaning against the railings that signalled the entrance to the play area Luke flicked open his mobile phone to check the time. It was past midnight. Agitated now he scanned the park again, checking the dusty tracks leading in and out, his eyes straining to see past the meagre light that splashed down from the single street lamp above.

Once more he considered moving towards the woodland and waiting in the shadow but with the hood of his dark tracksuit pulled up and the jacket zipped to the top only his eyes could be seen properly and anyway, he didn't want to get his trainers dirty. His eyes came to rest at the bag by his feet, a simple black rucksack unadorned by designer badges or colour.

It was the bag's contents though that had him on edge. Although Luke had had encounters with the police before and was no stranger to breaking the law, he had only previously committed, what he considered, small misdemeanours. He enjoyed getting wrecked and had done drugs, none of the harder stuff of course just weed, coke and pills. This had led, on more than one occasion, to vandalism or fighting but he shrugged away the thought. Isn't that what everyone does at sixteen? This however was the first time he had broken into anywhere and stolen something, and now the thought didn't seem to fit well with him.

Thrusting his hands into his pockets Luke remembered the conversation with Brassock. The brute of an ex-doorman had just sniggered at him, revealing crooked and broken teeth in a gash of a mouth.

"Well, if you haven't got the bottle to make a bit of cash from stealing a few rocks, I'll find someone else," he rasped, his gravel voice filled with mockery. Luke had tried to meet his gaze but one glance from the fierce dark eyes and he dropped his own.

"The alarm'll be taken care of," he coaxed, "nobody lives upstairs so no one will hear broken glass." He'd handed him a small axe and Luke had nodded his agreement. Brassock, an ugly snigger on his face, had strolled away. Angry now at the memory and at himself for being soft and feeling guilty, Luke kicked at the bag.

"Who cares about a few rocks anyway," he said to himself out loud.

"I do."

Luke immediately recognised the voice and turned to look into the shadows, his heartbeat racing. Sweat beaded his forehead, he had expected to see a car coming or at least hear the big man approach but Brassock stepped into the semi-circle of light at the park's entrance without warning.

Once again Luke took in the man's size. A few inches over six foot he was naturally big, meaning he towered over Luke, but it was the thick layers of muscle that sprang from his shoulders fattening the ex-bouncer's neck that added to the impression of size. Luke winced as he looked up into the older man's face. Completely bald the skin of Brassock's head was drawn tight over his skull, his features sunken and lined like one of the broken and dented knuckles that protruded from his huge fists. As soon as he was within arm's length Brassock, a contemptuous expression on his face, slapped Luke. His face stung as the calloused palm hit him, knocking the hood from his head and forcing him side-wards, immediately the youth's face flushed as he filled with rage.

"Don't kick my property." Brassock said his deep voice rumbling. Stooping down he picked up the bag, opened it and checked the contents. Appearing satisfied he turned and began to move back into the shadows.

"What about my money?" Luke called after him, not being able to keep the slight tremble of suppressed anger from his voice. The big man paused and turned.

"Temper, temper," the corrosive voice whispered dangerously and Luke's anger fled to be replaced by gnawing fear, but he stood his ground. Brassock laughed derisively and reached into his pocket to pull out a plastic bag the size of his hand that he threw towards Luke.

"Not bad for a trip to Pulton and an easy target like the Seven Rivers," he sneered.

Luke wanted to shout why hadn't he done it himself if it was so easy but the fresh and pungent smell of skunk reached his nose. Confused Luke looked at the bag at his feet, there was easily an ounce there, worth more than the money that that had been agreed for the rocks.

"That's not what we said?" he ventured, still not picking up the bag. The big man shrugged.

"I figured that's where the money would go, might as well miss out the middle man. Is there a problem?" he asked, taking a threatening step back towards the youth. Luke shook his head and picked up the bag. Brassock turned and walked back into the shadows, the stolen stones stored in the rucksack, one thick arm through one strap and the other hanging down like a noose against the broad expanse of his back. Pulling the hood back into place Luke pushed the cannabis into his pocket and walked back onto the estate.

Brassock watched the boy leave from just inside the woodland and smiled to himself. He had placed himself in the shadow of the trees, his long black jacket drawn around him and watched the boy approach. He had stood there in silence with his massive arms across his chest as the lad had nervously peered into the shadows. The brutish figure had waited in amusement, watching Luke become more and more agitated as the minutes went by.

He had taken the lad for a coward, not wanting to wait in the dark, which was why the flash of anger in the boy's eyes had genuinely surprised him as he had slapped him. He had also seen the anger fade and fear replace it but being a fighter Brassock knew it was that first emotion, that initial reaction that ultimately defined people. Staring along the road as the small hooded figure disappeared from view, he mentally revised his opinion of Luke but then the vibrating in his pocket interrupted his thoughts. Scooping out the phone he pressed it to his ear, a frown adding to the creases along his forehead.

"I've got them, on my way back now." He kept his voice even, there was a pause as he listened and then he spoke in slow grating tones.

"No sir, not seen him. Ungrateful little wretch. No, I'll tell the others and come right back with the stones." He ended the call and tapped in some numbers. "The lad's taken some things from the house, boss wants them back. Find him." He listened impatiently for a second and then angrily growled into the phone. "No, tomorrow won't do. Take Cross and find him tonight." Without waiting for a reply, he ended the call and stuffed the phone back into his pocket. Swearing he picked up the bag and moved into darkness.

Five minutes later when the park was deserted a massive oak shook its leaves and disgorged a lean figure that had witnessed the whole scene. Klim straightened himself up and headed after Luke, but his friend was out of sight. Catching his breath, his eyes searched the different paths that Luke could have taken. He decided they would leave him too exposed to his uncle's private henchmen. With movements as quiet and graceful as so many other hunted creatures, he turned and ran back into the woodland.

*

Klim was short for Michael Klimzcak; eighteen today. Brushing back his short black hair he wiped away the sweat that had beaded at his temples. His olive complexion was stained with dirt and the grey hoody and dark jeans he wore were splattered with mud. He had managed to evade pursuit until he had been seen buying water at a garage just out of town. They had almost caught him but were unable to match his speed as he ran towards the densely-forested area that rose high above Bankside.

Taking slow deep breaths, he tried to lower his heartbeat so that he could listen. At first there was nothing and a spark of hope began to flutter in his stomach, only to be extinguished moments later when he heard heavy footsteps drawing closer from beyond the tree line on the left.

"Great birthday," he muttered, then pushed himself to his feet and began once again to weave through the darkness, avoiding as best he could the trees that sprang out of the blackness around him.

Moving deeper into the wooded area, Klim didn't try to force his pace. The last thing he wanted was to trip over a root or stumble down a sudden drop. He knew that this was not an ideal situation, he had never ventured this deep into the woods at Bankside but, he reasoned, it was a better option than facing the two men that pursued him.

Klim cut sharply to the right, as he did so his left foot slid from beneath him. Quickly he corrected himself but a branch whipped across his face and before he could stop himself he let out a grunt of pain. Immediately he dropped down behind another thicket.

Peering between the tightly knitted branches he once again slowed his breath and listened for any sign that his pursuers had heard him. Reaching up to his face he felt blood leaking from a gash running along his cheek and down to his jaw.

At that moment, a wave of anger swept over Klim and he clenched his fists, trying to fight it back down. It was not in his nature to react to situations angrily but this was almost more than he could take, to be hunted in the middle of the night by men working for one of only two blood relatives left in his life. A man's face appeared in his mind with cold, hate-filled eyes and the rage threatened to engulf him. Abruptly the image of a woman replaced the man's face, kind features with soft brown eyes and long fair hair moving towards grey.

The anger faded and he breathed in deeply allowing the air to come out slowly. Calm now he could hear the leaves rustling as a slight breeze moved through the branches of the surrounding trees but there were no footsteps and he toyed with the hope that they hadn't heard him. As if summoned by this thought however a beam of light flashed through the trees aimed directly at him.

"He's here, I can see him!" came the call.

It was the hard-edged voice of Banks. In his twenties, he had gladly joined his uncle's team of ex-mercenaries that satisfied his vicious nature and paid him well. Immediately Klim lurched to his feet and broke into a run, this time he didn't hold back, the trees flashed past him, luck and quick reaction saving him from colliding with denser and denser woodland. Suddenly he found himself facing a wooden fence as tall as himself, only just managing to stop before crashing into it.

For a moment, he considered the absurdity of a man-made fence being this deep in the woods then he placed his hands atop the fence and with little difficulty pulled himself up and over to land lightly on the other side. Klim focused on the darkness around him, where the ground was clear of trees but seemed darker somehow and smoother. He edged forward and found himself moving downhill, after a few steps understanding dawned on him, it was water.

Casting a nervous glance behind him he could see the beams of light from his pursuer's torches flickering amongst the trees beyond the fence. Turning back to the pond he moved out into the water, wading slowly deeper and deeper until his feet barely touched the slippery bottom. Then he began to swim finding himself in the middle of the pond where tall green shoots broke the surface.

Grimly Klim drew himself up amongst the bed of reeds and clinging to them he did what he could to pull them around him. Once he considered himself hidden he stared at the fence he had climbed only moments before. Would they see the fence? Would they cross it? Time dragged out before him as he waited until his questions were answered by the heavy thud of boots on soft earth. Between the reeds, he could make out two tall shapes moving amongst the shadows at the edge of the water and recognised the leaner one as Banks. He was peering out at the water.

"You're here boy, I can smell you. Your dear uncle wants you back. Make it easy and come out now." The voice was as slippery as the mud that seeped into his boots.

"If you make this hard," another voice added, "you won't get back to him without, shall we say, a mishap." This time the voice was guttural and abrupt, the sadistic Cross, expelled from his unit for misconduct with women. On one occasion, Klim remembered overhearing his uncle's furious voice, 'don't ever touch my property' he'd told him threateningly, his black eyes assaulting the other man, "If you are unable to control your lascivious instincts I will have no further use for you." Cross had paled and rambled pathetically that it wouldn't happen again. As Klim had edged towards the open door of his Father's study he saw his uncle turn and then the other man was suddenly writhing in pain on the floor. The polished shoes had stepped over the doubled up figure, ignoring the breathless grunts of pain, meeting Klim's eyes with a look of sneering hatred.

The torches began to scan the water and Klim closed his eyes, frightened of a reflection. His pulsed raced; if they found him he would fight but he knew he would eventually be dragged back to the hunting lodge. And more than likely severely beaten along the way. Suddenly Klim experienced a new sensation. Even though his eyes were shut he became aware of Cross, recognising the older man's fear that they had lost him. Flashes of the jagged contents of the other man's mind broke into Klim's own consciousness and he became aware for certain that Cross was torn between searching the pond and heading back out into the forest.

Mentally he began to reach out further; a bright light broke his concentration. When he opened his eyes, he could see that the two men had tripped the motion sensor of a large lamp hanging over the door of a stone building. The pond remained in relative darkness but the two pursuers were illuminated as they stood in the middle of what his mother would have called a large wildflower garden.

"Can I help you?" Klim's view of the door was obscured but images flashed through his mind of pages of music notes, half written melodies, scores covered with annotations. He glimpsed the silhouette of a man no taller than himself but stockier. The voice sounded American. It was soft but direct and with no hint of fear although both the mercenaries looked what they were, their natural meanness obvious in their whole demeanour.

There had been no aggression in his challenge but it was a challenge nevertheless and Klim realised that he could sense Cross's reaction to the other man, a faint recognition and a reluctance to enter into conflict, he was uncharacteristically cautious.

"We're looking for someone," Cross said firmly, his eyes continuing to search the garden but glancing only fleetingly over the pond. "Our friend's nephew, the boy is sick with grief and we worry he may do himself some harm alone and away from home." The insincerity sang out loud and Klim was certain that the householder could hear it as clear as he could himself.

"Well if I see something that may help you I'll report it." The man had not moved from beneath the light and his voice remained neutral.

"Would you mind if we searched amongst your property for a moment?" Cross asked.

"As I said, I'll let you know if anything untoward happens, right now I'm heading for bed and I'd like to see you both on your way before I go." This time the man's reply was not neutral. A hint of hard anger crept into his tone.

"But surely..." Cross began.

Something passed between the men that Klim could not see but only sense. It stretched out for a few moments and then passed. He felt his pursuers' acquiescence as the unknown voice spoke again, softly neutral.

"I trust you can return the way you came." Klim saw his two pursuers walk along the path and exit the property, the silhouette under the light moved a little across the path and then he heard a bolt slide into place on a wooden gate. Klim was waiting for the man to enter the house but caught his breath as moments later he saw a shadow loom up in front of the pond. Panic hit him as he peered through the reeds and he felt his heart beat rapidly. After a few seconds, the figure turned and moved back into his home. Klim let out his breath hurriedly.

"The door is open. I imagine you're rather cold by now."

The words floated back out of the house. The man had known he was there. As the thought registered the stranger's words hit home and Klim did in fact begin to shiver. Although it seemed stupid to enter the home of a man he didn't know the options seemed limited. His uncle's two hunters would most likely be waiting beyond the fence, and tired and wet as he was he wouldn't get far. His decision made he pulled himself upright and began to wade towards the house.

The door was indeed open but Klim saw that it was solid and contained three mortise locks. Once closed it meant to stay closed. It led into an old-fashioned farmhouse kitchen that was sparse but clean.

'There's a towel and some clothes on the chair," came the American voice from another room. It was only at that point that he realised that he was dripping on the stone floor. Shivering he quickly dried and changed into jogging bottoms that pulled slack round his waist, and a grey oversized sweatshirt. He ran his hand over the gash on his face, wiping away dried blood. He was most grateful for the clean socks realising for the first time just how cold and wet he had become

There were sounds upstairs and Klim ventured into the next room, which was clearly a music room. It had a keyboard, guitar, stacks of sheet music on shelves and a sophisticated sound system. This led into the main lounge, which was large with bookshelves lining the walls. The furniture looked as if it was from the original farmhouse including a huge fireplace. Another guitar, an expensive looking one, sat in a stand on the fireplace. Klim reached out to touch it but drew his hand back as he heard his host putting more than the normal locks into place on the front door before returning into the main room.

At first appearance, the man stood before him was menacing, his head encased in a black wool hat. Klim's eyes flickered towards the kitchen door that still remained open, moving automatically back towards it. The householder laughed and removed his hat and suddenly his whole look changed. The man who appeared to have come to his aid was no more than thirty with long fair hair tied back in a ponytail. He wore an earring in his left ear and now Klim noticed he had the kind of soft features of an artist. As he came towards his unexpected houseguest the man peered at him carefully and Klim felt a jolt of recognition that he found hard to understand. It was the first time they had met. A hand reached out towards him.

"I'm Siskin." Klim's hand was shaken firmly but was not the test of strength that his uncle had always managed to make it. The accent was American and pleasant.

"Klim," he replied a little shakily. Siskin's eyes examined him as he offered a drink and the younger man realized he was suddenly parched.

"Water would be great thanks."

Siskin disappeared to the kitchen and once again he heard the sound of locks being put into place. Klim reached out with his thoughts and to his surprise found he was quickly able to get a feel for those of the other man. It was a mind that saw the world in terms of sound and melody, his whole psyche was filled with music and extreme contrast. The younger man was also able to understand that his companion had reciprocated the jolt of recognition that he had felt. Siskin had returned with the water and signalled for Klim to take a seat, making himself comfortable in the armchair opposite.

"So, what did you do to incur the wrath of the mighty Alex Jackson?"

Klim gasped in surprise that the stranger had made the link between his attackers and his uncle.

"Why do you say that?" he asked trying to regain his calm. Siskin held his eyes.

"Those two sadists look for the chance to torture and get paid doing it. They've been working for Jackson for the best part of five years."

"Who are you?" Klim asked, suspicious. Siskin smiled slightly.

"I'm an ex-soldier and you're Jackson's nephew if I'm not mistaken"

"How do you know who I am?" He was disturbed now. "Do you work for someone?"

"Only for a purpose and I promise you that I've no intention to harm you or any of your friends. Jackson however is another story."

"They may come here to look for me." Klim said apprehensively.

"I wouldn't worry about that," the ex-soldier replied and Klim believed him.

'Thanks for helping but I should go," the youth said, placing the glass on the floor and standing.

"My pleasure," Siskin replied and then as Klim started back towards the kitchen the man with so much music in his head added softly, "you look to me like someone who might need a place to stay. I've a spare room if you want it."

Klim automatically felt uneasy with the offer but there was nowhere to go except Gabbie's house and although he had always kept his closeness to her secret, he couldn't take the chance that his uncle hadn't found out about her and was even now spinning some story inside the small railway cottage. The thought of his uncle near Gabbie appalled him and suddenly he felt an unaccustomed relief that her Dad was back home. The other option would be to go back to his room in the hotel where he worked but that would be the first place they looked.

Klim looked up to see Siskin busying himself rearranging CDs as he mulled over his offer. His brain told him that to trust a complete stranger was madness, his gut told him otherwise. He had felt an instant liking for the other man.

"Thanks, I could do with some sleep," he said smiling. Siskin nodded, it felt as if they had both passed the other's unspoken test. Within ten minutes Klim was upstairs on a single bed and he barely noticed the simple bedroom as he fell into an exhausted sleep.

Chapter Eight

On Monday morning, busy roads soon gave way to deserted lanes as Kier headed towards the Dales in a hired jeep. The sunshine of the coast was replaced with an introspective white mist as she pulled on to a narrow track that edged along the side of a mountain. The engine deepened its hum as she lowered gear to negotiate a bend and then the road stretched into the distance. The mist seemed to fold the way ahead into a detached entity that continued much longer than she had expected from Gally's directions. There was a small parking area on the left-hand side and she pulled over to check the map and realised she was only a mile away from the Inn where Gally had booked rooms for them both.

The morning was getting hotter and the mist beginning to disperse and she realised she had pulled up at the start of a footpath that seemed to lead across the fields towards the valley edge. There was so little of her journey left and plenty of time before Gally expected her to arrive so Kier felt comfortable in giving in to the impulse to explore.

She grabbed a light padded waistcoat to wear over her shirt and grabbed walking boots from the back of the jeep. As she pulled on the boots sitting on the edge of the vehicle she realised that she had not seen another car for miles. Looking back down the hill, she saw that dry-stone walls lined the deserted road and that these appeared to be the definitive feature of the area. Kier climbed the wooden ladder that straddled the wall and as she stood at the top she was struck by the profound absence of human sound. The odd protest from nearby sheep and occasional warble of tiny birds was all that disturbed the silence and yet these sounds were so much part of the landscape that they seemed, if anything, to add to the sense of isolation.

The path was easy to follow across the field but soon she found herself on a wide stretch of grooved rock and had to concentrate on her footing. Reaching the edge, she stopped to catch her breath and then gasped with pleasure at the view that opened out before her. The limestone pavement on which she stood formed a cliff overlooking an imposing valley.

Green pastures rolled away in front of her down towards a river that was drained low, exposing part of its pebbled bed. The fields were interspersed and bordered by huge expanses of naked grey-white rock similar to the one on which she now stood. A gentle breeze tickled her neck and she breathed in the distinct air of the northern dales, the damp scent of river-soaked earth, the heady aroma of living wood and the unmistakable bouquet of animal life. Gally had once described this part of England as his favourite place on earth and she could understand why.

He had taught at the University in Manchester for a few years and made periodic trips all over the country to examine different landscapes, but she knew this location was special for him. The thought of her brother made her smile and the growl in her stomach brought home the realisation that she had yet to have breakfast. Kier lifted her arms to take off and replace the scrunchy so that her hair was firmly tucked into it once more. As she did so the mist fully cleared so that she could see across the river valley to the opposite side.

The hairs on her exposed neck tingled and a sense of dread blotted out the serenity of the morning. Two figures were becoming visible as they reached the far side of the opposite scar. She flattened herself on top of the rock and eased herself into a rectangular space between the patchwork of stones.

There was no way that she could be sure that the slim figure of the dark-haired man she had just glimpsed was her attacker of the previous morning. She closed her eyes and examined what she had seen, a man of medium height dressed in a red top and dark pants. For some minutes, she reverted to the paralysed state that had almost been her undoing yesterday, her limbs froze even in the gathering heat.

Eventually anger released her immobility, she was furious with herself for over-reacting. Just as she was about to pull herself up however a shadow fell across the limestone. Kier realised she was completely trapped, hemmed in the small space. The scuffle of boots came from directly above her inadequate hiding place.

"Hi, you ok?" The voice was female and warm, possibly with a touch of American or Canadian accent. Kier turned her face upwards and was dazzled by sunlight that seemed to thread itself through the woman's blond hair giving a translucent glow to her face. She held out her hand and Kier allowed herself to be helped back upon the limestone pavement.

A quick glance across the valley revealed a landscape void of human movement and she sighed in relief. When she turned back to the woman she realised that she was older than she had first thought, perhaps in her forties. Her hair was worn long and loose and her small face had a glow of health. Kier found herself smiling easily at the petite woman with cornflower blue eyes who completely ignored that fact she offered no explanation for being found prised between the rocks.

"I'm Marianne. I often sit on the edge of the scar looking at the valley, it's my daily fix!"

She smiled revealing a perfect set of teeth that confirmed Kier's idea that she was from across the Atlantic and yet she seemed completely at home in the landscape. To Kier she was like a rock sprite, wise looking and beautiful. The green shorts and t-shirt seemed somehow not to detract from her overall ethereal quality.

"Kier," she offered, "the view is certainly breath-taking." A wide grin spread over the other woman's face.

" Gally's sister!" Kier smiled with relieved surprise, realising who her new companion must be from conversation with her brother

"You own the place where Gally is staying."

"And where you're booked in tonight," she laughed. "Gally has told us so much about you." She hooked her arm in that of the younger woman as they made their way back down the path and chattered easily dispersing what now seemed to Kier the foolish fear of an overactive imagination.

The Inn of the Three Mountains was the romantic title given to the only pub in a radius of ten miles and was known locally simply as the Mountain. Kier pulled the jeep into the car park behind Marianne's Peugeot estate and was struck with the isolation of the building. The pub was stone built, etched into the side of the mountain and surrounded only by fields. The nearest of these to the car park was filled with tents and Marianne explained that the Inn was a favourite for cavers and hikers. The heavy front door was already open revealing a porch filled with leaflets and notices of local events. A door to the right led to the main room and this was smaller and cosier than she had assumed from the outside.

The floor was blue slate and complemented a huge stone fireplace by which stood baskets of logs and brass tools. The grate had been cleaned and logs laid ready for lighting. The building's original features had been preserved including solid oak beams and wood framed windows and the benches were cloister style with high carved backs and long flat cushions either side of heavy wooden tables. Two spacious window seats added to the welcoming character of the room but its most eye-catching feature was the bar that gleamed with old-fashioned pumps and a string of real ales.

It was dotted with sketches of people that appeared to have been drawn within the room while the walls to either side of the bar provided the backdrop for a series of black and white eighteenth century prints. Of pride of place however, to the right of the main window, was a large framed colour poster of a cave where the ceiling domed high above the heads of two helmeted cavers. The excitement of discovery in their eyes shone brighter than the lamps that illumined a bejewelled hall of encrusted minerals where daggers of stalactites froze in suspended fall.

The building was unique and authentic; a no-frills luxury for anyone who wanted to share the land around it.

"What an amazing place!" Kier was gratified to see Marianne's pleasure at a compliment she must have heard so many times before.

"It's converted from a farm that belonged to my husband's family."

As if on cue a man appeared from behind the bar carrying a crate of empty bottles from an underground cellar. His face lit up when he saw his wife who introduced their latest arrival. As he shook her hand Kier was struck with the complete contrast between husband and wife.

Matthew Allithwaite was well over six feet, large framed and completely bald. As if in compensation he had grown a thick black moustache that covered his top lip. He had the kind of raw and natural strength that came from generations of men who worked the land and although he looked older than his wife Kier suspected that this was not the case. His eyes twinkled but he spoke very little and she was later to learn that his reserve was pretty much legend in this part of the country. Gally later told her that a twitch of his moustache could signal last orders better than any bell.

After the introductions, Matthew nodded towards the far door from which came the wonderful aroma of home cooked English breakfast.

"Go straight in," Marianne encouraged, "I'll bring you a menu." The breakfast room contained four tables but only one was occupied. Gally sat with a coffee in front of him, his head, a mass of dark curls, bent over reading as usual. She pulled out the chair opposite and he looked up startled, his soft brown eyes still containing a look of sleep.

"Kier!" He stood up, a good four inches taller than his sister and enveloped her in a bear hug that reminded her that he had spent his university life and most of his free time playing rugby. Her heart filled with pride at the sight of him as it always did and she felt her eyes welling with tears of relief. She had not managed to wipe them completely without him noticing but with his residual tact he said nothing. The look of concern in his eyes meant that he would allow her to tell him in her own time.

Breakfast was one of the best she had experienced partly because of Gally, partly the excellent food and partly because the Mountain was the kind of place that would always lend itself to enriching whatever experience you brought beneath its roof. Content, she listened as her brother began to explain that he was planning to work on Whistmorden Scar that afternoon and that he had been prompted to come back to the Dales to examine some bizarre results one of his students had obtained.

Glad to have something to distract her from her own brooding thoughts she cheerfully volunteered to help. Gally looked at her speculatively, his head tilting to one side, his sister was not known for a keen interest in his work. She'd listened patiently enough to him over the years but her eyes usually glazed over after the third sentence.

"Hmm," he considered, stroking his chin. Gally stood up and threw her an apple that she promptly caught. "Come on then," he laughed and put his arm round her shoulder as they left the kitchen together.

*

Kier was saturated with a sense of pure unexpected joy as she accompanied Gally on the climb up Whistmorden Scar. She had walked for hours around the city and been involved in many sports but she had done little fell walking before now. The miles of dry stone walling seemed to signify the interlocking of man with a landscape carved by ice and filled with green moorland that had borne thousands of years of footprints.

There were rolling hills from the top of which it was possible to see distant contours of the ridge valley that spanned a river's length. At one point the aloof faces of the three mountains seemed to peer impassively with different profiles at the creeping life that traversed their surfaces.

Gally explained that Ravensmount, on the other side of the valley, was considered the hardest climb with some treacherous paths. The dark brooding mountain raised its pointed head in the North. Towards the East was Greenmasthow, flat topped, lending itself to visitors in its natural stepped ridges. The last of the three was Overidgetor, just visible to the south and the highest point in the landscape, calmly accepting the clear paths eroded into its Southern flank. Outside of these paths however, it was plain that a walker could become quickly lost. Up here there was little use for Sat nav and no signals on their mobiles. Even with his familiarity of the place Kier knew her brother had packed emergency supplies and carried an ordinance survey map and compass.

He explained some of the geological features of the landscape and she found herself fascinated by his description of how the different layers of rock held fossilised clues of the land's history. At the top of the scar they picked their way carefully over the crevassed surface and made for the shade of the long reaching branches of a single tree. The edge of the pavement lent itself easily to a seated picnic spot and Kier gratefully accepted a bottle of water and sandwiches unpacked from Gally's rucksack. They ate in silence, each absorbing the surroundings and the modest sense of achievement from the climb.

Shortly after they had eaten Kier found herself carefully holding a glass thermometer as her brother unravelled his athletic frame and laid aside the safety glasses. He moved his feet carefully to avoid the small crevasse from which he had just chiselled a sliver of grey-white rock. Taking a few steps backwards to his rucksack he wrapped the sample in newspaper and placed it in a labelled plastic bag and then gently added it to several others that he had already taken. He marked the area on his geological map and made detailed notes in his logbook

"Baffling," he said out loud, shaking his head.

"What is?" Kier asked.

Her brother looked up and gestured outwards with his arms to cover the length of Whistmorden scar on which they were standing,

"This. I've already tested around the perimeter and the samples I've taken from the middle today will probably confirm what I already know."

She walked towards him and packed the thermometer in its case and placed it in the rucksack. He was totally pre-occupied by whatever puzzle the limestone pavement presented and she had been reluctant to break his concentration working silently with him throughout the afternoon. Once prompted at the right time however she knew Gally would explain in detail.

"I have a student named Philip Challon. He came up a few weeks ago, his tests showed some changes but this is far more widespread. The samples all appear to be carboniferous limestone but have virtually none of its chemical properties. I don't even recognise some of the mineral compositions. And what's so ridiculous is I mapped this area two years ago, without anything unusual showing up. It's as if the rock is metamorphosing. Kier, this is limestone country and I can't find real limestone on this part of Whistmorden scar!"

Unconsciously he swept back the dark hair at his temple and focused troubled eyes on the surrounding countryside. White rock edged this part of the river valley imprinting its criss-cross pattern on the landscape and looking raw and bleak in the dusk. It was aptly called a 'scar' as if the land had been severed to expose its entrails that spilled out in rock screes across the hills that were now hardened and healed with the passage of time.

"Do you know what's causing it?" Kier asked him, her brother's anxiety transmitting itself.

He shook his head, "nope, and it's gonna take better brains than mine to figure it out. Come on sis it's going to be dark soon, we'd best get going."

They were on the same side of the valley that she had been on that morning but virtually opposite the Inn.

"Where's that?" Kier enquired pointing to the opposite ridge. Gally answered automatically his mind preoccupied with possible explanations for the strange phenomenon he had witnessed.

"Ravenscar," he told her, unaware of the consternation on his sister's face.

He turned towards her and sighed, "look I'm gonna have to get back to Manchester first thing tomorrow with this lot, sorry Kier, had hoped we could do some walking together."

She squeezed his arm trying to hide her disappointment with a smile.

"No probs, I could do to get back anyway."

On the way, down it took all her concentration for Kier to keep pace with her brother without losing footing on the difficult terrain. Gally's anxiety had subsumed her own, his sense of urgency heightened her deep-seated alarm that things had suddenly ceased to be ok. He had chosen a difficult short cut outside the normal paths that brought them down in half the time it had taken them to ascend to the top. Almost at the bottom she stopped and caught her breath turning towards her brother.

"Look if you want to leave tonight it's fine." She was dismayed to see an expression of remorse cross his already troubled face.

"I'm so sorry Kier," he hugged her, "I've dragged you up here, used you as hard labour and then rushed you back down." Her smile said such things would never matter between them; she raised her hands in the air.

"To say nothing of giving me a serious case of the heebie jeebies."

"What do you mean?" he asked, concerned.

"Hey, when someone as laid back and clever as you is this worried then, if the rest of us aren't, maybe we ought to be." Her words seem to produce a realisation in him. He tucked her arm inside his own for the gentler walk across a field down to the road

"Your right. I could end up causing a major panic and God knows what else, maybe I need to do a little research before I contact anyone."

"Isn't that what you've been doing?"

"Not that kind of research, I think I need to talk to Matthew and Marianne."

Brother and sister continued their journey without speaking and Kier was sure Gally was mentally going over his results, hunting for some logical explanation. Kier, on the other hand, realised she had not mentioned the thing that concerned her most, still little able to face the horrific concept that the forbidding stranger she had seen in Roust the day before had been able to tamper with her mind with such devastating effect.

The shock when she saw the dark figure on the scar that afternoon had left her immobile and fearful. Could it be that he was searching for her? Kier buried the thought away, shaking her head, suddenly glad she was heading back to Pulton the following day.

Chapter Nine

An old-style juke box was playing classic rock when Gally and Kier arrived back at the Mountain, probably the same sound, he told her, that he had listened to ten years previously. Matthew greeted the pair with a half- smile that would have signalled a heartfelt welcome in a less impassive character.

Kier was surprised to see a young man ascend from the cellar carrying boxes of crisps. He was very slim with pure gold waves of hair that he wore shoulder length and a face that was a male version of Marianne's. Gally introduced him as Matthew's son Josh and once he had put down his boxes the young man came across and shook her hand. Not for the first time that week she was surprised by a sense of déjà vu as she returned his easy smile.

Gally brought her attention to the coloured sketches that Josh had drawn and that dotted the stone walls around this side of the bar. There was one of himself, his brown eyes showing an expression of concentration as he sorted fossils on one of the tables.

"What an anorak," Gally noted glumly seeing his dark hair neglected and long. Josh had pictured him in his weathered cagoule that he so often forgot to remove before sitting down to work. He nodded towards his friend.

"You didn't exactly accentuate my natural good looks and muscular physique."

Josh lifted his hands either side, palms open.

"I see, I draw," he laughed.

The fire was lit as the evening turned cold and they settled to a bar meal that would have graced any of the fine restaurants she had visited in Manchester. A small man with glasses and curly hair picked up a guitar and played an Irish folk song. As she joined in the singing, the worries that had dogged her last few days disappeared in what she was later to remember as a precious interlude of warmth and relaxation before they became caught up in events they could never have previously imagined.

Later, when the bar had emptied, Matthew shut the main door and invited Gally and his sister to sit with them for a nightcap. Kier was struck by the closeness between the family of three as they chatted easily about the evening. The only note of tension was when Josh mentioned that he had seen Arthur Beeston on Ravenscar.

'There are dangerous aspects to that man Matthew," said Marianne turning to her husband. Matthew nodded.

"I agree that greed and stupidity can be a very dangerous combination but I've known him all my life, ever since school. At heart, he's a coward."

Josh turned to Gally, "you remember him? He owns the farm at the bottom of Ravenscar."

Gally looked rueful.

"Should never have let that old bully hang on to my things when I moved camp. I was young."

"What things? Why didn't you tell me?" Matthew asked. The landlord was angry and it was clear Gally had forgotten that he had never discussed that a rucksack of clothes and books had disappeared from his tent the day he had decided he wanted to change sites. At that time, the area was much less popular and someone like Gally, booked in for three months, was a reliable source of income, however small. The lecturer sighed.

"I couldn't prove he'd done it. At least he didn't get my thesis. That's all I really cared about." Gally shrugged his shoulders.

"Still, had I known..." Matthew blew through his moustache before picking up the glasses and moving across to the bar. "I best go lock up properly."

It was unusual for Matthew to be so vehement. Gally's expression was questioning as he looked over at Marianne but it was Josh who spoke.

"Beeston's always been a pain but since he linked up with a businessman in Roust things have got a lot worse. They've dug up some old document that says this whole side of the valley belongs to the Beeston family."

"I thought the farm had been in your family for years?" Gally queried.

"Course it has, but Beeston's always wanted it," replied Josh, his eyes afire. "They've hired some hot-shot, ridiculously expensive legal brains and they've had the cheek to offer to buy us out."

"What's worrying," added Marianne thoughtfully, "is the amount of money offered. It was surprisingly high." She shook her head. "It's all nonsense, they can have no right to this land but Matthew is worried, more than he'd like us to know." Marianne's voice had lost its lightness. She smiled as her husband came back over to the table and then turned back to Gally.

"Now what have you been doing up on Whistmorden to cause you to leave half your dinner? That's never happened before!" Gally grinned and Kier laughed.

"You certainly know my brother," she smiled.

"Well?" persisted Marianne. Gally sighed but launched into an explanation.

"I was going to talk to you about it anyway but first I need to ask you to keep it between us for now?" They all nodded.

"Whistmorden scar is changing its composition without changing appearance."

"You found a few new minerals lad?" Matthew half smiled but Gally shook his head.

"It's as if the rock is in a state of flux. The changes are happening rapidly and some of the substances are one's I've never seen before, I can't even identify much of the composition under a microscope."

"Global warming?" Josh suggested frowning.

"I really don't know but I doubt it. I've checked and re-checked the results- Whistmorden scar is no longer composed of limestone. Whatever that rock is it's something I've never come across before. But most puzzling and a little sinister is the fact that there is no visible alteration."

"Just Whistmorden? What about the surrounding area?" Marianne looked concerned.

"Well the tests I've done so far are very limited but the rest of the area looks normal." Marianne was fiddling with a pendant that she had removed from under her T-shirt. Kier was struck by its unusual striated pink; fine lines ran like capillaries throughout the small oval shaped stone. Josh looked thoughtful.

"Dad, what was it you once told me about an arrow on the scar?" Matthew looked solemnly around the table.

'There's been rumours about Whistmorden since I was a small boy." He looked at Marianne, who nodded slightly, and went over to the far corner of the room signalling the others to follow. Gally had never realised that this particular area of the main room always seemed in shadow, no lighting was set up in the small space and it was an area out of sight behind one of the tall cloister type seats. Only a black and white print of a solitary ash tree upon a limestone pavement occupied the space.

Matthew carefully removed the print. The picture had covered a stone that was larger than those around it. The landlord pressed the top right of the stone and its diagonally opposite corner dislodged allowing Matthew to remove it without difficulty. Marianne switched the main light on and revealed an inscription that was carved deeply and as finely as if it had been written with a fountain pen. Josh signalled to brother and sister to come closer and Kier found herself examining the inscription.

Matthew explained that it had been in place when the first farmhouse had been built almost four hundred years earlier and that it was reputed to have been found on Whistmorden scar.

"It's supposed to contain a warning that an arrow would break the surface and mark the beginning of some disaster," Marianne added.

Josh, who had never before seen the inscription, stared in wonder that it had been under his nose for so long without him knowing. Kier moved closer and examined the markings; she read out loud but haltingly, as she was unsure how to pronounce some of the words.

"Beneath the grooved and weeping stone of Whistmorden
lies abandoned Obason, the tainted land.
Let not the Perfidium carve its curse when
the bonds begin to wane,
for then the dank darkness of the deep
shall cast its shadow on Ordovicia's grave."

Kier stood back fascinated by the old inscription. Lost in thought it was a moment before she realised that the rest of the small group were staring at her in disbelief.

"What?" she asked alarmed. Gally put his hand out to touch the markings and turned to his sister.

"What language is this Kier? How do you know it?" She could see his question echoed in the eyes of the rest of the group and felt unnerved.

"But it's plain English," she said slowly. Marianne put her hand on the younger woman's arm.

"No one has ever been able to read that inscription Kier, or even identify the language. For the rest of us it's just about as far as it gets from plain English."

Kier stared at them in disbelief. She began to wonder if it was some kind of joke at her expense but Marianne's eyes were concerned and there was something else, suspicion almost. Marianne considered Kier for a moment more and then moved over to the bar and picked up a pen and paper. The inscription faced her, an indecipherable web of characters.

"Kier, please write it down."

The younger woman, a little shaken now, did as she was asked. As she placed the pen down she felt Gally's strong arm around her.

"Are you ok?" he asked concerned.

Kier tried to force a smile but couldn't keep how unsettled she was from her brother.

"Perhaps we should call it a night," he suggested to the small group. They all nodded agreement. Nobody wished to speak and each one left the room as Matthew carefully replaced the stone and re hung the picture of Whistmorden Scar.

A few minutes later the landlord turned off the light and looked out of the window to see Marianne sitting alone on a bench in the moonlight, her hand clasped tightly around the pendant she had always worn since he first knew her. She looked beautiful and fragile; age had made no difference to her attraction for him. She told him that when she married him and moved to the Mountain that she had at last come home and sometimes he felt that she belonged here even more than he did himself, that in some strange way, he and his family had been keeping this land for her.

He knew that Gally's findings had deeply disturbed her but his sister's reading of the inscription had done more than that. Marianne had been shocked to the core. And there she was with the stone he had given her, Echinod Deem, the man who had been part of her life before Matthew had ever met her. He sometimes felt that Deem was in the room with them even when he was nowhere to be seen. Above all he was certain that she was willing this man to be here with them right now, in the home that Matthew had developed and the land that he and his family had kept for hundreds of years. He waited until she had returned inside and the back door was locked before he quietly made his way to bed.

*

Kier awoke to the sound of sheep, lots of sheep. They seemed to be standing just below her open window. And the smell of earth. Not paved or tyre marked ground but rich soil that teemed with life and sun scented grass sweet with summer. The room had a clean,simple look in white and greens with a bunch of yellow daises on the windowsill.

. The window itself was small and latticed but was positioned at the back of an alcove that came level with her bed and formed a window seat.

Kier, in her oversized t-shirt, crawled into the alcove and drew her knees up to her chest savouring the view across the valley to Ravensmount. The pleasure that this gave her meant that it was some time before she was revisited by the sombre thoughts that had filled her mind the night before.

The reading of the inscription made no more sense this morning than when Gally had told her that she was reading in a different language the previous evening. At first, she was unable to believe even her brother but there was something at the edge of her consciousness, a hint of a memory unfound. And what could they mean those words? There were too many questions. A shower, she decided, would at least dispel the mood that was beginning to spoil a beautiful day.

Washed and dressed in shorts and yellow t-shirt she tossed her hair into a clip above her head and followed the sound of voices coming from below. It had never occurred to her just how early she had awoken and she was surprised to enter the back room of the bar and find the clock showing only 6.30am.

The voices were from the main room on the other side of the bar and the shutters were open, she identified Marianne's soft tone, hushed with intensity.

"I am convinced that she is genuine Echin, I found no lie in her or her brother. I think you are right, the Myriar begins to form." Kier stood transfixed as a man's voice with the hint of an accent she could not place resonated softly from the other room.

"We should speak to her then," he said. Steps moved through the small passage to where she was standing and suddenly, to her complete astonishment, appeared the stranger she had seen on the sands two days previously.

"Hello" he said easily, "You must be Kier. I'm Echin Deem." His hand went out and as she took it she felt as if his touch had innervated the densest reaches of her mind. Images of other worlds, other times, filtered across her vision. Disorientated she realised that he was still speaking to her.

"Marianne told me you had managed to read the inscription." His voice was rich and clear and different, having some quality of its own she was unable to identify. Then she realised that neither of them had acknowledged meeting in the bookshop a few days previously.

"Do you know what language you were speaking?" he asked her, his compelling blue eyes seeking her own. Close up his smell was morning grass and fresh spring water. She shook her head.

"No, I have no idea."

He smiled gently at her, his expression curious. Marianne was close behind him.

"Good morning. You're a bit early for breakfast but come through to the kitchen and we'll make some tea."

Feeling absurd Kier followed them through in to the bright room she had entered the previous day. The business end of the kitchen was large and well stocked and she and Echin perched on stools by a central workstation as Marianne brewed tea.

"There's juice if you prefer," she said to Kier nodding towards the large American style fridge.

"Tea's fine," she replied.

Marianne chatted easily as she passed hot mugs of tea to them both.

"Echin's an old and dear family friend," she explained, her light blue eyes smiling affection for this enigmatic visitor.

"You're from Canada then?" Kier asked him and Echin smiled.

"I certainly spent a lot of time there but this is the place I always come back to."

"England or the Dales specifically?" she asked.

"Well, he's virtually part of the landscape in the Dales," Marianne commented. "knows it even better than my Matthew."

His nearness was a magnetic force for Kier but she found no trace of unease or any sign that he felt the same. With an effort, she quelled the response she was feeling and her words were direct and addressed to them both.

"What is the Myriar?" she asked simply.

Marianne looked slightly uneasy and moved as if to speak but it was Echin who replied, placing his mug of tea on the worktop and holding her eyes with his own. As a result, Kier had enormous difficulty concentrating on anything but their oceanic depth.

"The Myriar is a promise." Kier squinted her eyes, prompting him to go on.

"For the future," he continued, gauging her response, "in part it involves someone who can understand the language you were able to decipher last night."

"I didn't know I was doing it, "she told him, disturbed. "There was nothing different from ordinary English for me. How do you mean involves?"

Marianne looked uncomfortable. "It's possible that you are specially chosen Kier."

"How's that? "she challenged, replacing her mug on the counter. "And by who?"

"No one else has been able to do what you've done," Marianne told her. "It may be that you are one of a few people who have tremendous potential to make the future a better place for all of us."

"Woa!!" said Kier, stepping backwards, "you've definitely got the wrong person! There's nothing special about me."

"I think you are mistaken," was Echin's comment as he lifted his eyes towards her.

Kier smiled weakly and turned to Marianne.

"Thanks for the tea. Look I'm afraid I have to get back to work this morning so I'll skip breakfast." She nodded to Echin, "Nice to have met you."

"I hope we meet again," he said simply.

Kier turned and made her way back up the stairs, her heart racing. The events of the past two days had unnerved her and she felt an overwhelming need to get back to the Seven Rivers. At a deeper level, she acknowledged the impulse to put some distance between herself and the disturbing presence of Echinod Deem. It was with frustration that she realised she had found herself unprepared. The conversation in the kitchen had left her feeling uncomfortable in so many different ways.

A few minutes later Gally's tussled head moved restlessly on the pillow as she shook him awake.

"I'm going," she told him. Her brother struggled to wakefulness and then as her words penetrated he perched up on his elbows.

"What? Where?" he asked sleepily.

"Pulton," she said smiling. Her expression turned serious.

"Come with me Gally, we can get breakfast on the way." She tugged at his covers and her brother struggled to sit up and then he put his hand down over hers.

"Hang on Kier, what's up?" He had adopted his big brother voice and it always calmed her.

"They're freaking me out," she told him in a hoarse whisper.

"Who?" he asked gently and she relayed the conversation she had just had in the kitchen with Echin and Marianne.

"I've never heard of this Echin," he told her "but I'd trust Marianne with my life. Let me go down and talk to them, have breakfast."

"I'm going back to Pulton now Gally. Please come with me." Kier was adamant, Gally sighed but gave in.

"I can't offend them. Look I'll go pay the bill and explain that you need to go back early."

She nodded.

"I've already told them."

"I need to tell them I'm going with you ok?" His tone told her that she was being irrational and emotional and he was going along with her because he loved her. It was a tone she knew well.

"I can set off and meet you back at the Seven Rivers?" she suggested. Gally looked at her knowing that he would be unable to change her mind.

"Ok. I'll be right behind you." She leant over and kissed him and in five minutes she had gathered her things and was in the hire car heading back to Pulton.

Chapter Ten

The 'bottom park' covered an acre of land between the farmland and the shore. The younger ones had been playing manhunt all evening chasing each other through hedges and streams. Gabbie had joined in but all the time she had thought about Klim. They hadn't fallen out and there was no reason he shouldn't have phoned. If his phone was broken why hadn't he turned up? Gabbie suddenly recognised that she was afraid for her friend, really scared something had happened.

And who would notice apart from her? His mum was in a care home and, poor thing, had no idea what day it was. She didn't know his uncle but Klim would only go to him as a last resort. Reg, the hotel owner where he worked, had just shrugged his shoulders and told her Klim was a grown lad and not to worry. But Gabbie was worried and then she thought if he wanted to meet her alone he would go to the den they had built as kids. Where even now they sometimes went in the summer after dark.

It was pitch black on the path that led down to the shore from her house and Gabbie felt unusually nervous. Finally, she reached the lamppost as the road turned inward and could see the eerily lit green expanse of grass with its football posts, and the brightly coloured play area. She yelped with fright as a voice came behind her.

"Hey Gabbie, thought you'd gone home." Luke came out of the darkness and she was positive he had seen her pass his house and followed her silently on to the shore road.

"Thought you had too," she replied. She checked her watch and it was almost midnight. Maybe Luke had been worried too and shared the same idea.

"Thought I'd see if Klim was down here," she smiled.

"Yeah me too. You heard from him?" Luke smiled back, his eyes off focus, looking strange in the reflected lamplight.

Gabbie shook her head, "nope" she answered, "have you?"

"Nothing. Been texting him all night."

The park was empty but it was towards the small copse behind that they were heading. It was invisible from the main park and surrounded by a thick hawthorn hedge. Gabbie and Klim often curled up together in the hollow of a massive tree in the far corner of the copse that fronted on to a field filled with sheep. Young lambs huddled against their mothers at the far corner, bleating in the dark, and then they spotted a small orange glow beside the tree.

It seemed to annoy Luke that his friend always managed to build a fire first time but Gabbie knew that Klim took pride in remembering what his Dad had taught him, how to lay the paper and the dry twigs and make a triangle to keep it controlled. The paper was usually cigarette cartons but Gabbie didn't care, it was yet another thing that Klim seemed to be able to do so much more easily than any of the others.

Klim came towards them and Gabbie realised that she'd made a mistake letting Luke come with her. Klim told some tale about being away for a couple of days in Roust standing in for someone at another hotel that his employer owned. He told them he'd left his phone at home. Gabbie knew he was lying but said nothing, Reg would have told her if he'd been in Roust. Gabbie chatted easily about Danny and the others, covering the tension between her two friends. Eventually she became tired of talking and Luke sighed as he leaned forward to light a spliff. He shrugged his shoulders as Klim shook his head in response to his friend's offer to share.

'Time you got rid, Luke," he told him seriously.

Gabbie nodded and laughing she added, "mashes your brains and you ain't in a position to lose much."

Luke jumped up angrily and kicked up part of the fire onto them both, sparks flying. Gabbie leapt backwards patting down the fleece top that hung loosely on her slight frame.

"Stop it Luke, you idiot."

Luke, sullen now, turned and swore at them both. Pulling up his jacket hood he crossed the field to leave. Gabbie turned to Klim.

"What's got in to him?"

Klim shrugged his shoulders feeling guilt and sadness. Luke's family had let him stay over when his mum had been admitted and even now he knew they would offer him a bed if he needed it. They were good people. Luke and he had been together since school and they'd both flirted with drugs like most of his friends. Neither he nor Gabbie wanted any more than that and watching Luke it scared him to think how easily it took hold of everything. Worst of all was the knowledge that Brassock had targeted his friend.

"Best let him go," he said, watching the retreating figure striding angrily across the field. Gabbie came towards him and put her hand in his.

"How've you been?" she asked gently, her eyes shining in the moonlight.

He squeezed her small fingers and brought her to sit beside him in the hollow tree. Gabbie saw the grim expression on his face in the firelight. He often went quiet when his mum was particularly bad, on the days she didn't even recognise her son. It was why he worked long hours in the main hotel in Bankside, usually in the kitchen. Reg allowed Klim to sleep in one of the rooms. He had hardly been home since his Mum had been taken into care.

"I went to collect my things from the hunting lodge." He never called it home nowadays.

"I'm eighteen now so he has no hold on me."

"I thought you had everything already." Gabbie nuzzled her head under his arm and some of the tension left him.

"There are a few family heirlooms I wanted back."

"Such as?" she asked. Klim straightened up releasing Gabbie and burrowed down into his jeans pocket.

"Such as this," he told her holding his hand out towards the fire. In his palm was a milky white stone.

"It's called adularia, a moonstone." In the centre of the stone was a single line that moved across the surface like a pupil in a cat's eye, Gabbie peered closer. "It's called adularescence, it's an optical effect when I move the stone." Gabbie raised her eyebrows.

"An *optical effect* hey. Very technical." Klim grimaced at her mockery.

"Do you want to hold it?" he asked.

"Sure." He handed it to her and Gabbie ran her fingers over the smooth surface. "Where did it come from?"

"Dad said it was originally from Switzerland. It's been handed down in the family for years. He called it his lucky stone, it was on his key ring in a little leather sack." Klim's voice became choked but he steadied himself and then continued. "On the day he died it was nowhere to be found. It turned up much later in the hunting lodge inside a locked drawer. I saw it once when my uncle was putting away the deeds to our house." He looked up into the distance and Gabbie saw the firm line of his chin jut forwards and his eyes harden. "My mum's house."

"How did you get it back?" Gabbie asked.

"I took my chance and made a copy of the drawer key and on my birthday, I went and got them both. The deeds are stowed away and the stone is right here." He threw it up in the air and caught it again, for the first time that night he smiled.

"I wish I could have seen his face when he opened that drawer."

"But why would he open it if he thinks they're safe?"

"He took it out every night, like some ceremony. Heard Brassock talking to Cross once, they thought it must be worth a fortune. It's not though, only to me."

Klim pocketed the stone again. "Now he wants them back and he's sent his hard men to find me."

"Klim!" Gabbie looked alarmed and he put his arm around her again. Gabbie shivered, the fire was nearly gone. Klim leaned forward to see if he could save it but as he stared into the dwindling flame he became aware of movement in the field beyond.

The figure of a girl was outlined by the meagre splash of moonlight. She wore jeans with a light t-shirt, her hair was dark and hung to her waist. Klim reckoned she was about the same age as him but if she saw them she took no notice.

It was clear that the field was just a short cut to get to the shore and she was all but running. He called to her and she looked across, first at him and then at his companion. Gabbie had that 'don't even think about it" look on her face so he wasn't surprised that the other girl carried on without answering. In a moment, he was up and moved quickly suddenly realising where the girl was heading. Seeing her pursuer however, she started to run and soon became entangled in the hawthorn hedge that lined either side of the small gap where there was a path leading down to the shore. Klim caught up with her to find her tangled by her T-shirt.

He slipped through the gap, blocking the path she wanted to follow. Finally, she freed herself and turned wild eyed towards him. Her arms were scratched and twigs were sticking out from her straight hair. Seeing him she looked around for another way through the hedge. There was none to be seen and she started to edge backwards once more. It was with a jolt Klim realised she was scared of him. He was, after all, a lot bigger and chasing her in the middle of the night. He stood away from the opening to let her pass but she was too nervous of him to move.

"I won't hurt you. This way just leads to the shore, bit dangerous right now with the tide coming in. Come over and sit with us?" The girl's face was visible in the moonlight and it was streaked with tears. Her dark eyes looked out from thick natural eyelashes and it was obvious that she wasn't local. Her features were like the striking South American family who had visited the hotel recently. Klim felt he wanted to protect her but knew he daren't put his arm round her> He wasn't sure if she could speak English. An electric current in the pit of his belly had switched on and with a shock he realised this girl was somehow very important.

Gabbie came around the corner and the agile limbs shifted, ready to bolt. Klim smiled gently, looking directly into her eyes and it stilled her. He stopped Gabbie behind her with a raised glance. At that moment, they all turned at the sound of an engine on the road. A Land Rover was just visible as it took the bend past the field and headed up the shore road. The girl's body jolted and she would have run if Klim had not grabbed her and pulled her behind the hedge.

"There's a five-foot ditch ten yards away," he whispered, "stay still." Instinctively all of them had ducked down behind the hedge.

"What's going on?" demanded Gabbie. As the sound of the engine died the girl slumped to the ground on her knees and shivered. Klim took off his jacket and gently put it around her shoulders, ignoring Gabbie's laser-eyed stare.

"What's your name?" he asked. The girl was breathing heavily and looked exhausted. Words tumbled out as she pulled against Klim's arm, it sounded Spanish."

"Tengo que escapar . tiene que ir, vuelve!" The sound of the car engine on its way back stopped her words with a startled intake of breath and she sat straining to hear.

"Who's coming back?" insisted Gabbie.

Klim looked at her with surprise. "Can you understand her?"

"A bit," Gabbie shushed him

"Him," was the tremulous reply, her rich Spanish accent making the word an accusation. The girl was shaking now, pointing at the road. Gabbie put her arm round her, maybe to stop Klim doing it, he wasn't sure. She soothed the frightened girl and stroked her hair like a young child. The sound of the driver's door banging sent a bunch of crows cawing in a tumble of feathers from the big Oak. The den was well hidden and the small fire consisted merely of a few embers. The copse was not visible from the park but the firm stride of the driver took him straight to it. Had they still been at the tree they would easily have been discovered. Picking up the leaves around the fire where the group had been sitting he let them fall and turned to scan the field.

"They've gone." Klim immediately recognised the harsh rasp belonging to Brassock and it struck him that his hold on Luke was even stronger than he'd thought. How else did the ex-wrestler know where to look? The small gap in the hedge was hidden from the oak tree. The bullish figure stood stock still listening for a few minutes, a disturbed ewe bleated protectively as she nestled her lamb. Klim and the two girls, by silent agreement, were picture still, ignoring the uncomfortable position of their limbs as they squatted behind the hedge fifty yards away. Finally, Brassock trudged back out of the copse and across the park to the car. Gabbie went to move but Klim held her back until they heard the engine of the four-wheel-drive drum to life in the silence.

Cramped and cold the three of them started to make their way back across the field. They were almost at the oak tree when Gabbie caught her foot and cried out. Klim turned to help and by the time he had hauled his friend out the rabbit hole the dark eyed mysterious girl had disappeared. They searched the field and the park and even the nearby shore as far as they could in the dark, both of them tired and cold. Klim suddenly realised the girl was still wearing his coat. Gabbie shrugged her shoulders.

"Look Klim, she's gone. Maybe we should ring the police or something?" Klim could see she was relieved as he shook his head. Her eyes were shutting with exhaustion and they were at least a mile from her house.

"Come back with me ok?" he suggested." Stay in my room at Reg's tonight?"

"Don't be daft, come to mine," she replied but Klim was adamant as he put the key in her jeans pocket.

"Where are you going?"

"Don't worry about me, just stay in the room until morning and then head back home. Ok?" Gabbie was too exhausted to argue. "You can go in the back door, no one will even know you're there," he instructed.

The two friends took the back way to the hotel along the shore road; Klim was relieved that no one drove past. He suspected that Cross and Banks would be out looking for the girl and would not be watching the hotel. Anyway, he figured that Gabbie's slight figure going in the back entrance would be taken for one of the early morning cleaners. Once in the small town they steered along the back streets and he watched from the railway bridge as she entered the hotel.

Once Gabbie was safe Klim made his way back along the shore road watching for any sign of the dark eyed girl. There was none. He thought of Gabbie and felt that she was ok. He could snatch images of her fighting with her anxiety for him and at the same time could feel her mind ready for sleep.

Klim never talked about his random telepathy to anyone, his instinct about what others were thinking and feeling. Since his birthday however, it had become amplified beyond anything he had ever previously experienced. In the last two days, he realised that he could search and find what he had already come to call individual "mind prints" and he could home in and pick up an idea of where they were and what they were doing. He was almost certain that this was because of the moonstone he carried. There was a vague memory of his dad telling him that it made people more of who they already were.

Klim flinched as the stab of grief found its mark, as it did every day. He missed his dad. Sometimes he felt as if someone had punched out his middle and left a hole that only Gabbie seemed to see. Now that he thought of it, his uncle had grown more dangerous since his Father died. Klim had reckoned that the reason for this had been the removal of the only check on the natural greed and violence of the man that his father had supplied. Now he wondered if, after all, it had been the adularia that had made him such a potent force of evil, more adept than ever at twisting things to his advantage.

The fact that Jackson might be chasing the girl made his stomach turn. Klim was glad that he no longer shared even a name with the man who had destroyed his life. The family surname, he had heard him tell his father, "would not be politically astute for a man in my position." He had paid to change it by deed poll. The day his Dad had died from a heart attack Jackson was in another country but Klim had never lost the feeling that somehow, for some reason, his uncle had played a part in that awful day. He wondered how it would change things for his uncle now that he had taken the stone away.

Klim was exhausted as he headed back to Siskin's house where he had, perhaps stupidly, begun to feel at home. And yet a voice inside him whispered that he had not been wrong to trust the man with music inside his head. He shivered with cold and tiredness and continued through the maze of back streets instead of the main road. The musician had offered him a room permanently, said he'd been looking for a lodger but wanted to wait for the right person. Klim let him lie, this man loved his privacy but he could sense nothing sinister in his kindness. Already they had arranged a rent that even Klim could afford and now, only two days since that first meeting, he already had his own key.

All of a sudden, a sense of impending doom engulfed him and despite his caution he slammed his foot into the wooden wastebasket nearby.

"No!" Waves of panic filled his mind, and he felt the pain of Brassock's rough fingers as they clamped on the thin arms of the girl they had met in the park earlier that evening. Never before had he felt so overwhelmingly a part of another's mind. He saw there the memory of an exhausting journey along the shore and her relief as she found that she was in Pulton. There had been distress when she could not find the person she was seeking, a woman, and the girl had braved the boulders that formed the sea wall, squeezing herself between them to hide.

Undoubtedly it was the same girl he and Gabbie had tried to help, he saw how she had pulled his fleece around her trying to keep out the cold but she could not stop the tide as it lapped over her feet and forced her higher on to the rocks. Brassock had found her and Klim felt her terror as the Land Rover had pulled up and the brutish figure had descended towards her. Stiff with cold she was appalled to find one of her ankles wedged underneath a boulder and in her panic, she scraped her skin trying to escape. Then Brassock's massive hand had caught her hair, and pulled savagely, wrenching her free. In another moment, she had been thrown in the back of the Discovery. Even as he felt her tremble, Klim saw also the fierce determination that lay underneath. And something else that he was unable to define, something that alarmed him.

Wide-awake now he took the same route to Siskin's house as he had done on that first night to shorten the distance. Once he had dropped over the fence he was surprised to hear voices from the front of the house. A coldness clutched at him as he recognised the oily voice of his uncle. Klim edged around the corner and there he was, his black hair gleaming in the lamplight, his faultlessly featured face turned towards Siskin smiling. To Klim's father Alex Jackson had always been 'the handsome one." To Klim and his mother it was their Father's face, his dark eyes always kind and ready to laugh, which had been truly handsome.

"Deal?" His voice was full of the sickly charm that Klim had come to detest.

"Deal," agreed Siskin smiling back. The two men shook hands oblivious of Klim's presence and silently he made his way back to the garden and over the fence. In the dark of the forest a tear trickled down his cheek. For the girl, he told himself, for the girl.

He was cold and exhausted but made himself think how his uncle would think. It was obvious that they wanted the girl back urgently and Jackson had bent his resources to finding her. Maybe he had even enlisted Siskin's help for that reason, he thought bitterly. Klim was sure he had seen no watch by the hotel in Bankside and carefully he made his way along the empty back streets to where he had stood earlier that evening, on the bridge overlooking the back door. Tentatively he sent his awareness out and found himself picking up different patterns of thought. He found he could identify those who slept, some easily and some uneasily but he had no desire to intrude further. Here there was a subtle lack of definition that distinguished sleep from waking thought, he was also aware that his presence was somehow more potentially visible to the sleeping mind.

Reg was on reception at the other side of the building and Klim had a defined image of newsprint and horses as he identified his employer. As far as he could he scanned the bushes and streets outside of the area but could find no trace of the vicious mind print of Cross or Banks. Exhausted he made his way quietly into his room where Gabbie's tousled head stirred for a moment as he entered and then relaxed back into slumber. Tenderly he smiled at the softly breathing form knowing how deceptive her angelic face could be. He had too often seen it break into sudden storms of emotion that left him bewildered. Quietly he sat in the armchair and sipped from the bottle of water on the bedside cabinet. He was asleep in minutes.

Chapter Eleven

Kier had been working mechanically in the gift shop all morning since Gally had left to head back to Manchester. Hannah had phoned to say she would be in late and she was happy to fill in serving customers and hoping that the busy tasks meant that she wouldn't have time to think of anything else. Yesterday she had avoided all Gally's attempts to discuss what had happened in the Dales until finally he had sat her down and looked over with his best big brother expression.

"There's some things I want from my office so I'm going to head back in the morning." He stopped to gauge her response but Kier had said nothing. He sighed.

"I'll come back, or you come to me when you're ready ok?" His eyes, so like her own, were tinged with anxiety.

"Right Galahad." She replied in what she knew was a pathetic attempt at humour. The use of his full name always infuriated him and usually brought a playful cuff round her ear but he chose to ignore it, he was not going to let her distract him. Kier had wanted him to stay but she knew it wouldn't have been fair to ask. Adam had gone back to the city the previous day and once her brother had left a wave of loneliness swept over her that even the sounds and smells of the Seven Rivers could not dispel.

When Hannah arrived, she took over in the gift shop and her employer went to help in the café. Gina whispered to her as they worked behind the counter.

"They've been here for ages. He doesn't need his hood up indoors like that." Kier focused on the young couple that faced each other in the last booth.

"They had breakfast two hours ago; those mugs of tea must be stone cold," the redhead told her.

At first Kier did not recognise the girl, she looked young and vulnerable without her make up. The usual trendy clothes were replaced with an old fleece and jeans and it was a few moments before she placed her as the assistant from the bookshop. It was impossible to see the boy's face from the counter. Kier went over to collect the mugs, which were still half full, and Gabbie nodded for her to take them. The boy looked up and she realised he was older than she had first thought, perhaps eighteen or nineteen. He had a continental look about him, something in the angular set of his jaw, and his eyes were soft and brown and tortured.

Gina had been concerned that he was another potential burglar but Kier could see at a glance that this would not be the case with this young man and her heart went out to him. Whatever the cause, his suffering was keen. On impulse, she put the mugs down and pulled a voucher from her apron.

"We have an offer on this morning- you get a free meal for two any time this week." She always kept a few for families she thought needed them and her instincts were usually good. He looked at her and Kier felt once more the absurd sense of recognition that she had first experienced with Siskin and Josh, and then again, only more personal and more strongly, with Echin Deem. The dark-haired youth reached out his hand and put the voucher in his pocket.

"Thanks," he smiled, holding her eyes.

"Klim, we'd best go." The girl stood up and gathered her things. Kier picked up the mugs and walked back to the counter. Gina nodded and her smile was a congratulation on getting the couple out of the shop but Kier shook her head.

"They were no threat. If anything, I'd say someone was threatening them." Her eyes followed the young couple, the boy still wearing his hood on the warm summer's day as they disappeared among the crowd on the stone jetty.

The morning had been busy but there were few customers in the afternoon and still restless, Kier made her way down to the bookshop. The Welshman was busy serving but there was no sign of the girl as she made her way towards the reference room.

The rocking chair was no longer present but one of the ornately carved chairs had been moved to face the stained-glass window. Kier turned to the shelves where she noticed that on one of the binders a beautifully cut lapis stone had been inlaid. The books constantly altered in the reference room and no matter how many times she went to take them to the desk to make an enquiry she found that somehow, by the time she got there, she had left the book behind. Mostly she had left the shop before she remembered that she had intended to ask something about the material she had studied. It had become her habit therefore just to enjoy whatever treasure she found available in the time she had.

She wondered why she had never thought of sitting this way previously, as the light of the window seemed to glow directly onto the pages. It illuminated the rich texture of the book in which the lapis lazuli was encrusted.

The book she had chosen was atlas sized and full of pictures. The detailed sketches seemed like paintings at first, so vivid and full-bodied was the colouring. On close examination, however, she could see that the strokes were made with pencils and not brushes though she had never seen such rich and diverse colour in a pencil drawing. Many of the drawings showed tall elegant men and women with honey coloured skin that glowed with the suggestion of athleticism and health. The men wore their hair in a knotted stallion tail down their back, the women dressed their long dark hair in an intricate weave of star shaped flowers. The page that lay open showed a particularly detailed drawing that fixed her attention.

*

The scene depicted was of a futuristic town; the buildings were different shapes, some tall and others conical. The richly coloured plants and animals were totally unfamiliar more suited to a tropical rain forest than an imagined alien planet. It was a place built around a lake and the sky and water were drawn with such purity and clarity that for a moment she felt as if she were stood on the edge of the lake watching the breeze ripple along the surface. Underneath was written

"Ordovicia before its jewel was cast beyond the stars and its land buried in the grey ash of betrayal".

The name slammed against her consciousness and she gasped aloud. The stone inscription had talked about "Ordovicia's grave." She could feel her heart beating faster as she continued, could it be that "Ordovicia" referred to a place and not, as she had first thought, a person? She skimmed through the rest of the pictures that depicted views of beautiful foliage and brightly coloured birds on unusual trees. The wood was pale and smooth as if the bark had been stripped and yet they were fully alive with green shoots and bright, multicoloured blooms.

Carefully she closed the book and placed it back on the shelf. There were too many things alien and yet disturbingly familiar. The young entrepreneur clung on to the smooth wooden shelf as she experienced a moment of complete disorientation. It was as if her world had suddenly tipped to one side and then awkwardly righted itself again. Kier decided that right now she would secrete her thoughts in the still place inside her mind where she stored those things she would discuss only with herself. Trembling a little, she quietly made her way back to the corridor and out into the late afternoon sun.

A little time after she had left, the lapis jewel in the spine of the book she had been reading glowed brightly before it transmuted into the form of Echinod Deem. He walked into the passage where Evan bumped into him.

"Where did you spring from?" The Welshman shook his head in confusion. Echin smiled, he knew that the room from which he had just come was invisible and inaccessible to Evan and all those who visited the bookshop.

"Let me give you a hand," he offered taking some of the books that his friend carried. Evan leaned against the solid wall that reached across the doorway to the reference room as he divided his load.

In hundreds of years only Echin had crossed its threshold and now Kier Morton had strolled into its confines, not for the first time, to read material no other human being had been able to read since it had first been penned in Ordovicia.

Chapter Twelve

The sun was setting as Klim began walking eastwards towards the Hunting Lodge that stood high above the Bay with a view right over to the Lakeland hills. The only stretch of road he needed to take was the one between the crag and the village and on which Luke's van went past travelling in the opposite direction. To Klim's ears the failing exhaust was unmistakable and he moved out of sight long before the vehicle rounded the corner.

Klim was agile and quick, he was confident that the dozens of off road paths he knew would allow him to arrive at the site of his old home without being seen. The use of these routes however, meant he had been walking for two hours before he reached the forest that surrounded the lodge and where Klim and his dad had walked so many times.

He had learnt about the ways the animals behaved, their distinctive movements, and about the land, how it grew and changed, giving and taking as it did so. Klim approached the edge of the property that his uncle had enclosed within a six-foot stone wall and made his way quickly past the huge wooden gates and further up to where the land bordered on to a path that was not well known, even to locals. Klim followed the path that took him to a place where the forbidding stone wall was partially hidden by an overhanging tree. Here there was a gap where Klim had removed the interlocking stones so that it was easy to sit on top and still be invisible from the main house.

Klim had sat watching from this place when his mother had been first sectioned, his mind filled with the desire for revenge. The hotel where he had helped out offered him thirty hours a week once he reached sixteen and Reg, with his gruff kindness had given him one of the cell like staff rooms "for when it was too late to get back home." It had been too late to travel back home from the moment his mother had been taken into hospital.

The story was that Jackson had purchased their home and the money now paid for his mother's private care. The anger welled up inside again, an over-ripe fruit that was filled with bitterness that threatened to burst him. He let it go as he had taught himself to do, relaxing the way his dad had shown him, slowing the breath, thinking past the emotion. One day, he told himself, the house would be his again and maybe he and Gabbie could make it their home and bring his mum back here to live.

The few occasions on which he and his uncle had met in the last two years were short and filled with undisguised loathing on both sides. As Klim's legal guardian and his mother's power of attorney, Jackson had been careful not to let the outside world see his real character. Within the walls of the Lodge he had been his cruel and vicious self. Klim bit his lip and ran fingers across the jaw his uncle had punched more than once. It had provided the impetus for the youth to seek martial arts lessons and months later several times he had sat on top of the wall waiting for an opportunity to take his revenge. He realised now how naïve he'd been. It would take more than a well-aimed punch or kick to tackle the amount of evil of which his uncle was capable.

Construction workers were there every day at the beginning converting the outhouses at the back of the property into a small cottage. Watching from the wall as the lodge had been rebuilt to his uncle's design he had barely seen him. Carl Brassock had often been there however, his mouth half full, shouting orders at the labourers. The memory of the girl being thrown roughly into the car by the brutish ex doorman brought him abruptly back to the present.

Klim turned and eased himself up over the wall and for a few moments sat in his old hiding place scanning the lodge for any signs of activity. The house was in darkness. The design of the property meant that the main drive from the gates cut through a large lawn and led up to the front of the house where there was now a fountain. Behind this was a landscaped garden about the size of a small field. Sitting on the wall he saw the row of tall leylandii trees that had been planted to divide the main house and garden from the small cottage that Jackson had built at the back of the property.

Carefully he crawled further along the wall to position himself on the other side of the trees. He jumped down and Klim saw that the tall evergreens completely masked the existence of the cottage from the main house. Jackson's nephew was certain that if his uncle was hiding the girl then it would be in the small deliberately hidden building, carefully constructed to be as invisible as possible. The outside stonewalls had been painted green so that even from the air he suspected that the existence of the cottage would be difficult to detect.

Klim kept parallel with the tall trees as he moved. He brushed away the soft feathery branches that filled his nostrils with the strong sense of pine and memories of kinder times. At the edge of the trees was a garage that had been fitted with doors at either end. It meant that when the doors were closed there would be no sign that the drive came around the back of the house and continued through the brick garage to the cottage at the back. At that moment both front and back garage door was open forming a square window that peered into the garden area behind the main house.

He glimpsed wooden frames and trailing plants in the moonlight and watched as a hedgehog raised itself on thin legs to run across the gravel drive. There were still no lights on in the big house but he saw a dim glow from the back room of the cottage.

Klim realised that he would be most in danger of being caught on the slope of lawn that that led up from the trees to the smaller dwelling. He lay on the grass and started crawling slowly, peering upwards under his hood, elbows and knees dimpling the soft earth. He edged towards the side of the building and then settled into the slope, watching for movement. After a while he risked the brief flash of his watch display, it was almost midnight and he was starting to feel the cold. Soundlessly he crept towards the right-hand side of the small cottage. A moment later the front door opened and he slipped down flat into the grass where it was shaded by trees, only just in time to escape being caught in the glare of a flashlight that swept across the lawn.

Klim buried his face in the grass, praying that his dark clothes would render him invisible amongst the patchy darkness of the moonlit night. Heavy footsteps, undoubtedly belonging to Brassock, crunched on the narrow gravel path that led from the door of the small building to meet the adjoining drive. The flashlight changed direction and fell on his uncle's expensive black boots as Jackson came out on to the drive and gave his instructions.

"I'll take the torch. Bring up the car and park it as near as you can to the door." His uncle's voice was a harsh whisper, his mind searching, and Klim imagined the surface of the lawn covering him, making him invisible to his uncle's probing mentality. He dared not try to link with Jackson's mind for on some level, at a very young age, he had recognised attempts by his uncle to dominate his thinking. It was, Klim realised, different to his own sense of another's mind. Jackson seemed able to impose his thoughts directly on others. It had never happened when his father was near but it meant that early on Klim had developed defence mechanisms to keep his uncle from bullying his way into his thoughts. He imagined that his mind was enclosed in a hard shell and soon it became like a coat he could pull on and off at will. On one occasion, soon after his Father died three years ago, exhausted with shock and grief, he had let his defence slip. In those moments Klim had insight into the cesspit that was his uncle's psyche, not long enough for him to probe deeply but sufficient to confirm the man's abounding malice. And beyond this was the shock of his uncle's link to another mentality, a tsunami of utter malevolence, an alien presence from which he had quickly retreated, utterly terrified. He banished the disturbing memory. After that Jackson had never again tried to invade his nephew's mind but his sinister heightened awareness was still more effective than any flashlight.

The young man held his breath until he heard Jackson turn back into the cottage. He could feel the vibration of the ground as Brassock lumbered down the drive to the main house. Klim scrambled up to the right-hand side of the building where underneath the window a black charring was visible in the moonlight against the dim stone. As he crawled along hugging the stone, the reek of rotting meat seemed to seep through until Klim felt himself gagging with the stench. Moving quickly and keeping low he reached the back of the cottage where, to his dismay, he saw there was no back door and the three small windows were high off the ground. He reached the end of the building just as his uncle's flashlight swept a line from the side wall to the rear hedge. Klim darted around the opposite side of the cottage and heard Jackson follow along the rear wall. A flashlight was now illuminating the spot where he had been standing two seconds previously.

Klim suddenly realised this might be his only chance to get inside the building without being seen. He darted silently across the space between the edge and front door and moved inside, feeling his way along the walls of the narrow hall. There was a door to his left and he knew that this was the main room. He wondered fleetingly why the front of the cottage was in darkness and he slipped inside the first doorway almost falling over a long sofa. He felt along this and positioned himself behind the door, Seconds later small slaps of designer leather sounded on the wooden floor of the hallway.

Klim felt a trickle of sweat in front of his ear. He remembered the number of times his uncle had known just where to find him. Somehow, he suppressed the urge to run as Jackson moved on down the hallway. Klim tried to remember what he knew of the cottages as he had watched them being built. The construction had incorporated the existing outhouses and he realised he was standing in the main room which was the first on the left from the hallway.

A little lower down on the right was a bedroom and Klim realised that this was the source of the foul smell on the other side of the building and from where he could now hear sounds of movement. Lower down, at the bottom of the hall were the entrances to two further rooms and a bathroom. He flattened himself against the wall at the sound of a car and risked carefully moving to the window, this time avoiding the sofa. The curtains were open and the moonlight meant he could see enough to edge himself nearer the sill and slip behind the curtain at the far side of the room.

Carefully he positioned himself to see the front door. A black estate car with only it's side lights on drove right up against the arched entrance of the cottage and Brassock got out, slamming the door in his heavy way. Alex Jackson gasped in the hallway as he pulled something behind him.

"Be quiet you idiot- give me a hand with this."

The high-pitched scrape of plastic screamed as it was pulled along the floorboards. Klim wanted to retch as he glimpsed the outline of a polythene bag, long and black, body shaped. Even as he registered that the weight of the bag was too heavy to contain the young girl, he was unable to stop the wave of despair that brought him close to the edge of panic. Klim steadied his breathing as he watched Brassock move to the front of the vehicle. The bullish features were now inches from the unknown visitor as Klim carefully avoided any movement. He worked out that when the two men were at the rear end of the car they would be unable to see the front door. Brassock's broad back turned towards the rear of the vehicle. As he passed the front door he gestured towards the hallway.

"Where's the girl? She still out?" he asked, his caustic voice loud in the silence.

"Quiet," Jackson hissed, as the two of them lifted the soulless polythene bag into the boot. As the sickening thud registered on Klim's hearing he dived out from beneath the curtain and moved towards the hallway. Turning, he followed the glimmer of dim light at the end of the narrow corridor and saw that it came from the room a little to the left of the hallway. His heart dropped as his uncle's voice sounded from only a few feet away. "Check on the girl and stay with her. We can't take the chance she runs again."

The car door was banged shut and a few moments later came the sound of the car backing down the drive and Klim slid into the bathroom just as Brassock re-entered the passageway.

Heavy steps vibrated on the floorboards in time to Klim's palpating heart. He became aware of the same sickly smell that had been in the bedroom and turned to see the outline of soiled sheets piled in the bath. A door banging outside made him jump but then he realised that this must be the garage door shutting so that the driveway to the cottage would be completely obscured from the main house. Brassock moved down the corridor, past the bathroom and entered the room Klim was intending to search. Despite his distaste, he climbed in the bath and pulled the curtain. w he recognised the foisty and gut-wrenching smell as dried blood. He heard a key turn in the lock as the big man came out of the room moments later. He pulled his muscles taught as Brassock came in to relieve himself without turning on the light and then sighed with relief at the sound of footsteps labouring the hallway once again. It was only when he saw light shining from the main room and heard the TV that he climbed cautiously from his hiding place. As the TV flicked from channel to channel Klim moved to the bedroom door and said a quiet thank you that the key was still in the lock. He turned it as slowly and quietly as possible and let himself into the room.

The shrouded glow of a small lamp revealed that the room was small and cell like with another door off to the right. Klim checked out the small toilet room with a sink where there was a toothbrush and toothpaste but no cabinet or any other of the vast array of toiletries that Gabbie would have had spread about the sink. It surprised him that the room had obviously been carefully arranged for the girl. It was decorated in pinks and purples, there was a CD and DVD player.

The bed covers and curtains were modern and bright and the furniture was what he would call "girlie." The armchair by the single bed was covered in brightly coloured spots and the wardrobe had a vanity mirror with inlaid gold trim. Quietly he crept quietly towards the bed.

There could be no doubt that it was the same girl who had run from himself and Gabbie in the bottom park. She was breathing deeply, her face a pale mask under the olive skin and he could see a bruise at the top of her forehead. He remembered that Brassock had pushed her roughly into the Land Rover, knocking her head against the passenger door. It confirmed for him that it had not been a dream or imagined event, he had definitely linked telepathically to the girl's recapture. The link was broken now however, he realised he was unable to gage any idea of her current thinking.

It would be difficult if he couldn't rouse her, he wasn't sure how he'd manage to carry her down the hall without attracting Brassock's attention. Whatever it takes, he told himself, certain that he had to move before his uncle returned. Klim bent over the bed, unable even to call the girl's name as she had not given it to him. As he reached across to touch her shoulder, her eyes flew open and with a grunt she attacked him with a razor-sharp blade that hissed across his left earlobe and would have pierced his chest were it not for his quick reactions. Then girl cried out in horror seeing Klim and the blade dropped to the floor.

Immediately they stared at each other in shock as they heard the sound of the TV increase in volume as Brassock opened the living room door. Klim picked up the blade by its unusually shaped round handle, a bit like a pink doorknob he registered somewhere in the back of his mind, and then remembered that Reg had something like it in the hotel for opening letters. He squeezed himself carefully behind the chair as the girl once again pretended sleep, somehow making her breathing slow and deep. Klim's heart sank as he realised that he had unlocked the door and knew Brassock would figure out that someone, apart from the girl, was in the room.

Slowly the doorknob turned and then the door was pushed open, banging against the wall. Klim held his breath as he heard heavy footsteps enter the room, the girl had not moved. His fist clenched around the odd-looking knife when he heard Brassock opening the wardrobe door. Instead of checking behind the chair however the heavy steps approached the bed where the girl's breathing had remained deep and regular in contrast to Brassock's laboured wheeze as he bent to look underneath.

A sudden crash and a yell from the girl brought Klim out from behind the chair and threw the room into to darkness. A dim light from the living room leaked its way in through the open door and he could just make out the girl pinned to the bed, a huge and brutal fist around her throat. Brassock's other hand was pressed against his bleeding head where she had crashed the lamp against his skull. Klim leaped forward, both legs connecting with other side of the kidnapper's head and the floor shook as he went down unconscious.

The girl reached over to the other side of the bed to pick up the jacket Klim had given her on that first night and then they were both running as fast as they could over the unconscious figure and out through the door. Klim suddenly turned on his heel and the girl cried out in alarm but then understanding dawned in her eyes as he locked the door and pocketed the key. There was a fierce satisfaction in her face as she waited for Klim to take her hand once more and guide her out into the fresh air.

Chapter Thirteen

A car engine rumbled behind as Klim and the girl, strides matching, walked doggedly along the shore road. She reached for his hand and he pulled them both off the road before it came in sight. At least he had a name,

'Sylvana," she had told him in English, "but I am known as Swift." Another bird he thought. Siskin and Swift, but the thought of Siskin was quickly banished from his mind.

"Thank you," she said simply, her voice a little slurred as they hunched together under the rim of the river, just below the grassy embankment. It was the first time she had spoken since she had told him her name for they had been concentrating on speed as they darted through the woods and through the back streets on to the shore road.

"It's ok," he told her.

He sensed the fog in her mind that the drugs had created and her struggle to clear it. Klim wished he could risk a taxi but he dared not leave any trail of where they were going. Besides, Brassock rarely walked anywhere and on foot they could take routes that he was unlikely to follow. Cross and Banks were another matter however, the youth continually widened his awareness to catch any hint of their presence. The car passed and Klim sighed as he thought about his aching legs. It was still about a mile down the shore road to the small railway cottage that Gabbie shared with her dad. Her mum had left years ago, a subject never mentioned between father and daughter. Once Klim had asked his friend about her mother but Gabbie's face had contorted into an expression of grief and she had shaken her head; they never spoke of her again.

*

Gabbie looked up midway through filling the washing machine that Klim thought must be working on pure willpower by now. It heaved and gurgled its way through each cycle so much that they always went out when it was on because they couldn't hear each other. She tilted her face towards him, empty of make-up. The blue grey eyes hadn't yet got dressed up to tell the world how tough she was. He always felt she looked more beautiful without it. Then her mouth compressed into a tiny line and Klim guessed Swift had come in to view.

Gabbie stood up and banged the machine door shut but before she pressed the start button he caught her hand and pulled her into the small living room. Swift slid in beside him and Gabbie folded her arms, her eyes fixed on the tiny sofa covered in an old orange bedspread where she and Klim had spent so many evenings huddled together. It was no surprise that she was up doing these things at silly o'clock, she had been waiting for him. Her eyes fell on Swift who looked nervous and pale.

"He found you then," she said bluntly, more statement than question.

"Sí. me llamo Swift."

Gabbie raised her eyebrows, unsmiling.

"That's my name," the girl stated simply in English. "My grandmother told me I was like the agile bird that found the tall places in the city. All my family," her eyes clouded, "all my family, they call me that name." She seemed unperturbed by the other girl's hostility.

Gabbie looked directly at Klim and then back at Swift.

"Why'd you run then?"

Before Swift could answer Klim pulled Gabbie on to the sofa and Swift perched herself on the red leather armchair on the other side of the room that was pock marked with cigarette burns. As he was about to speak Gabbie turned angrily towards him.

"Where have you been all night?" she asked through gritted teeth, "I 've been waiting ages. How come you didn't phone?"

"I had to ditch the phone," he told her "look Gabbie, we're in real trouble, all of us." He sounded exhausted and for the first time she noticed the darkness around his deep brown eyes.

"What happened?" she asked, the rancour gone from her voice.

Klim told her about the events at the hunting lodge. Gabbie kept looking to Swift who nodded in confirmation of his story.

"Why were they holding you? We should phone the police," Gabbie said, getting up and moving towards the kitchen.

"No" the girl stood up, her voice in high-pitched panic. "One of the men, he knows the police, we cannot trust them."

Gabbie turned and Klim was also on his feet, coaxing her back into the living room.

"There's no time for this Gabbie, none of us is safe right now. Jackson is on the police committee, she's right. They know we're close and if they don't know already they'll find out where you live. I know somewhere we can hide."

Gabbie frowned but said nothing as Klim continued.

"Brassock saw me, they probably won't take long to figure out I'd come to you."

Gabbie's voice quavered a little but she shrugged her shoulders.

'Don't be daft. Where would we go? We should wait here till my Dad gets back."

Klim said nothing, both of them knew her Dad wouldn't be a match for a man like Alex Jackson.

"Well maybe that would be too long to wait," she offered and Klim nodded. Then Gabbie stood up and pulled her jacket on.

"What's the plan then?"

Klim guessed she was motivated not so much as fear for her own safety as not allowing Swift and Klim time to be alone together. Klim looked at Swift- he could see her eyes weren't quite right yet; the drugs they'd given her had still to wear off. He said to them both.

"First of all, you have to swear never to talk about this place to anyone."

"Yeah right!" Gabbie went to pull him from the sofa but he held her hand and brought her down beside him again.

"I mean it. I promised not to tell anyone and I have to tell you two but that's as far as it goes. Right?" Gabbie, still not in the best of moods, was getting angry now.

"What's all this about! Tell us what?"

"My dad named it 'Alcedo Athis'."

"Edo what?" She asked him irritably.

"It's another name for the kingfisher."

"Since when did you become friggin David Attenborough?" Gabbie rolled her eyes.

"It's a place of safety," Klim said seriously. "He meant it for my family to give us a clue how to find it. I think he knew that bad things were going to happen." Gabbie looked at Klim's dark exhausted eyes and sighed.

"Where is it then?" Klim took out the stone she had seen the previous night.

"Dad showed me how to use it. The place is only a couple of miles away, towards the crag. But first..." He looked around the room, "you have to both swear."

He picked up a DVD with a cross on the front and held it out for them to put their hands on. Gabbie frowned, the DVD was a horror movie and probably the least holy thing she had in the house. She put her hand on top of Swifts and Klim covered them both with his own.

"We swear," they said together. Klim carefully replaced the DVD.

"And no mobiles," he looked directly at Gabbie who was in the process of producing hers.

"No way." She snatched back her hand as Klim held out his. He lowered his voice.

"Please Gabbie. They can track us with them." Gabbie was about to laugh but the anguish in his face made her turn off the phone. She ignored Klim's hand but placed it behind the bread bin on the way out.

"Wait!" she said at the door. Klim saw there would be no arguing about this as she turned on her mobile and left a message on the bookshop answer machine to say she was sick and wouldn't be in for the rest of the week. Then she rang her Dad, knowing he would have the phone turned off, he always did. Gabbie told him her phone was playing up and not to worry if he couldn't get in contact. He was due back in a few days.

"Done?" Klim asked her pointedly but Gabbie looked carefully around, ignoring him. She turned off the washing machine at the wall socket.

"Ready," she said, finally satisfied.

In less than ten minutes they had locked up the house and were heading out on the crag road. Stricken with a sudden sense of urgency Klim's pace was such that the two girls struggled to keep up with him as he took a path towards the crag. They crossed two fields and then took a left downhill, holding hands as they scrambled downwards through a forest of beech trees.

At a small stile Klim crossed and then signalled for both girls to be quiet and keep out of sight behind the trunk of a particularly big tree. Gabbie wanted to giggle as the leaves tickled her neck but suppressed the impulse in light of the serious expression on Klim's face. He made them stay down for at least ten minutes, until he was completely sure that no one had been following them.

"Paranoid," whispered Gabbie under her breath. Swift's adoring eyes as she looked at Klim were getting on her nerves. A few hundred yards further on Klim started examining the tree trunks and Gabbie burst out laughing, "Oh come on!"

Klim ignored her, carved into one of the trunks was the distinctive figure of a small kingfisher. He headed right and continued in that direction across a maze of footpaths until they arrived at a part of the crag Gabbie had not known existed. She hadn't realised how high they had climbed until Klim brought them out on to a ledge at the end of the path they were following.

There in front of her was a magnificent view of the bay in the moonlight, the dark water reflecting the lights of a hundred hillside homes. Here they were at the top of the horseshoe looking out towards the sea that formed a vast darkness beyond. All three were tired now and Klim guided them to the left of the ledge, which then turned out to be a roof as he dropped down and entered the cave underneath. As the girls followed Gabbie's heart sank, the cave would be a cold place to wait.

Klim pulled a torch from his jacket and moved to the back of the recess, the girls followed. There was a gap in the rock that was just wide enough for a person to pass and all three edged their way into the second cave that was now revealed, passing the torch between them.

This cave was much larger than the first. Klim looked around the wall until he found a coloured painting of a bird. He brought the small stone he had taken from his uncle's desk out of his pocket and inserted it into the eye of the pictured Kingfisher. The girls gasped as the door that was solid rock opened out in front of them and all three entered Alcedo Athis, his dad's bolthole.

They were in a kind of porch. On a ledge, was an oil lamp. Klim took out a lighter and in a few seconds had the lamp lit. He placed the torch where the lamp had been. A second wooden door led to a living area and Klim quickly lit the lamps set into the cave wall. He then found a kitchen, a porta-loo and another room with some fold-out beds with bedding still in the packaging.

The small dwelling seemed to be very old. On one side of the living room the wall was lined with books of all kind from philosophy to romance. On the other were murals of a time long past. The clothes of the village people depicted were similar to those they had looked at in history classes about the middle ages. One of his dad's wooden sculptures stood in the corner, and tears welled in his eyes as he realised his dad had made a carving of his son as a small boy. The pure untroubled smile of his own younger image as he examined a fossilised rock brought back a sudden grief that left him gasping for air. Gabbie, who had been about to exclaim her surprise closed her mouth and turned away.

A huge stone fireplace dominated the room but this was now home to a calor gas heater. It was as if the crag had grown around the small dwelling. There were two deep wooden armchairs with cushions and Swift sat on one of these. The floor had been scattered with rich rugs and Klim couldn't help wondering how his Dad had managed to furnish the place, he imagined him secretly ferrying the contents a little at a time.

"I'm frozen," said Gabbie, hugging her shoulders. She lit the calor gas fire with the matches that had been placed in a tin on the fireplace and then she followed Klim into the kitchen. At least she thought it was a kitchen. In really looked more like a storeroom. The walls were lined with cupboards all of which had been stocked with tins, packets, dried milk, and in the lower cupboards, bottled water. In the middle of the room was a small table and a couple of chairs, the kind that were bought flat packed and then built up. Besides this was a small stove that ran on bottled gas. Gabbie pulled out three bottles of water.

"Wow, how come your Dad had a place like this?" Klim shrugged his shoulders; he'd been thinking the same thing. His Dad showed the entrance to Klim once on a walk but they had not entered and he had made his son promise to keep the place and the stone a secret between them.

"There may come a time when we need to come here without anyone knowing," he told Klim who had never really understood but agreed gladly to anything they would share together. They went back into the living room where Swift was looking exhausted and uncurious, seeming content to have found a place to rest. Klim thought she looked fragile and lost. She gratefully took the bottle of water he handed her and drank quickly, the plastic bottle shrinking inwards as she slaked her thirst. He was about to suggest they sort out one of the beds for her when he saw that Gabbie had already started unfolding the mattress and was putting on covers. Gently she came over and took Swift's hand, guiding her under the covers. After that she made up another two beds and turned to sit opposite Klim who had sunk into one of the armchairs.

"Do you think she's alright? They drugged her," he asked.

Gabbie looked at the sleeping girl, and tried not to feel jealous at Klim's concern. The edge in her tone told him she had not quite succeeded.

"I don't like it, none of it. It's too much for us to handle on our own."

Klim didn't reply, his eyes had closed and already he seemed deeply asleep. Gabbie removed the water bottle and covered him up, then gratefully climbed into one of the other beds and drifted off to sleep in a matter of minutes.

Chapter Fourteen

The dream came to her again, so familiar now that she sometimes struggled to distinguish it from memory.

Standing on the highest point above the lake, her eyes hungrily followed the far away form of the Mourangil. A hollow place had opened up inside her, the vacuum created each time he ceased to be near. Suddenly a stab of pain ripped through the muscle of her left shoulder and she turned placing her right hand over the area. The alu cloth was intact, there was no wound but her body felt as if she had been stabbed. Her eyes searched the crowd and stopped as they met the dark brooding turbulence of a face she had not seen before. He was taller than most, his clothes tapered closely to his lean form and his dark hair loose. Her breath stopped as he raised his eyes to look directly at her, oil black pools of viscous hatred.

Suddenly the ground gave way beneath her feet and she was falling towards the lake, willing herself away from the walls of the cliff and between the rocks below. Cold sliced her limbs as she descended beneath the water until she was choking on silt. She tried to push upwards but her body was caught in tangled fingers of foliage. In her mind, she screamed a cry for help that seemed hopeless as the lake sucked her further down and down into its depths. And then suddenly she was not in water but in the fluid arms of her Mourangil and lifted beyond danger. Then she awakened, as always, trembling and bereft.

*

The weather had broken, rain poured in great swathes across the sea and Kier wondered how visitors to England coped with the fickleness of the weather. She hoped it would pick up again for the weekend, the town would be full and there were many small businesses depending on the trade the Light and Water Display would bring. For herself though, she loved the unpredictably and changes the seasons brought. Gally had rung after breakfast to say he was heading back to the Mountain Inn. The face of Echin Deem had never been far from her thoughts since she had left the pub and even before her brother had rung she had decided to return to see Marianne.

"I'll come with you," she told her brother and there was a silence that told of his surprise before he arranged to meet her that evening. Once she had put the phone down she decided not to wait, to go across on her own that afternoon and speak to Marianne and perhaps Echin, if he was still there.

Kier was gathering a few clothes into her rucksack when the banging of the flat door downstairs startled her. A few moments later Adam entered the sitting room, his laptop strung across his chest and his face unusually solemn.

"Hey," she said, "I didn't know you were coming. What national emergency has brought you back to Pulton then?"

Adam removed his laptop without replying and Kier's stomach lurched.

"Is something wrong?" she asked, "is Gally alright?" Her voice shook.

Adam nodded.

"Everything's fine," he told her sitting down, but his expression was still grim. He waited for her to sit beside him before continuing.

"You asked me to check out Jackson. I did."

She nodded and waited and was then completely taken aback by his next words.

"You never asked what happened to bring me to Manchester that very fortunate New Year's Eve?" His voice was hoarse, as if the words scratched his throat.

"I knew it was something that caused you a great deal of pain in every way," she said softly. His face was almost as pale as the first time they had met in the shelter. His eyes were green shards that did not connect to the self-mocking grin.

'There was a man called Alec Klimczack. He was the most charismatic person I ever met. I was a skint student and flattered that someone so clever and sophisticated should befriend me. Before I knew it, I'd moved in to his flat near the castle and given up my studies to help him in his work. He bought and sold everything from property to antique pieces.

"Bit like me, no wonder you were so at home with a business portfolio!" Kier commented.

"Nothing like you," Adam's voice was tight with emotion, "nothing ever like you. Where you buy to nourish and develop a community he used his wealth to cause division and destruction, building his own fortune at the expense of those around him. I told myself you had to be hard in the world of business and that I had to hide my sensitivity.

"I was too infatuated to care that my friends had disappeared. I was living the high life until I found a folder I'd never seen before."

He glanced at Kier whose eyes, filled with compassion, did not leave his face.

"Alec had a personal lap top that I never touched but one day I noticed he'd left it on and went over to turn it off. Knowing how naive he was with computers and being both jealous and curious minded I started to root around a little."

"He was trafficking Kier, not only in drugs but in young people, girls and boys. They were from all over the world and his laptop contained the details of where they had come from, their real names. Photos of them, graphic photos, pieces of meat he intended to sell."

Adam's voice was filled with anguish, "the arrogance of him to leave them on his lap top. He was never too bright with computers and always lazy in the little things like logging off."

Kier touched his shoulder, "what happened?"

"I copied the contents to disc and packed my bags. There was actually very little that was truly mine, most of the stuff I wore was his cast offs, some cast offs! Armani, Gucci, I left the lot"

He sighed, "I was a complete narcissistic fool. I came back into the room and logged off his computer hoping he wouldn't realise I'd found it. And then I went to the police and asked to see a senior officer. That was my big mistake. When the man came in I vaguely recognised him but wasn't sure how. It was only later I realised he'd been to some of the Soiree's I was forever being asked to arrange. I waited a long time at the station, given tea, all the usual. Oddly no questions …. well perhaps not so oddly."

"When I left a couple of hours later being reassured that I'd done the right thing I walked straight into Alec." His eyes hardened and he fiddled with his glasses, his eyes glossing with memory.

"Well you know the rest…he left me for dead but I crawled into a truck and some blessed angel brought me to your door."

Kier put an arm around his shoulder and gently kissed his cheek, "blessed for both of us Adam."

Adam smiled his thanks and sighed, his voice tight with strain as he continued.

"Klimzcak had an obsession with the occult and a particular artefact. An obsidian stone."

Kier looked at him sharply.

"From what I know this object was originally a spear. It was thought to have endowed those who used it with enhanced power but always for evil. According to legend it's been used through history to enable massacre and torture on a huge scale. Then miraculously it was reputed to have been changed to a harmless stone and hidden after the Second World War. My erstwhile mentor was fanatical about tracking it down. Hoping to please him, I started researching the subject. I decided it was nonsense and a dead end and as he didn't know I'd been trying to help I just left him to it."

"And now you think it might exist after all and that I carried it home from Peru?" said Kier walking towards the window, suddenly needing some air.

"I think Alex Jackson is really Alec Klimzcak" he told her, "and will not be many miles away from that stone, if that is indeed the case. And I wish that neither you nor myself, ever have the misfortune to come into contact with him when he possesses it."

Kier stared out at the grey blanket of sky.

'I think you should come back to Manchester with me tonight," Adam suggested but she shook her head and turned back towards him.

"There's no need, I was just leaving to meet up with Gally in the Dales. Besides, from what you're telling me it's you who's in most danger." Adam was biting his lip.

"What else Adam? What else is there?" she said.

His eyes held hers, uncertain, and he stood up and paced across the room,

"He's dark Kier, cruel and dark but there's someone else- even darker and more vicious."

"Another person?" she asked.

Adam looked uncomfortable and she heard the dread in his voice.

"When I first knew Alec, I swear he wasn't that bad. Then he became more secretive and I was pretty sure he was seeing someone else. One night I followed him up to a small pub towards the castle. I watched through the window as he went to sit at a table opposite another man who had his back to me. He had blond hair and seemed young by his dress. Adam's face was lit with excitement- well, so I thought. It was only later I realised it was fear.

"Later?"

"I'd packed my bag ready to leave when I heard him come in and go to the bathroom. He was whimpering, in an appalling state. His body was covered in marks, like animal scratches. He just kept repeating one word 'the Perfidium.' It was only later that I realised that this was the stone he was looking for, the spear of atrocity." He sighed, "you know the rest."

Kier nodded.

"I'll come and find you in Manchester," she told him, "watch yourself."

Adam nodded, "I'll go back tonight."

Chapter Fifteen

Kier drove the hired jeep most of the way without noticing much as Adam's story played itself over in her mind. She realised her encounter with the man Jackson had been in keeping with what he had told her. She had felt the dark-eyed man's presence as she went to pass the narrow, cobbled street that morning, had known with absolute certainty that the toxic stranger was nearby. Kier had never seen his face before and yet she recognised the taint of corruption, a primordial recognition of malice so deep that its touch on another resonated in a way that left her physically shocked.

It was obvious to her now that she had been attacked when Alex Jackson had locked eyes with her in the rear mirror of the Mercedes, passing on the insidious impulse to end her life. Anger coursed through her as she acknowledged that she had been completely unprepared. How could she explain such a thing to anyone else? She had left herself naively vulnerable, forgetting all that she knew, pretending that only the visible and acknowledged could be real. Constantly she had pulled herself back to an inward reality, an awareness that she was following some internal impulse that she could never afford to ignore. That had been the instinct that dominated her whole life. If it hadn't been for Eamon Keogh that life would now be ended.

The change in the landscape when she reached Gladdendale brought her attention back to her surroundings. Ravensmount was a dark shadow to the left and the rain had beaten a bleak path across the valley. The sound of the window wipers sweeping rhythmically across the glass loomed loud in the silence of the place. There was a river crossing at the foot of the valley and Kier dropped a gear and slowed the jeep to manoeuvre across a small stone bridge. A vehicle nudged at the edge of a gate just over the crossing on her right-hand side and as she passed Kier saw the driver clearly. Dread fixed her hands tightly on the steering wheel and her limbs stiffened as she willed him not to follow. She was sure he had been veering towards the left to go back in the direction from which she had come.

It was the same man she had seen in Roust, the same car and the same eyes as they once again tried to catch hers in the mirror as the dark vehicle slid behind her own. Kier was determined that whatever menace he intended she would not allow. The road was completely isolated and visibility in the rain became even poorer as the jeep tackled the steep climb up the winding lane. Fighting down panic she put her foot on the accelerator and prayed that she would soon see the Inn. To her horror, the outline of an animal blocked her view and it took her a moment to realise that a chain of cows was part of a herd crossing the road from one field to the other.

The jeep squealed to a halt as she pressed down the brake and the animal in front grunted a rebuke and gave her an irritable nod for her noise and proximity. Kier felt trapped and her instinct was to jump out and run. Steadying her breathing she berated herself for overreacting, realising that she could find herself even more vulnerable. Instead she flicked on the central locking switch and felt for her mobile ...that was in the boot in her rucksack!

A glance at the wing mirror showed the door of the Mercedes open and a highly-polished designer shoe step on to the road. Kier hunted in the glove box, having no idea what she was trying to find but in moments she was conscious of a dark shape at the driver door. She gasped as the locks undid themselves clicking into the off position. She knew she had not touched the mechanism and automatically her face turned towards the menacing shape beside her.

The smouldering black eyes burned into her though somewhere she registered that they had lost some of their fierceness since the first time she had seen them. Even so, this man felt to her profoundly evil and for some reason she had no doubt that he wanted her dead for there was utter contempt and hatred in his eyes.

"Whoooah...get across...come on now." The voice was light and the Canadian accent unmistakable. Marianne, wearing green wellies and looking every inch a farmer's wife, came in to view. Kier went to open the door, her relief overwhelming, but the man still stood there looking at her and she shuffled across to get out on the passenger side.

"Marianne!" The older woman who had been concentrating on getting the herd across the lane turned towards her surprised and smiling. Then her glance fell to the dark figure standing on the other side of the car and her expression became one of deep anger. The last of the cows entered the field and they were three points of a triangle shrouded in a thready drizzle.

Kier's hair was damp against her face but she remained still as she realised she was now primarily a spectator of the intense unspoken interchange between the other two. It was eventually Jackson who moved away.

"Mrs Allithwaite." The voice was urbane and smooth, like the Armani suit he wore it was out of place on the raw surface of the Dales.

"Jackson," Marianne nodded, her voice thick with contempt. He smiled and his gaze moved to Kier.

"Your friend has a rear light out of action, I was just going to let her know." The fixed smile directed at Kier was a challenge. "It's dangerous conditions up here," he added. Turning, he walked back easily to the Mercedes.

"My regards to your husband," he said to Marianne with a cold smile as he opened the door.

The two women closed the gap between them as he performed a faultless three-point turn and headed back down the valley. Kier was in a cold sweat and Marianne's arm went around her shoulder though the older woman was also trembling slightly. Together they walked towards the field where the full herd was now munching fresh grass.

"The cows belong to Martin and his wife," she explained. "They rent our field. I'm just helping out." The gate clanged as she pulled it towards her and secured it into position and then Marianne turned to Kier, "can I pinch a lift back home?"

Kier nodded, relieved and started up the car as soon as Marianne had jumped into the passenger seat. Once they had travelled a little distance she questioned her companion about how she knew Alex Jackson.

"Who is he?" she asked, her hands gripping the wheel more tightly for part of her did not want to know the answer, as if further knowledge would bring him nearer. Marianne looked as if she had eaten something sour, her expression contemptuous.

"Beeston's business advisor. He's the one causing all the trouble. He makes my skin crawl." Kier remembered the conversation the last evening she was here when the Allithwaites were explaining the attempt by the old farmer and his advisor to oust them from their property.

"I'm travelling up to Roust tomorrow to meet our lawyer," Marianne continued, "Matthew should have gone but he loses patience too quickly. It seemed so ridiculous at first, all this about them having some claim to our land but last time I spoke to Geoff, that's our lawyer, I knew he was seriously worried. I'd even go so far as to say he's been spooked."

Kier felt Marianne's eyes on her as they approached the most treacherous part of the journey. At the bottom of a steep hill the road edge curved sharply above the river valley with a sheer drop below. Kier was unaware of her foot pressed hard on the accelerator until a scream rang in her ears as the other woman pushed the steering wheel and the jeep swerved across the road onto a patch of ground used by visitors as a viewing spot. Kier hit the brake and the car came to a skidding halt on the grass just before they reached the dry-stone wall. She released the wheel, trembling with shock. Without Marianne's intervention, she would have driven straight over the cliff edge.

Marianne, shocked, looked at her companion in bewilderment.

"What on earth!" she exclaimed breathlessly.

Kier leant both hands on the wheel and buried her face within her arms. She had so nearly killed them both. Lifting her head, she turned her face towards Marianne's, she saw the deep concern in her cornflower blue eyes.

"You drive Marianne, please." She jumped down from the driver's side as the older woman nodded and slid across from the passenger seat. Neither spoke again until they reached the Inn.

Chapter Sixteen

Marianne parked the jeep in the garage at the back of the pub where she kept her own Land Rover. Kier found herself unable to speak, so deep was her sense of outrage and self-abnegation that once again, after seeing the man called Jackson, she had unwittingly tried to end her life. And Marianne's life. The full sense of the almost tragic accident brimmed to the surface as Marianne stopped the engine and Kier, tears in her eyes, turned to the other woman.

"I'm so sorry, I didn't know what I was doing." Marianne put her arms around Kier who allowed the tears, finally to fall.

"It's happened before," she mumbled.

After a few minutes, when Kier's emotion had spent itself she straightened up and Marianne said gently, "come on, we need some brandy, both of us. It's been quite a morning."

The kitchen was empty and the two men could be heard working in the outhouse moving furniture. Marianne signalled Kier to take a chair and returned shortly from the bar with two glasses of brandy waiting until her companion had downed some of the amber liquid. Kier choked slightly as the spirit burned in her throat but she was glad that it had somehow kick-started her back to herself.

"You said it happened before. What did you mean?" Marianne looked concerned and slowly Kier gave a full account of what had happened earlier that week in Roust.

Once again Marianne seemed to find reassurance in holding the pink stone on the chain around her neck that appeared to pulse as she turned it. Matthew and Josh came in and for a moment Kier thought the look of disapproval in the big man's eyes was aimed at herself.

His characteristic flicker of a grin soon abolished that sense however, and Josh told her how much he was looking forward to seeing Gally that evening. Marianne told the two men about meeting Jackson but not about Kier's attempt to drive the car off the road. An almost imperceptible shake of her head was signal enough for Kier to do the same.

Kier was exhausted and the brandy had made her sleepy. She realised she was now feeling the fact that she had been awake most of the night before and went to the car to pull out her rucksack. Finally, the rain had stopped and the cloud was clearing, Ravensmount winked at her between the wisps of cloud and some of the tension left her face. A few minutes later she was fast asleep in the small clean room she had left so abruptly a few mornings earlier.

*

The sound of a car pulling up in the courtyard brought Kier back to wakefulness. Gally's voice came from the front of the building and she climbed into the window seat to open the window as her brother pulled an overnight bag from his car boot. Shocked, she realised that it was almost dusk and she had slept away most of the afternoon.

There were shadows under her brother's eyes. He seemed older and she guessed that his initial concern as to how the pseudo limestone could have been formed had grown to become a tick burrowed into his consciousness, eating away at his sense of the rational, causing continued unease. Gally had told her that his analysis of the samples he had taken confirmed there were substances unknown in his geological experience and this added to the sinister tone he had come to associate with Whistmorden, a place that until now he had held in affectionate memory. The lecturer had explained to his sister that he had been on the verge of communicating with his closest colleague when he decided in the end to come back and re-sample key points of the Scar once again.

She noticed the rain had cleared altogether as she shouted down to him.

"Hey handsome!"

Gally raised his head and smiled, his worried expression wiped from his face.

"I'm in the same room as last time," she told him. "Come on up."

As he bustled into her room he looked surprised to see she had been sleeping.

"You ok?" he asked, looking worried.

"Sure," she told him, "just catching up on some late nights. You go down and I'll follow you after I've showered."

Gally nodded, "I'm famished," he told her wearily as he dropped his bag in his own room. Kier breathed in the delicious smells that wafted up from the kitchen suddenly realising she hadn't eaten since breakfast.

"Will you order for us both, please?"

Gally, as she knew he would be, was more than willing, and she needed time to change and think how to explain to him what had happened that morning. She should tell him about Roust as well she decided.

Half an hour later Kier made her way down to meet her brother and was aware of a profound change in the atmosphere of the Inn. Terse lines pulled around Matthew's mouth and his expression was more implacable than ever. She said hello to Josh who was waiting on tables and saw he was quickly distracted and his movements seemed filled with tension. Gally signalled her over to the window seat and explained he had ordered her some 'goat's cheese stuff' and a steak and ale pie for himself. She laughed, making the decision not to speak about the morning's events, or what Adam had told her until after they'd eaten.

Instead she chatted easily to her brother about the Seven Rivers. After a shower and change of clothes she was beginning to feel almost normal again when a distinctive voice called from the doorway.

"Alrite Gally!" Its owner was a farmer with whom Gally had spent many evenings chatting about the land. Martin Cave had changed very little. He was a big man in his forties and his only concession to the passing years, were the grey flecks showing at his temples. He had regaled Gally with Dales stories born of the long farming history of his family. Martin had told him of the Greenhow Miners who had been saved by a ghostly shift that brought warning just before the mine collapsed. He also told the story of the crystal child, a beautiful white-haired girl who was seen to emerge from caverns locally when cavers were in danger to guide them to openings they had been unable to find.

Gally had been entranced, not only by the stories but also Martin's passion for the area and its history. He took the older man's outstretched hand and made room on the bench.

"This is my sister." He introduced Kier and Martin took her hand easily.

"Wow, you're way too good looking to be related to this reprobate," he told her.

Kier told him that Marianne had spoken about him that morning as she was herding the cows in to the fields. To her surprise, Martin's expression was troubled but it was only for a moment. Before long he and Gally were filling in the events of the last couple of years building once again a sense of warmth and familiarity.

Martin's son and daughter were clearly flourishing at the local primary school and Gally remembered Sandra, his wife, with a smile. A buxom brunette, she had once floored a man for pinching her bottom.

"T'was Sand's idea to open a farm shop, she's made it work too," he told his friend proudly, "come and see us while you're up Gally, she'll be well pleased." Gally nodded and fished in his pocket for his phone.

"Put your number in my mobile will you Martin," he passed the phone to his friend as Kier glanced towards the bar. The landlord seemed even more reticent tonight. There was no occasional grin to change Matthew's face from a hanging judge to Father Christmas which was how his wife had described the transformation that came about when her husband smiled. Tonight, the idiosyncratic moustache barely flickered and his eyes carefully examined every customer in the room. Martin followed Kier's expression of concern and seemed to come to a decision. He lowered his voice.

"Bit of a bust up, Matthew and Marianne, this afternoon. Marianne came across to the house, Sand said she'd been crying and they spent half an hour together. Anyway, she headed off back this afternoon but didn't turn up for evening opening. It's her night off from the kitchen but she's usually here helping around the bar or just chatting. Car was back in the shed, and she often goes on the fells alone but she would normally be back by now. Matthew's worried."

It was only as Martin spoke that Kier realised how much she had been looking forward to Marianne's benign presence putting right all the things that had been out of place since she had come down to greet her brother. She felt her insides lurch with apprehension that something had happened to her friend.

The food arrived with hardly a word from Josh but Gally happily cut into his pie. Trying to bring back some normality she picked up her knife and fork only to realise that her appetite had abandoned her after all. Martin stopped talking and Kier followed the farmer's eyes as he looked through the window at the two men just arriving.

"Arthur Beeston," whispered Gally through a mouthful of food, "no change there." Kier saw that he was referring to the first of the two men who had entered the room. Flat capped and heavily built he dangled new Range Rover keys from sausage-like fingers. The second was a tall red bearded boulder of man who followed Beeston towards the back room.

Matthew signalled to Josh to take over from him and he went after the two men, closing the door behind him. Josh leaned towards the shutters that had been pulled across the bar on the back-room side. Martin picked up his pint, excused himself and joined a group of locals at the bar.

The jukebox had stopped playing and the room seemed far removed from the haven it had been only a few nights previously. Josh was tight lipped, his eyes constantly looking out of the window for any sign of Marianne. Gally turned to speak to his sister but he was silenced by the sound of raised voices coming from the back room. Martin, quickly followed by Josh, moved to enter. As they did so the door banged open and the two visitors exited. Matthew Allithwaite stood red-faced and furious, moustaches quivering in rage.

"Get out and stay out Beeston!" The other man's face was aflame, his laugh a cackle of discomfort as he looked over at Martin and his friends. The big redhead turned to Matthew, his voice a malicious growl.

"Best and only offer you'll get for this old museum, Allithwaite. It's a fool who don't take notice of Alex Jackson."

The two unwelcome visitors banged the big oak doors and swept the old ornamental bottles from the porch shelves by means of a lift of their coats. The crash of broken glass started Matthew moving towards them but Josh signalled for help to hold his father back. Gally moved to support his friend and eventually it took four of them to hold the huge landlord. An arrogant tear of wheels signalled the departure of the two men and Josh sighed his relief.

"Dad, that's what he wants. He'd have you up in court and stripped of this place as soon as he can." Matthew was still shaking with rage.

"He said your mother's left, not coming back. How the hell does he know anything about Marianne?" Misery filled his eyes and gruffly he turned from the hall and disappeared into the kitchen to be quickly followed by Josh and Martin. About fifteen minutes went by and all three men returned with outdoor gear and headlamps.

Martin told the group of locals at the bar they were going to search for Marianne. In unison, they put down their pints and were quickly organizing themselves into a search party. Gally looked at Kier who nodded and they went across to join the group.

"I'll get our things," she told her brother who was joining in with the organisation of search routes. A deepening dread filled her as she climbed the stairs to her room. The thought of Marianne in danger brought back a picture of her face that morning confronting the despicable Alex Jackson. she feared to think that the encounter had been to blame for Marianne's disappearance. The thought of her own actions, almost driving them both to their death, chilled her If Jackson had really been the instigator of such a thing happening, then who knew of what other terrible deeds he might be capable. She was now certain that Adam was right and that Alex Jackson was the Alec Klimzcak responsible for her friend's attempted murder.

Chapter Seventeen

Klim's eyes opened suddenly to the sound of a cupboard opening. It took him a moment to realize that he was in the cave his father had prepared in secret and that he had fallen asleep in the armchair. Gabbie's long blond hair hung over the side of the mattress, she was still fast asleep. Gradually he recalled the events of the previous evening and pulled himself up, checking his watch as he did so.

It was 3.00pm, they had slept for twelve hours. Serious dark eyes peered warily around the kitchen door, Swift had a bottle of water in her hand but Klim thought she looked little better for her sleep. The dark shadows under her eyes had got bigger if anything and her skin had taken on an unnatural yellow sheen. Klim thought of her name, long dark hair, pale throat, hard to find unless on the move. The Swift was his favourite bird. As they had walked the shore road the night before she had told him that her grandmother used to watch the tiny birds in the chimney stacks in South America. She liked the English name of Swift. In Lima, she told him, she had learnt English to help make money from the tourists. Mainly she sold small bracelets that she and her grandmother had embroidered.

"I'll get us some breakfast," he told her getting up, "you get some more rest. Couldn't you sleep?"

"I slept all the time," her slight smile transformed her face and for the first time she looked to him like a normal girl. Her words were no longer slurring and her almond shaped eyes, even darker than his own, were clear and direct. She paused for a moment and then walked over to him reaching out her hand and taking his.

"You were very brave last night." Her Spanish accent made him feel ridiculously like Zorro. Klim shuffled uncomfortably, embarrassed he dropped her hand as he noticed Gabbie's eyes open, two sparkling daggers.

"No problem," he stepped past her into the kitchen "I'll see what I can find for breakfast."

Gabbie sat up, her long hair tussled and her eyes afire.

"So, what's your story Swift?" It was a demand rather than a question and the other girl ignored her, turning back to the kitchen.

Gabbie was infuriated, she stormed into the makeshift bathroom and Klim could hear her banging things unnecessarily as he rummaged through the cupboards pulling out a tin of beans and a packet of dried egg. Swift, at the kitchen door, told him quietly,

"Don't think your girlfriend likes me very much."

"She's not my girlfriend." As soon as the words were out Klim knew it was the wrong thing to say. His face reddened as Swift's eyes registered her surprise and pleasure at his statement. The reply had been automatic, he'd always been afraid to call Gabbie his girlfriend, to expose anyone he cared about to his uncle. Gabbie stepped into view behind Swift with a toothbrush in her hand, she'd come in for a bottle of water. The hurt in her eyes left him in no doubt that she'd heard him and quickly he moved past Swift to speak to her. Gabbie was too quick, already she was picking up her things and heading for the cave door.

A small gasp from behind them made them both turn in time to see Swift fall to the ground. Klim dashed back to pick her up and Gabbie reluctantly turned to help him put her on the bed. The girl's eyes flickered open for a second and they helped her sit up.

"I'm so dizzy," she told them holding her head. Gabbie picked up the unopened bottle of water and pulled off the cap.

"Drink this," she told her. Swift had so little strength that Gabbie ended up holding the water bottle so she could drink and then she leaned back against the pillows, her colour a little better.

"Don't fight because of me. Por favor." Her voice was weary.

"What's happened to you Swift, what's going on?" Gabbie asked her question again, this time gently.

"She doesn't have to tell us," Klim began but Gabbie's eyes were flint and he sat back and allowed Gabbie to adjust the bed so that Swift could sit up properly. Once settled, the troubled eyes looked at Klim and Gabbie in turn. She sighed.

"I'll tell you everything but it's not my fault if you don't believe me. Poka. OK?"

Klim was puzzled and Gabbie looked suspicious but once Swift started the words tumbled out and they both sat by the bed listening intently to her story. Gabbie couldn't help but acknowledge that her musical Spanish accent made her even more exotic.

"A few months ago, my grandmother died." Gabbie instinctively reached out for the other girl's hand but after a long intake of breath Swift stifled the tears that rimmed her dark eyes.

"Lima is tough for the poor and those with nobody," she told them. Klim saw the pain in her eyes as she spoke about the way Mateo had handed her to the foreigner, whom he knew even before her accurate description, was his uncle.

"How long ago was this?" he asked her.

"I'm not sure. It felt like years in that place, but I think it was only weeks. That was one of the worst things, not knowing what day it was. Sometimes I couldn't tell if it was night or day. There were no windows but I got a glimpse of light and dark when Sarah came in and out. There was a window opposite my room in the hallway."

"I'd have been terrified," Gabbie told her. All her aggression vanished as she realised the horror of what had happened. "Were you on your own the whole time?"

Swift shook her head.

"I could hear other girls talking next door. There was a toilet attached to my room and it backed on to some kind of shower room because one of the girls tapped on the pipes until I went to see what was happening. When I took off the top of the cistern there was a tiny hole and we could talk through it. The girl called Georgia was the one who spoke to me most, she was Albanian. She told me not to be scared, that they were really looking for one girl and that once someone she called 'the shadow man' had been to check me out then I would be moved in with the rest of them. She was so scared herself but she wanted to help me."

Swift choked with tears and Gabbie reached in her pocket for tissues, handing them to the other girl. Klim realised that this was the first time Swift had told her story to anyone and she was struggling painfully with the memories even though he knew she needed to tell them. It was like lancing a boil he thought, remembering the pain and release he had felt at the same time as his mum pierced an infected insect bite on holiday.

"They gave us drugs so we wouldn't try to run away." Her eyes swam. "To tell you the truth I was glad to take it after a bit, then at least I could be somewhere else even if only inside my head. She looked at the other two, willing them to understand and Klim smiled reassuringly.

"But it made me enfermos, sick," she added, "and Sarah got angry and made me clean the vomit." Swift's head turned and her hand came over her mouth, "the smell never went away." Klim was aware of a sensation of nausea and passed the water bottle to Swift who took a swallow and a deep breath before continuing.

"Then one morning it seemed like the whole building stood to attention. It was him, the shadow man. I could only see a dark shape but I was more afraid at that moment than any other time. I felt him touch my hand and it was if a jolt of electricity went through me. He said something to Sarah about needing to look at me more closely."

"After he left it was as if some bell had been rung and they began cleaning me up. She took me out into the corridor and I saw a dormitory full of girls my age and younger, they looked mostly drugged. There was an older girl with dark hair that I was sure was Georgia, she caught my eye as I passed. I think they were taken out at night and sold..." her eyes were full of tears, "they were beaten if they tried not to go."

"The shadow man came to see me. I was surprised when he offered me a job in England if I would do a 'small service' for him. I felt only relief when all he wanted was for me find a stone for him that had been buried at an old place outside of Lima."

"Wouldn't boys have been better for that job?" suggested Gabbie.

Her lips trembled but her eyes were clear and determined, searching those of her companions.

"My grandmother would have understood, she protected me."

The increase in her breathing and the way her eyes flickered everywhere worried Klim. He understood how raw the wound of her grandmother's death must be.

"Understand what?" he asked gently.

Swift said nothing then, sitting still, staring at the carving that Klim's Dad had made. A shadow fell across her face and Gabbie offered her some more water. Her eyes drifted to the cave door. Gabbie put her hand on hers, her face was angry, but now it was anger on Swift's behalf.

"The shadow man knew my secret."

"Who is he?" Klim asked.

"Mateo called him Mr Jackson once," she replied. Gabbie gasped, looking at Klim but saying nothing. "In the house, he came and left in the dark." She bowed her head, "just to meet him brings despair."

"What secret?" asked Klim. Swift had become pale again and her lips trembled, her words a quiet murmur.

"He told me that the Swift was the devil's bird. That's why my grandmother had given me the name."

"Is that all?" said Gabbie. Swift shook her head.

"It's true. In older times. He showed me on the computer"

"Do you feel like the devil's bird?" Klim asked gently.

"He made me feel like that at first but no, I'm not like him. Though I'm not normal either," she told them with a hint of defiance in her voice.

"Go on," Gabbie told her, "it's alright." Swift took a deep breath.

"I can do strange things. Pass me that piece of granite," she asked them pointing to a stone that Gabbie had found on the floor and placed on the table. She retrieved it and put it on the bed in front of Swift. The dark eyes closed and slowly she extended her long fingers to softly cover the rough stone. Swift sat unmoving and Klim focused again on the pale knuckles stretched over the granite. At first, he thought the light was changing but then realised that a pinkish glow was emanating from her hand. It became a pulsating orange light and then suddenly back to normal skin. Swift opened her eyes and the other two gaped as she removed her hand from a perfect round of smooth marble.

"How'd you do that?" He looked around for the original granite.

"It's not there Klim, I changed it. I can also find rocks that feel alive. Some rocks have something about them, some other presencia, another life inside."

Gabbie's expression was one of disbelief, her lips tightened in suspicion. Before he realised he'd done it Klim had stood up and moved away. Swift's face was streaked with disappointment, she looked more exhausted than ever,

"I told you don't blame me for what you cannot believe."

He came back to sit beside the bed.

"I believe you," he told her and the wall between himself and Gabbie was back in place. "Is this something that you've always done?" he asked her.

"No, that's just it." Her voice had become tinny and Klim glanced over at Gabbie who avoided his eye contact, watching Swift with concern in her eyes.

"I have always known stones, been drawn to the different types, but this other thing started just before Mateo found me on El Silencio, a beach." As simply as she could she told the story of her first encounter with the Stone of Silence, then she reached into her waistband and brought out the shining diamond. Klim had never seen anything quite like it. It caught the light from the lamps and he lost himself in its radiance. Gabbie stared in amazement.

"Wow," she looked closer, speechless. "I mean really." Swift nodded as Gabbie made a gesture to touch the stone. As she handled it her face was in awe and the other two laughed. It broke the tension between them and Swift's voice was lighter as she continued.

"Why didn't they take the diamond?" asked Gabbie.

"They never found it – I can make it disappear, look!" Again, she passed her hand over the stone and it became invisible although Klim could see the outline faintly. "You can see it a little because you know it's there, but if you don't then it's invisible. No one knows I can do that except you two. Also, I have a special pocket in my waistband that my grandmother made."

"Cool." He tried to smile but didn't quite manage the expression he'd intended. He stood up, looking at Gabbie, uncomfortable.

"So why did," he hesitated and then went on, "why did the shadow man want you?"

"At first I thought it was money but then I realised there was something much bigger." There was a haunted look about her and her eyes became unfocused and then closed. He looked over at Gabbie,

'Enough," he said firmly, though he wanted to hear more. "We can talk another time."

Gabbie echoed his concern but then Swift opened her eyes and looked directly at Klim, her voice strong.

"How did you know they'd found me again after I got free? How did you know where to come?" she asked and Gabbie frowned puzzled, adding her own unspoken question.

Klim saw Swift's eyes starting to close again, as if that last effort had used up any store of energy she had left.

"Come on, we should let you sleep," he said ignoring the question. He adjusted the top of the bed, as Swift's breathing became deep and regular. Worried he looked across at Gabbie.

"D'you think she'll be ok?" Gabbie shrugged her shoulders.

"Maybe she just needs to sleep. I don't know." She stood up and Klim followed her into the kitchen.

"So how did you know?" She repeated the other girl's question.

Klim knew nothing but the truth would do.

"I saw it happening in my head, Brassock finding her by the rocks in Pulton. She'd got all the way there along the shore. I think she was waiting for the woman Sarah to arrive. She helped her to escape I think." Klim's face became grim as he remembered the body bag his uncle had taken away. Surprisingly Gabbie said nothing about him being daft but stood with her arms folded, looking thoughtful. In Gabbie's case he never tried to enter her mind apart from the ordinary knowing of her and that usually didn't help much.

"Look I didn't mean…. earlier on," he began, but Gabbie stopped him.

Coldly she told him, "It doesn't matter. This is too big for us, we have to get to the police."

"No," he said simply, shaking his head, his own arms folded.

"I know he's your uncle but,' she left the sentence unfinished.

"It's not that," Klim was adamant, "I don't know who we can trust. He has arms like an octopus, you've no idea He sits on some committee that decides who gets the top jobs in the Police. And they'll be looking for her, for all of us." His dark eyes were anguished and Gabbie sighed in exasperation.

"But we can't stay here forever. We don't even know what's going on out there."

"Look," he said, "let's eat. Then we can figure it out." Gabbie unfolded her arms and began searching for a tin opener, she handed it to Klim with the can of beans and went to put the kettle on to make up the eggs. At least, he thought, she was still with him, for now.

Hours later Klim sat staring at the ceiling wondering when his dad had come up here to plaster the roof of the cave and make sure it would stay snug and dry. He'd found cleverly placed vents here and there and wished he'd been old enough to share the work. He stifled the awful sense of regret, reminded himself that he had to live with what he couldn't change, but his jaw set as he also remembered his promise to himself that he would change what he could for his Father's sake. Looking over at Swift he saw she was resting more peacefully although she'd had only water to drink all day and that worried him.

He stood up and went towards the entrance that had been so cleverly concealed and that Gabbie had left open so, she said, at least Swift could feel some fresh air. For a horrible moment, he thought she had decided to leave after all and then he spotted her as he came out from the outer cave, her small figure perched further up the path, her feet hanging over the ledge.

The blond hair had been combed and her hand reached up to push it back over her ear as he settled himself on the ledge beside her.

"Gabbie," he said softly, reaching for her hand. She let him take it though her eyes remained on the golden disc of the moon that shimmered on the sea and trailed rippling lights back across the water.

"I'll go and get some help tomorrow, ok?" he said pulling her round to face him.

Gabbie's eyes were the grown-up ones, the responsible ones that made him sad and glad at the same time.

"Who?" she said, "like you said, there isn't anyone we can trust."

"I can trust Reg,"he said quietly.

"Reg?" she repeated. "You've got to be joking!"

"He'll get us out of the area. Then we can go to another police force."

Gabbie shook her head, "and what if your uncle finds you? Then none of us will be safe. And what about those poor girls he's stolen? There might be some over here too." The sob in her voice made him tighten his hand but she released herself and stood up.

"We'll all go together when Swift is better tomorrow," she decided, striding back to the cave. Klim hoisted himself up with a last look over the Bay and quietly followed her back to the cave.

*

Klim was surprised he had slept so quickly in one of the pull-out beds that Gabbie had made up for him. It was just after midnight by his watch. Gabbie, her blonde hair hiding her face, was steadily asleep not far away. Something had pulled him from his sleep. Klim had found Swift's mind print as they settled into the cave, its sadness and turmoil was equal to his own but now he sensed something else, something very wrong.

She was a doll like figure on the bed and there were huge dark circles under her eyes. He tried to give her some water but she moved her head away. He could see the outline of the diamond around her neck, it seemed to give her skin an unreal look, as though she would never quite belong among ordinary people. He wasn't quite sure what he felt for this girl but whatever it was Gabbie would never understand.

Klim sensed that in the few hours since they had been asleep her condition had deteriorated. Gabbie was right – they needed help. Quickly and as quietly as he could he put on his trainers and jacket and grabbed a bottle of water from the kitchen. Gabbie would be furious if she knew he was going without her. He found the pen and paper his dad had left and made a note telling her he would be back in a couple of hours with some help.

The hotel wasn't far. Reg was working nights this week and Molly, his sister, was a nurse. If he could borrow the hotel van he could get Swift down to the hotel and he knew Molly would help them if he asked. Klim glanced over at Gabbie as he went to open the door, if he were lucky she would still be asleep when he got back. The key was still in his jacket, it was possible to open the door from the inside without it but not from the outside so he made sure it was safely tucked away. A few minutes later he was outside, climbing back up to the remote shelf of path that hid the opening to the cave and that led into the middle of the forest.

Chapter Eighteen

Gabbie squashed down the feeling of guilt at leaving Swift on her own as she made the decision to follow Klim. Living on her own for so long she was a light sleeper and the careful closing of the cave entrance had brought her fully awake. The note he had left confirmed her fears but the rush of determination she had felt on leaving the cave had disintegrated in the wooded darkness.

She had no idea where Klim was and no clue how to get back to the cave but she was sure that he would be walking into danger. He had been too quick for her, already part of the dark forest when she left the cave he had taken so much care to find. She sat on a stump of wood listening to the small animals scuttling around her. If it were not for the moonlight filtering through the trees she would have been unable to see anything. Looking up her eyes fastened on a small marking on the tree by which she sat. Straining her eyes to make it out more clearly, she reached up to follow its contours. It was a small bird.

"A kingfisher! Thank you, God!"

Instead of following the beak of the figure as Klim had done on the way to the cave she followed the tail to find the path backwards. Once on the main paths she knew her way down and despite the speed at which she now ran she barely made a sound. As she rounded the final corner she spotted him crouching by a boulder, watching the road just below.

He reminded her of a beautiful picture she had seen once; his face intense, his jaw lifted, and his dark eyes moonlit jewels. Gabbie toyed with the idea of shouting to him but he was clearly taking a lot of trouble to be unnoticed so she continued quietly towards him. Before she could reach him however Klim stepped out on to the road, pulling up his dark hood as he did so. As Gabbie reached the spot where he had been watching the road she saw Luke's van pull up on the other side. Some instinct made her step back into the trees. Luke was wearing a green camouflage jacket and baseball cap. He locked the van and pocketed his mobile, his eyes on the road ahead.

Gabbie noticed that even if he'd looked around Klim wouldn't have seen Luke pull up due to the bend in the road. She thought at first the other youth would shout his friend but as she dropped down it was obvious that Luke had no intention of letting Klim see him. Gabbie was puzzled but decided to follow quietly behind the pair.

Gabbie had decided that there was no way she could carry on without being seen past the old railway bridge at the edge of the town where the road became long and straight and lined by the wall of the Industrial estate. It was here she had planned to tell Klim she was coming with him. Just before the bridge however she almost ran in to Luke who was speaking in to his mobile.

"He's just gone past the estate, no, can't see no girl. No, she in't here neither. Ok, I'll catch up with him, course he'll tell me, I'm his best mate."

He turned to see Gabbie's wide eyes looking furiously at him.

"What the hell you doin Luke?" He looked back at her, and she thought it was as if the hard edges of his body had punched holes in his eyes.

"Mind your own business" he snarled, and she realised that somehow, he was glad she had seen him, like a cat finding a mouse. Anger rose like bile in her throat, she snatched the mobile out of his hand and turned away, her thumbs working to see whom he had been phoning. Luke was furious, his hand caught against the stone Jackson had made him take with him. His fingers reached inside his pocket and curved round the obsidian. At his touch, it elongated and seemed to mould itself to provide a carved handle for his grip. Gabbie was still tapping furiously into the phone. A moment later the touch screen images blurred and the mobile crashed to the floor as the knife blade entered her exposed back.

*

Klim lurched as he felt pain rip through his back and the image of Gabbie's collapsing body, her face pale as death, flashed across his mind. He had reached the shore road, was half way along the riverside when he sensed that she had been attacked. Klim hunched over in shock and pain but quickly he gathered himself and headed back along the road towards the edge of the small town.

"Where've you bin?"

Luke's voice rang out from the small passing place just before the railway bridge. He stood beside his father's van and looked to have been waiting for his friend. Klim was suddenly so glad to see him he flung his arms around the taught body of his friend, his distress banishing all caution.

"You wasted?" Luke pulled away with an uncomfortable sound between a laugh and a cry. Klim sank to his knees. It took Luke a second or two to realize that "Klim the almighty" as he often phrased it in his own mind, was crying.

"What the hell's up?"

Klim was distraught now.

"It's Gabbie, she's really badly hurt. I think she's dying."

He did not look up to catch the cold expression on his friend's face.

"What happened? "Luke asked, backing away a little more.

Wiping the tears from his face Klim continued, "someone attacked her. She looked almost dead."

He covered his face with his hands.

"What d'you mean – when did you see her?"

Klim was too distressed to notice the accusation in Luke's words, he continued.

"Her face was so white Luke. I saw the road. Come on, we've got to find her."

"Why'd anyone want to stab Gabbie?"

The words were a low drawl and it was if cold water had been poured over Klim's face. Carefully he stood up, reaching to the nearby wall to help him. Luke's face was almost insubstantial in the pre-dawn light.

"I never said she was stabbed Luke."

The blow was vicious and without warning. Luke crashed the bottle he had been holding into Klim's skull and jumped out of the way as his friend slumped forwards. He wondered if he had killed him. He hadn't meant to kill Gabbie and he hadn't meant to kill Klim. The knife in his pocket caught at his flesh but instead he reached for his mobile to text the man who Klim called uncle that he was bringing in his nephew. The phone had cracked when Gabbie had dropped it but the message confirmed as sent. Any remorse he felt was soaked up by the cocktail of drugs and alcohol he had taken.

He dragged Klim over to his dad's van and opened the doors; there were still a few logs in the back. Klim was far heavier than he looked and Luke grunted as he heaved him into the back of the van. He moved to the driver's door and turned the key. Nothing. He cursed and tried again. Only the clink of the key turning, the engine was completely dead. He took out his mobile to ring and the screen was black. He swore again and threw the mobile out of the window in to the bushes. He got out and fiddled under the engine but could see nothing wrong. He kicked the tyres and slumped in the front seat, he'd have to walk to the Hunting Lodge and get Brassock to drive them back.

The thought sent fear shooting through the fog in his brain. He looked over his shoulder at Klim, the blood now dried on his left cheek. Getting out of the car he got into the back of the van and rummaged in the pockets of Klim's limp body to see if he could find a mobile.

"Who the hell would come out without a mobile!" he shouted at the unconscious form. He slammed the van door and realized there was no choice but to walk

Even if he found a public phone the numbers were all stored on his mobile. He tucked the keys inside his pocket and headed out towards the main road. Klim opened his eyes and focused on the echo of footsteps passing underneath the railway bridge after the bend in the road. The glass had barely missed his eye and his temple throbbed with pain. The skin on the left side of his face felt stiff with dried blood that cracked as he moved the small muscles into a grim expression. A metal bar fell to the floor with the force of his kick and the van doors flew open.

Klim stumbled into the road and steadied his feet with fierce determination. Luke's betrayal was a sour taste in his mouth. Weariness, thirst and even pain were, for the moment, forgotten in the white-hot anger that coursed through him, he had to find Gabbie. Just before he hit the railway bridge was a spot his Mum had called the Goose Parliament. Walking home from primary school they used to lean over the wall and watch as dozens of geese all congregated together by the bridge where the river widened and curved towards the east. The noise level as they passed every day rose as, one after another, the birds trumpeted their annoyance until they were a chorus of angry sound. Tonight, he could hear the gaggle of birds muttering further down river as he clung to the wall for support.

Edging slowly along, nausea made him stop and he leaned over the wall and vomited. Suddenly his eyes could no longer focus and the spurt of energy had disappeared to be replaced by a sickly dizziness. The damp vegetation prickled at his nostrils and he fought down another wave of nausea. Slowly he forced himself further along under the railway bridge where the road turned sharply.

He leaned his back against the damp stone under the bridge to help him keep upright. The sounds of the river meant that the first Klim knew of the car approaching the bridge was the glimmer of headlights on the far wall. Fear shot through him and in that split second, he made the decision to hide in the trees on the far side. His injured body was unable to follow his intent however and as the car turned the corner he was caught in the full glare of the headlights in the middle of the road. Klim fell to the ground unconscious.

*

"Leave him Jo, he's drunk."

The man was in his thirties, tanned, with dark gelled hair. He was slim and well-groomed and the company car that had stopped under the bridge was a BMW. "Drag him over to the side, we can't leave the car there."

Jo was feeling Klim's body for any signs of broken bones. She was a petite brunette in her early twenties who was also the company first aider. She ignored her companion's words trying to rouse the young man on the ground and she watched with satisfaction as he stirred slightly in response to her squeeze of his ear lobe.

"We need to call an ambulance, he's got a nasty head injury."

Steve bent over and hauled Klim by the shoulders over to the long grass at the side of the road, ignoring Jo's protests.

'Trust me Jo, he won't thank you in the morning. Drive the car into that lay- by further down the road before someone comes around that bend and hits it."

Jo stood up but could see the injured lad was breathing ok and maybe it made sense to get out of the middle of the road.

"Try and keep him on his side," she shouted back, getting into the car and switching off the hazard lights.

"Jo." Steve had a card in his hand and was giving orders again.

"Get your mobile out and dial this number. It's all I can find."

Jo took out her mobile and looked steadily at her companion. He was holding it together but the wine had left him bleary eyed, and it was nearly dawn. Neither of them had slept since yesterday morning.

"We need to call an ambulance," she turned away and began to punch in 112 but Steve had covered her hand before she could finish.

"Look," he was staring straight into her eyes with his sincerest expression.

"If I thought he was really hurt of course it would be worth it ok? But I've dealt with hundreds of lads in this state. He just needs to sleep it off."

"His head," she reminded him.

"Ok he's had a nasty bump. I agree it needs watching. Look this is a mobile number, it must be important, it's all he has on him apart from some kind of pendant," he lifted the smokey stone to the light but seeing the anger in Jo's face he slid it back inside the lad's pocket.

"The best thing for us is to call someone who can look after him. Say we spotted him at the side of the road ok? That way he doesn't spend hours in the hospital that he doesn't need."

Silently she added 'and you won't need to explain to your wife what you were doing coming back from a night club with your PA at four O'clock in the morning.'

It felt wrong, like the whole fake business trip, but she felt herself backing down.

"You call," she said handing him the phone and going back over to where Klim lay still unconscious. There was a faint smell of alcohol about him, maybe Steve was right, and he had more experience than she did. There was even a slight anger towards the unknown guy lying in the road, she could have done without all this.

"Right Jo, he said he'd be here in ten minutes." His tone was one that made her feel he had sorted out her mess.

"How did you manage to tell him where we were?"

"He seemed to know from my description of the bridge, said it was a favourite short cut of the lad coming back from the pub."

"At this time in the morning!"

Her arms were folded around herself, she could smell the sea on the breeze and she shivered. Steve shrugged his shoulders and came over to her, wrapping his arms around her and kissing the side of her neck

"Who knows, local lock in probably. Come on we're out of here"

Holding her hand, he tugged her towards the car.

"We should at least wait till he comes," but Steve was at the driver's door as she spoke.

"He'll be here in five minutes," he insisted, "come on."

Klim, almost invisible in the long grass stirred momentarily before lapsing once more into unconsciousness.

*

The mobile he kept for only personal matters rang as the dawn light was reaching in through Siskin's open window. Glancing at the display screen he noticed the number was withheld and lifted the phone cautiously to his ear.

"Hi" his tone was neutral

A man spoke, his words a little slurred and his tone arrogant.

"Look we found your number in the pocket of a guy who's passed out on the road. You need to come and get him."

Before Siskin could question him, the voice went on, "he's on a road that sides onto a river in Bankside, just past the railway bridge."

The call ended and Siskin thought back to the mobile he had given Klim, he had put his own number in the phone but also written it out for Klim on a card to keep separately in case he was unable to use the mobile. He had only given the number in that way to two people and the other was female. He moved quickly and was starting the CR-V within minutes.

The roads were almost empty just after dawn as Siskin turned towards Bankside. There was only one road by the shore that he knew and it was one Klim would be likely to use. He pulled in before the road curved under the railway bridge surprised to see a van already parked with its doors loosely open.

Siskin's practiced eyes checked the area as he moved behind his vehicle and then alarm rose as he saw there were bloodstains in the interior and on the road. Walking towards the bridge he noticed other spots of blood and in the middle of the road a large stain that tallied with the caller's story of the boy passing out underneath the bridge. Cautiously he edged his way along the wall following the bend in the road and then he saw the outline of a body pushed roughly into the long grass beside the river, hardly visible in the morning light.

Gently he ran his hands over the unconscious figure in the grass and pulled a small light out of his pocket. With one hand, he softly pushed open the boy's right eyelid and passed the light across his eye and then repeated the procedure on the other side. He sighed deeply, both hands coming up behind his head. It was barely a whisper, a mixture of anguish and relief.

"I'm so sorry Klim, I should have looked for you before."

A discordant melody filled his ears and he blotted the sound out as he turned his head in the opposite direction from which he had come. Brassock, his vehicle left on the main road was searching for Luke who had not answered his mobile. He gave a cesspit of a grin when he saw Siskin bent over Jackson's nephew.

"Hit and run? Shame!"

The rough grating voice echoed on the lonely road. Siskin's eyes hardened and his body tensed ready to spring. Brassock took another step away from the shadow of the bridge and the stretched skin on his head and face was a sickly grey in the half-light. His small insipid eyes sparred with Siskin.

"I'll take it from here," he told him.

Siskin looked down at the limp form of the unconscious boy. He was caked in mud, blood streaked the side of his face and his breathing was shallow.

"He needs a hospital," he told Brassock, "the boy's seriously injured".

The big man hesitated, 'there's a doctor at his uncle's. Help me get him into the car, I'll bring it down."

Brassock turned and Siskin looked around planning how to deal with the big man. No doubt he wanted Siskin's help to get him into the car and then he would probably strike. He concentrated on making Klim more comfortable for the move, trying to support his head and neck using his jacket.

It was the return in his ears of the distorted melody that only he could hear that signalled Brassock's movement behind and Siskin leapt to his feet just as the other man aimed a lethal rock at the side of his head. Swerving and trying to steer the fight away from Klim's unconscious form

Siskin allowed his momentum to carry him through, bringing his feet up in a fierce roundhouse kick to the middle of the big man's chest. He felt his legs jolt against the layers of hard muscle as he made contact but the kick forced Brassock into the middle of the road where he lost his footing and toppled backwards. Surprisingly quick for such a big man he was up before Siskin followed through. Brassock caught his foot and only the younger man's athleticism saved his ankle as he twisted his body in line with his foot. Brassock was then forced to release it as his wrist buckled, then before he could recover, the massive head was locked between Siskin's lower legs as he rolled bringing the other man toppling over his head on to the road. Brassock's skull cracked on the stone and his eyes flickered and closed. A quick check told Siskin all his vital signs were ok before he pulled him to the side in the grass.

The light had teased its way through the grey furl of mist as Siskin carried Klim to his CR-V. Gently he laid him on the back seat pillowing the youth's head with his jacket.

"Gabbie," Klim whispered, his eyes open and panic stricken, "Gabbie's been stabbed. Please…" and then his eyes closed again.

Siskin rubbed his sternum to try and rouse him and Klim's eyes flickered,

'Tell me where Klim," he urged.

"The road by the Bridge," he mumbled, "next one."

Siskin climbed in the CR-V and drove the short distance to the next bridge on the outskirts of Bankside on a road that was rarely used at the weekends. He parked in the gateway of an office that looked unlikely to open on a Saturday morning. Siskin took out a torch and searched the ground finding bloodstains near the side of the road.

It wasn't long before he located the small body hidden in the bushes that had been planted to hide the industrial estate at the edge of the small town. Inadvertently her attacker had dumped her in a position where the moss had slowed the bleeding. Even so the girl was barely alive as he applied a field dressing to the ugly wound above her waist on the right side of her back. A noise to his left brought him upright; ready to make battle and knowing at the same time that if he had to do so it might cost the girl her life.

Siskin had no idea where he had come from. Later he reasoned that concentrating on the girl's state he had simply not heard the other man approaching. He tried to catch the melody of the other man whose blond hair and pale skin gave him an ethereal look. It was alien, sounds he had never heard before and yet they filled him with hope.

"My name is Faer," the newcomer told him "I am one of the few that can help her. Please trust me."

Siskin hesitated, aware that the girl's vital signs were diminishing with every second A moment passed and then he followed his instinct and stepped back from the dying girl, his eyes fixed on the other man. Faer approached and gently touched the site where she had been bleeding and Gabbie stirred in pain. In a swift motion Faer gathered her in his arms.

"There is only one place of healing that can help her," he told Siskin and then, still carrying the girl, he seemed to melt into the stone rockery that had been placed around the bushes. Siskin gasped. He looked around searching the ground, unable to find any trace of the two figures. Finally, he went back to the CR-V to check on Klim who was still unconscious. He checked the youth's vital signs as his mind raced. Jackson or Brassock would almost certainly make for the house, it would be foolish to head back there with Klim. How, in god's name, he asked himself, was he going to tell the youth what he had just allowed to happen to Gabbie! Exhausted, the musician climbed into the driver's seat but just as he was about to turn on the engine a Land Rover, driven at speed, passed the driveway.

Clearly visible, Brassock's grazed face was fixed in concentration and rage. Siskin waited a few minutes and then pulled out, heading in the opposite direction.

Chapter Nineteen

Kier sat opposite Gally around a table in the main room of the Mountain Inn. Josh had made hot drinks for them both, Gally poured a brandy for himself and Matthew. The others had all gone home to their families but none of the four remaining was ready for sleep. They had searched until it was too dangerous and pointless to do so. Beeston had told the police that he had seen Marianne with another man getting into a car in Roust, looking relaxed and carrying a suitcase. It was a lie, there was nothing gone, not even her purse but Matthew was unable to convince the force, now based in Roust and knowing little of the local people, that this was an impossibility.

The big landlord sat amidst the wooden tables and stared sightlessly at the solid oak panels that separated him from the outside world. Bar towels draped hopelessly over most of the pumps, the wooden floor had been swept clean. Music and company were but echoing memories within closed doors. Matthew buried his head in his hands and looked up, his eyes gazing somewhere across the room.

"This is my doing," his voice was anguished and unusually hesitant, his head hidden in the huge shovels he called hands. Looking up he wiped his eyes.

"We argued about…"

"Echin!"

Josh shouted out his greeting to the man who had just entered the room and was moving in fluid strides towards the table. Marianne's son embraced his friend and then his expression turned to consternation as he looked at his Father's rigid face. Kier saw the anger explode within the big landlord as he leapt towards Deem.

"Dad, what are you doing?" Josh jumped in front of his Father only to be thrown roughly aside.

"You. You're to blame," shouted Matthew his fist battering across the intervening space, easily avoided by Echin who stepped calmly to the side. Gally moved in front of the huge landlord, his solid and athletic figure not so easy to overcome. Matthew shouted over Gally's shoulder at Echin.

"You and your unnaturalness. That's why we argued. Where is she? What've you done with her?"

Echin said nothing, he was stock-still but Kier felt his presence fill the room. Matthew suddenly became quiet and stepped back but Gally remained between him and the new arrival. Echin's soulful eyes measured each person in the room and then turned back to Matthew.

"Marianne is a jewel that shines within the circle of your goodness and love."

The words brought Matthew's tear-filled eyes up to meet those of the man whose periodic appearances he had long ago chosen to ignore. He looked around for his son and reached out his hand in a rare physical gesture. Josh took it and was suddenly more afraid than when the huge man had been charging at his friend.

"I let her down," the big landlord continued. "I didn't want her to call you back."

Echin lifted his eyes and it seemed to Kier that she had never seen that colour of blue before; the colour of sky and ocean and rich sapphire all rolled into one. He bent forward.

"Tell me what happened," he asked gently.

Matthew was gruff voiced.

"After lunch, the rain had stopped and Marianne went to put away the stores in the outhouse. When I came in she was fiddling with the pendant you gave her. I could see she was thinking about you, wanting you to come back."

He hesitated, shamefaced.

"Something snapped inside. I said things I've never said to her, accused her of ...all sorts. I told her I wanted no part of someone who never aged, who turned up at odd times and from odd places. I was jealous," he added, his voice a hoarse staccato. He buried his head, "but I thought you'd know all this?" he added bitterly.

Echin shook his head, "I don't intrude into Marianne's life. She contacted me to come and see Kier," he glanced towards her as he spoke. "She also told me Kier was exhausted and safely asleep."

Kier nodded and Gally looked puzzled.

"I have things I need to say," she told them.

Kier hesitantly explained the events of that morning that now seemed an age ago, she also recounted what had happened in Roust a few days previously.

"Why didn't you tell us earlier?" asked Josh.

Kier turned her palms over and shook her head in apology.

"I was waiting for Marianne to come back," she said, her heart tangled with guilt. "I suppose I didn't want to connect the two things together because that means I put her in danger."

Gally looked profoundly disturbed as Kier continued, "and either what Jackson did was very real and he was inside my head or I'm losing it and I deliberately tried to kill myself and Marianne."

Echin spoke, holding her eyes. 'This was not your doing. Marianne has been taken."

The simple statement shook them all. No one doubted the word of this man who was so clearly much more besides. However, Gally's objective brain demanded more evidence.

"How do you know this?" he challenged Echin who took out a small pink stone.

"Mum's pendant." Josh cried out. 'She never takes it off."

Echin sighed.

"It called to me as soon as I arrived, it bears the imprint of her capture, she left it for me to find."

"Where did you find it?" asked Matthew stunned, "we looked for her on each of the mountains"

"I found it just now," replied Echin, "on the ground outside the back door." Matthew looked shocked, Gally looked uncomfortable and suspicious.

"You're saying that this pendant has some kind of recording device that can tell us what happened?"

Echin looked at Kier, "let's say it's the prototype of all recording devices. It belonged to Marianne, it will tell its story to only a handful of people."

He walked over and held out the pink stone in the centre of his palm for Kier to take. She felt herself tremble and then, with a firmness she did not feel, reached for the pendant. The stone was actually a colourless crystal-like form with pink striations running through it. As Kier touched the stone it glowed red. It was hard, like rock but it also pulsed like a living thing and gave off a soft warm energy that immediately brought to mind Marianne. Kier, who wore little jewellery, was fascinated by the unique stone. She looked into the pulsing centre where a spectrum of flickering colour held her eyes. As she concentrated she saw clearly the coloured shapes become a clear picture of what Marianne had seen and thought merely a few hours earlier.

Kier was able to see that her friend had come in quietly that afternoon, still upset about the row with Matthew but relieved that it had come to the surface where she could deal with it properly. Then with a shock she saw herself sleeping upstairs in the Inn, everyone else was downstairs. Her heart leapt as Alex Jackson moved down the hall towards her. In his hand, he held a syringe on the end of which was a sheathed needle. Marianne had come out of her bedroom behind him, anger stronger than fear at seeing the dark malignant shape scurrying around her home. All her will focused on preventing Kier being harmed. She lunged at

Jackson from behind and knocked him sideward into an empty bedroom, smashing the syringe. Marianne opened her mouth to scream for the others but a leather-gloved hand slapped across the front of her face, suffocating her. Then the assailant freed her nostrils and she could breathe again. There was a whoop of laughter from below and Jackson, exasperated, took hold of Marianne's kicking legs.

"Let's get her out of here. I'll get to the girl later."

Marianne felt herself efficiently bundled down the back stairs, helpless to call her family who were a few feet away. Even then Kier saw that her main concern was the fear that Jackson would return to attack again.

The pendant dropped from her neck outside, Marianne simply willed it to fall off and it did so, the moment chosen carefully when her head was nearest to the floor as they bundled her into her a white works van that had been parked unnoticed at the side of the building.

Kier let out a cry of anguish and Gally was there with his strong arms comforting her.

"It was here," she told the startled group, "she saved me. They took her but he came for me."

Gally was horrified and both Matthew and Josh were stricken as she recounted the events the stone had revealed to her. Gally was angry now.

"But this could all be implanted in your brain! We already know that you're
  susceptible, who's to say it hasn't just happened a third time?"

Josh ran upstairs and came down a few minutes later with the fragments of a syringe gathered in a towel. Gally picked up a fork from beside the bar and went over to examine it, he turned to Kier, his face a pale mask.

"If what you saw is true then my guess is we're looking at attempted kidnap," he looked at his sister, his eyes wide, "or even murder." He reached his arm around her shoulder.

"Why? I don't understand," Josh was ashen, "Why would Jackson want to kill Kier, she's nothing to do with the Inn?"

Before anyone could answer Martin Cave slammed through the door. He came straight over to Matthew his face taut with the news he had come to deliver. He looked around and his eyes fell on Josh, they were tear filled.

"I'm sorry, a body has been found on Whistmorden. The woman has Marianne's colouring and size."

An atavistic cry of anguish curdled around the room leaving the big man with his head in his hands being comforted by Martin. Gally went over to Josh who had shrivelled in his chair.

'The police are on the way," Martin told them.

Kier wanted to step out of this terrible day, her knees buckled and she would have fallen were it not for the arm of Echin Deem who appeared beside her. His touch did more than support her, for the first time that night she felt a surge of hope. In her hand, she still held the pink stone. It continued to pulse as she passed it back to the man whom, Kier had decided, may finally be able to answer some of the questions she had been so hesitant to ask.

"You need some air," he told her guiding her through the kitchen and out of the back door. It was the same spot that the stone had brought her to so vividly, in daylight, a short time before. It was a warm night, the sky lightening in preparation for the dawn as Kier stood listening to the sound of cars pulling up on the courtyard at the front of the pub.

"Do you trust me Kier?"

His voice was unadorned by any attempt to cajole or persuade, his face was turned away and the white stone in his ear glimmered in the half-light. Kier gasped as she saw the lapis jewel on his left index finger so like the one she had seen in the reference room.

"Yes. I believe I do trust you," she said softly.

He turned towards her.

"In case we get separated I need to stop this man getting inside your head."

She nodded.

"By you doing it instead?" It was Gally's voice. He was standing at the door but Echin seemed unconcerned and carried on talking.

"He has had two attempts to kill you by what you call suggestion or hypnotism but it is stronger than that. He has marked you by mensira."

"What? demanded Gally drawing near to his sister who looked in alarm at Deem.

"To those who cross the planes of reality there is a shadow on your mind that he will be able to access whenever you are in close proximity."

Kier shivered and Gally came out to stand beside her.

"I can remove it and help you to block another attempt."

"No way," Gally was furious, "I don't like this Kier."

Kier gently held her brother's hand.

"I can't think of anything, other than Marianne's return right now, that's more important."

She dropped her brother's hand and Echin reached out with his fingers to her forehead as Gally watched both of them, his fists tightly clenched. Echin's touch made her think of blue glittering crystal and then within the crystal was a diamond light, dazzling in its brilliance. The light then faded so that each facet slowly darkened.

"Place yourself within it, quickly," Echin told her. Perhaps because she had no time to think she sent her breath into the small remaining unclouded part of the crystal and as she did so the whole of her seemed to follow. The shadow that had almost occluded the dazzling gemstone was obliterated by the powerful light that was once again revealed. Echin removed his hands and she felt as if she had bathed in a mountain spring.

"It's gone," he told her. "And now I want you to learn how to keep yourself safe." Kier nodded that she was ready.

"Close your eyes," he told her as Gally looked on nervously, "pretend your mind is inside a large shell. No one can penetrate it unless you remove the outer cover or give them permission." His hands came up to her temples and Kier felt as if she had put on a bicycle helmet.

"You learn quickly" he commented, "that's a difficult skill to acquire."

Kier was intensely relieved, she felt sure that she would not unwittingly endanger another again.

"It's so evil what he did" she was near to tears, "how can anyone be so evil?"

Gally put his arm around her; he was still not sure about Echin. Kier on the other hand was completely sure, for the first time since the incident in Roust she felt like herself, and she had always known that self could be a formidable force. On the other side of the building they could hear the mournful sound of the dogs whining and Marianne's small family climbing into the police car.

"How do we find her?" she asked Echin.

Gally turned towards his sister "what do you mean? - Matthew and Josh have gone to identify her body." He looked alarmed and sad, "there's no point in filling our heads with false hope Kier."

He dropped his arms and turned away but Echin's firm voice made him turn back.

"Marianne's alive. The Chalycion stone would have given away her identity immediately to the man you call Jackson and the trace from the stone is closely linked to her. Her life is preserved for seven days until the residue of the Chalycion has been removed from her blood."

'So, she is unharmed?" Kier looked relieved.

Echin's eyes were filled with compassion.

"Sadly no. He can cause physical pain and suffering but he will not be able to kill her unless she chooses it. Until then she can be held between body and spirit."

Kier was shocked; she and Gally looked at each other in horror and she saw her brother was warring between belief and ridicule.

"Then how do we find her?" she repeated her question.

"I am hoping you will tell me," he replied softly.

Chapter Twenty

Kier was happy to drive, she felt refreshed from her sleep yesterday afternoon and from whatever Echin's touch had done to clear away the grey depression she had been feeling since her fist encounter with Jackson. Gally, on the other hand, had been exhausted and after a feeble attempt to stop his eyes from closing was now deeply asleep across the back seat. Beside her was Echin, a man she felt she would never be capable of truly understanding, so unusual did he seem. There was no denying his charisma and she was fiercely aware of the magnetic pull she felt towards him. At the same time, however, his difference from anyone else she had encountered made her feel uncomfortable and plunged her into a world for which she felt unprepared.

The sun was rising as she drove along the ridge, parallel to the river below. The rain had completely disappeared and the day looked to be warm and dry and this meant there was a clear view over to Ravensmount and Whistmorden where long stretches of limestone pavement glistened in the orange glow of a new day.

"What's happened to the rock at Whistmorden?" she asked Echin, "why has it altered?'

Echin looked at her carefully before answering and the thought passed through her mind that he would tell her nothing less than the truth, if he answered at all, however disturbing. She continued to drive, her expression calm as she waited for his answer.

'The agent of change has arrived," he told her cryptically, "it could not be used without altering the mineral fabric of Whistmorden. A long time ago a terrible crime was committed here and there is still a link between the land, racked and distorted in that moment, and the evil that brought it about. Over the ages, it has built itself to beauty once more but now it has been prepared so that the spear can be used to win passage for the enemies of man."

'No worries then," she replied, her hands trembling on the steering wheel, "glad I asked."

He smiled a wry smile in response. Kier's mind flew to the strange inscription at the Inn.

"The spear, it's the Perfidium," she stated.

Echin nodded and there was a tightness around his lips that made her feel sad for him.

"In my foolishness, I did not think to see it again used by any human being. I never thought it would return here."

Her heart plummeted and the jeep slipped out of gear as she manoeuvred the vehicle over the bridge. Her hands gripped the wheel as she concentrated on her driving, fearing to ask any further questions.

To her surprise Echin changed the subject and asked her about her parents. Relieved, in one way, though disturbed in another, her mind pictured a woman with long dark hair like her own, always tanned, a mother she hadn't seen for over five years.

"Our parents are abroad," she told Echin, "one in America, one in Australia."

Often, she felt that she and Gally had been accessories to the two "beautiful people" as she came to call them in her thoughts. Most of her life she had felt like a prize exhibit for the two high flying academics. Her father was a historian and had taught American History at the university, her mother specialized in early-years education. Once she had left home they announced an 'amicable divorce.' Each had found another partner and both felt they were still young enough to seek a fresh start abroad.

The inference was that their parenting lives and the reason for staying together had come to an end. A few months later they had sold the shabby-chic detached house in Cheshire where they lived as a showcase family. Every Christmas she received separate word-processed letters that were remarkably similar. It kept her informed of their new lives and families but neither parent had been back to England since. The guilt she felt never left her, whatever the cracks in their relationship, she knew it was her leaving that had torn it apart.

A parting gift was given to each child of £10,000. Gally used it as a deposit for his flat and it bought the small market stall that was Kier's first business venture. Neither parent seemed to have any interest that Gally was now a young principle lecturer or that their daughter had amassed enough wealth to allow her to sponsor the charities that had previously provided the purpose for the benefit balls they had often attended.

"They're not together any more" she said out loud, "they both seem happy though."

Echin nodded.

"And yours?" she asked.

"Set in stone," he told her, "never alter much."

"Oh" she smiled back and nodded, not really knowing how to reply to his unconventional answer, but then nothing was conventional about Echin Deem.

The castle came into view high above the river as Kier steered over the bridge and down towards the quay. Had it really been only a few days ago, that she had run down from the castle at much the same time in the morning and seen Jackson emerging from the house. Gally was still rubbing sleep out of his eyes when Kier gestured towards the road on which she had been running when she had seen Jackson emerge. Under Echin's instruction she parked the jeep further down the quayside and the three of them walked back towards the town.

"There," she told them, her finger directed towards the building that was positioned a little back from others.

"Ah," said Echin but Gally looked utterly confused.

"There's nothing there," he told her, "you're pointing to open space."

A figure that Kier had seen once before, crossed the footbridge over the river and came to stand beside them. Echin introduced him as Tormaigh. "Stay together," he told brother and sister as the two men walked across the road. Gally gasped, as the building, clearly visible already to Kier, came in to view. He looked shocked.

"I can see it!" he looked at Kier, "it's really there."

Kier was confused but was more concerned with what was happening as she watched Echin and Tormaigh enter the building.

"Come on," she told Gally," let's go." She pulled him across the road only to be met by the man who had saved her life on that very spot a few days before. Once again, he was in his jogging gear, his blond hair tied back from his face where a look of grim determination had replaced the softness she had initially seen. He looked at her and the building in front of them.

"How the..."

Screams came from inside the building and Siskin leapt forward closely followed by the other two. The doorway was old and narrow and led into a dim corridor where she was assaulted by the smell of sweat, blood and vomit. There was a kitchen to the left where a group of Asian children, looking unkempt, were huddled together. There were bowls on the counter ready to be filled and a vat of what could have been porridge on the hob. Tormaigh was speaking in a far eastern language, he gave the children whom, Kier guessed, were around five to nine years old, sweets from his pockets.

The ground floor had a couple of other big rooms; one was an office with several locked filing cabinets. Kier suspected that this floor was used mainly by those who had brought the children to the building. Horrified she had no doubt that she was witnessing the results of human trafficking and anger welled within her as she climbed the stairs to the first floor and saw a makeshift surgical theatre with empty cases specifically designed for organ storage. Nausea gripped her and she turned away only just managing to quell the impulse to be sick.

The sights became more pitiful as she looked in the rooms seeing children as young as five laying listlessly, staring at the ceiling. Tears sprung to her eyes, as she spotted pathetic attempts to make toys out of bits of cushions, and socks. They helped Tormaigh round together those who could walk and brought the children into the room with those who were most seriously damaged. The tall man's eyes were green fire as he reached into a cot of an infant obscuring her sight of its contents. Gally took her hand and led her up a further flight of stairs.

The screams had come from this floor where dormitories of young women and girls of all nationalities herded together.

"Juliette!" Siskin shouted as he entered another room further on and as Kier caught up he was holding a little girl of no more than four who was burying herself fiercely in his shoulder. The children in this room were all white and blonde haired.

"We'll get you back to your mum soon, I promise," she heard him say, his voice choked with tears. He carried her with him as he followed Kier in to the bedroom at the end of the corridor where a group of young men aged between sixteen and twenty had been gathered together. All looked towards Echin who stared at them impassively.

Juliette buried her head in the musician's shoulder, "don't like," she muttered.

They were a multi-national group of six youths. Kier read shock in their expression but there was also an arrogance that told of their perception that they were invulnerable in a world that had allowed them to dominate the unfortunate victims.

Kier couldn't understand why they had not run. Siskin handed the little girl to Kier and walked over towards the half a dozen male faces.

"Where's Jackson?" he demanded.

"They don't know," Echin told him, "they've been exploited in a different way. Without Jackson's influence, none of these boys would be here. He grooms them to cruelty"

Siskin looked at the other man suspiciously but Echin was calm.

"And not one had the moral courage to defend what they knew to be right,"

The faces of the young men became edged with anxiety and the tallest, his streaked hair jelled in spiky waves, leapt towards the stairs. Siskin shot after him and caught him before he reached the stairwell. He spoke in French and the ex-soldier answered him in his own language. Whatever he said brought the youth to panic and he struggled to free himself from the other man's iron grip.

Echin motioned the remainder of the group down the hall to where the girls had been incarcerated. Reluctantly they filed in to the grimy room and once Siskin had, none too gently, deposited the last one, they locked the door. Echin turned to Siskin.

"Call your organisation and the police. Speak only to Michael Barnes."

Siskin opened his mouth to speak but the little girl reached out her arms towards him and he held her tight.

"Siskin, one arm around Juliette, pulled out his phone with the other and tapped in speed dial. Walking slightly away from the others he reported the morning's events. Coming back to join them he turned to Echin.

"How do you know about my organisation?" he challenged.

"He set it up," Tormaigh told him ascending the stairs, "and now we must leave." Kier and Gally protested that they would like to stay and help but it was Siskin who spoke.

"I'll be fine," he told them, "back- up's minutes away. Best go before it arrives."

Juliette reached out her arms to Kier and Siskin transferred the little girl into her arms, seeing her snuggle into the crook of her neck. Siskin gently picked her up again after a minute or two.

"You should leave," he told her.

Still hardly able to take in the depth of depravity she had witnessed Kier descended the stairs unconsciously holding her brother's hand. The atmosphere in the room on the next floor had changed. T

he children were now responsive and she realised how malnourished they were. Echin spoke in what she thought was Albanian to a beautiful older girl, obviously leaving the others in her care until the police arrived.

At the jeep Echin and Tormaigh told them they were heading in a different direction to search for Marianne. Kier and Gally protested that they wanted to help but Tormaigh shook his head.

"You cannot follow us, there are places we can reach that you cannot go."

As Gally started to argue Echin gave them firm instructions.

"I advise that you discuss today's events with no one, Jackson has long arms. Go the bookshop tonight," he told them. "Tell Evan Gwyn that I've asked you to stay. We will join you later. Keep near to each other."

Before either brother or sister could object the two men had disappeared towards the river.

Once in the jeep Gally drove and Kier sat beside him, her eyes filled with tears. A flock of police cars, their sirens racing, passed them as they hit the bridge and made their way back to Pulton.

Chapter Twenty-One

The pain had forced Marianne out of her body so that she could clearly see the diminishing thread that held her to life. Down below, as she lay unconscious, the man called Alex Jackson was trying to rouse her, finally realising that the prize they had in their grasp may be as valuable as the one they had lost.

Jackson had been furious at her intervention to prevent Kier being taken. Marianne, already bruised from the rough handling she had received at the Inn had winced as the man Cross threw her into the small bedroom. After a sharp bark from Jackson she heard the distinctive sound of tyres on gravel as Cross left the building.

The room in which she was being held seemed to belong to a teenage girl with its pinks and purples and multi-media devices. There was no phone or computer point however and it felt empty and staged, missing the give- away signs of personality such as photos and posters. It appeared that it had been as much of a prison for its last occupant as it was now for her.

Marianne looked down at the bare hollow at her throat where she had worn her pendant. The decision to leave the Chalycion behind had been made in a split second when she knew that the greatest danger would have been to have given away her true identity. It's loss however had a profound effect for it weakened the connection between herself and Echin and made her feel even more vulnerable to her captors. A huge bear of a man Jackson referred to as Brassock had replaced Cross; on his arrival, he had entered the room and looked at her as a dog would a piece of meat. He threw a bottle of water on the bed and then exited, locking the door behind him. A little later Jackson came in, his rage abated but his malice just as alive.

"You needn't worry about your husband and son fretting about you anymore," he told her, "they found a body on the scar that has remarkably similar features. Her accidental fall on the rocks has made her unidentifiable. It will take a while, of course, to confirm dental records but by that time …well let's say the matter will be of no importance."

He came closer until his dark eyes were next to hers, his false perfumed smell filling her nostrils.

"Tell me about the woman," he had instructed.

It would have been useless to pretend she did not know to whom he referred.

"Just a guest," she had told him, 'she stayed with us earlier this week."

The blow had been vicious as he struck her across the face and she remembered the taste of blood on her lip.

"You can do better than that Marianne," he had told her, seating himself back in the armchair.

At that point, she had leaped for the door only to find herself entangled in the brutish arms of Brassock. He picked her up without effort and threw her back on the bed. She had pulled herself upright and faced Jackson whose venomous eyes held hers and he attempted to search her mind for the information she was unwilling to give. There had been confusion in his expression as he realised that she was protected and that he could not hurt her in that way. In his attempt, however Marianne had felt the touch of mind on mind and she, in that fleeting moment, was aware of his link to another terrible influence that had made her shrink back in alarm.

Jackson signalled to Brassock who had no such mental subtlety and she had endured his brutality until the violence had reached an agonising crescendo and she had fled in the only manner left to her. Echin had taught her long ago how to travel on this plane of energy, leaving her body sleeping elsewhere. It still came easily to her although she had not practised it for many years. At first, she wondered if her persecutor would follow her beyond the flesh, but he was a man of this age and could not. Jackson had ordered Brassock to stop his beating when he suddenly realised that the cut on her lip had already healed. Marianne saw the hint of panic in his eyes as he began to suspect that she might be someone to whom he should have paid more attention. However, his discovery came too late, her consciousness had fled and was now housed in the invisible form that could no longer feel pain.

Marianne watched the two men and saw the turmoil of hatred and lust that held them together as they left the room. There was something in this place, in its makeup, that blocked her ability to connect with Echin, she could sense it; she doubted that even he could find her here. Her unsubstantial form went to follow her two adversaries but she found herself unable to leave the room. This then, was the power she had felt, the creation of an unyielding wall on several planes of being that she feared had been created by a malicious non-human, what Echin named a Devouril. Effectively it meant the place was invisible even to those who were able to move in and out of these planes such as Echin, unless brought there specifically by those who knew of its existence.

Space and time became distorted as Marianne waited. The residue of the Chalycion stone that she had worn for so long would heal her broken body in another few hours and with any luck, left for dead or dying, she could escape. A door banged with force in the building and she heard shouts, a tirade that went on and on though she couldn't make out the words. There was movement in the hall and she heard Jackson's voice, taut and twisted, outside the door.

Suddenly he came crashing into the room, his faced flushed with rage, his distorted mentality plain in furious black eyes. He slapped Marianne's face, and delivered what should have been a fatal punch to her chest. A look of satisfaction crossed his designer features before he followed the others out of the room and then she heard him slam the outside door as he left the building.

Marianne saw the Chalycion residue working to repair her body but she was unsure, without the stone itself, if she could survive that last killing blow. Something, some major event had occurred, she was sure of that. The rage and fear of her captors still vibrated in the empty house. Even at that moment, when her own life hung in the balance Marianne felt a surge of optimism and allowed herself to hope that Kier had been the cause of whatever downfall had occurred to the monstrous individual who went by the name of Alex Jackson.

A sudden dread filled her awareness. Towards the south, a dark shadow was building, gathering speed and hurling towards where she was being held. It was terrible in it's black, undiluted evil and would swallow even her strong flame. A dreadful cry of distress screamed her re-entry into a broken body. Blood trickled down her throat and her spleen bled, swelling her abdomen. The choking shadow filled the room but by the time it had coalesced into human form her conscious awareness had fully departed to a place even that dreadful energy could not follow.

Chapter Twenty-Two

The music, rich and playful, drummed across from the prom as an African band played to a gathered crowd on a patch of grass on the other side of the road from the Seven Rivers. Gally was just behind her as Kier slipped through the side door and upstairs to the flat.

"He's right," her brother said as soon as they entered the living room, "Echin is strange, intimidating but also right. It's not safe for you here, Jackson has already made you a target twice and we have to presume it won't take him long to trace you to the Seven Rivers if he hasn't already done so."

"I leave you alone for a day or two and you get into more trouble?" The Edinburgh accent rang out from the kitchen.

"Adam," Kier ran over to him and hugged him tight, "what are you doing back?"

Gally came behind Kier and shook Adam's hand.

"Another visit to Pulton in the same decade!" he laughed, "why?"

"Apart from the fact that you never answer your phone?" Adam replied looking pointedly at Kier who fished in her pocket for her mobile that displayed nothing.

"Out of juice, sorry."

They made their way to the sofa and Kier looked at her friend carefully.

"There's something different!" she told him, scrutinising his face. "It's your glasses," she decided, realising the purple frames had been replaced by his old black ones.

"I broke the others, "he told her. "Anyway, how about filling me in on the excitement I've obviously missed while back in the land of civilisation."

Gally nodded.

"You start Kier, I'll make us something to eat"

'Toast," said Kier but Adam shook his head.

"Not for me thanks," he replied and Kier 's eyebrows rose in surprise.

Gally brought coffee and toast as Adam listened to the story of Marianne's disappearance and the role Jackson had played in trying to oust the Allithwaites from the farm. Kier wanted to tell Adam that they had been able to track Jackson's horrific crimes to the house in Roust that had been clearly disguised in a fashion that she could not explain. She decided to follow Echin's firm instructions however that neither of them speak about the events at Roust until Jackson could be found.

"It appears that my attempt at suicide was really that," she told her PA, "I tried it again in Gladdendale."

Adam bent over, his brows furrowed, waiting for her to continue.

"Apparently, Jackson is now into mind control, Marianne saved me. I nearly drove us both off the road into clear space."

Expecting to see a sceptical expression on Adam's face she was surprised to see him nod understanding. He questioned her closely about Marianne's disappearance and gave her a scrutinising look when she glossed over the events revealed by the Chalycion by simply explaining that she had slept until Gally's arrival.

"Everything you've told me confirms that we should all three head back to Manchester," he told them, "it's not safe here for any of us. Why don't I drive us back tonight?"

Kier started to express her surprise that Adam was using his car but Gally was already nodding.

"Good idea. You take Kier and I'll follow later."

Adam began to stand but Kier was up on her feet first.

"Hey big brother!" she told him, "I can't change my plans."

She glanced at the crowd that was beginning to gather on the stone jetty.

"Kier be reasonable," Gally said quietly.

"I promised I'd help out tonight," she said truthfully, "we're running a stall on the jetty."

Many of the shop owners had been offered the opportunity to advertise their business on the jetty that had been regaled with rows of multi-coloured bulbs that would look spectacular against their reflection in the water that evening. Kier had told Gina that if she was back from the Dales she would give a hand. Thoughtfully she looked at her personal assistant.

"Adam, you head back to Manchester. If anyone has to be in danger of Jackson it must be you."

Adam's face darkened.

"How about you Gally?"

Kier's brother sighed, "I'll stay with Kier and keep her out of mischief."

There was a moment when she felt that Adam was going to object but then he sighed.

"Ok," he told them. "I'll head back."

Kier disappeared upstairs and came back down with her rucksack.

"I need to collect some decorations for the stall," she told Gally, "some shells," she added as he looked at her quizzically.

"I suppose you need some geological advice for that mammoth task?" he said lightly.

"Of course,"

As they prepared to leave a few minutes later Kier went over and hugged her friend, his unusual stiffness made her feel guilty that she had not told him the truth.

"Watch it Scraggy," she told him, "give me a ring when you get back ok?"

"Charge your phone," he told her.

Kier looked at her friend and smiled.

"I promise," she said going out of the door.

Out on the prom Gally looked over at his sister.

"What was that all about? Why didn't you tell him what we were doing?"

Kier shrugged, "why worry him even more?" she replied, unable to explain her sudden instinct not to share their plans with the man she had, until this moment, trusted more than anyone except her brother.

*

The display was set against the backdrop of mountain and sea. The moon shone a perfect circle beneath which jets of multi-coloured lights danced to the sound of classical music. Families crowded along the promenade and children clung excitedly to adults, their screams of amazement lost in audio-visual bombardment. Finally, to loud applause, the spectacular show came to an end.

Alex Jackson allowed his features to show a satisfied smile as he received the congratulations of those he had come to impress. The local councillor, David Neil, whose bald head shone with sweat, heaved his round torso from a stone bench and went to put his arm round Jackson's shoulder and then thought better of it. His voice however was warm and enthusiastic.

"Great show Alex, fantastic organization."

Jackson nodded modestly, he had sub-contracted a team of people from outside the area to arrange the event. The red shirt he wore was made of silk and his suit was perfectly cut. His dark hair was jelled back from his face and he wore leather boots he had picked up in Madrid. Other members of the council came to congratulate him and he smiled his perfunctory thanks, quickly turning his eyes back to the now dispersing crowd. There had been no hint of his nephew, no sign of the girl. He was furious, not only had he lost what he thought of as his property but the raid in Roust had ended his most lucrative business. At least he had taken his revenge on Marianne. It irked him to have failed three times to finish the girl Kier Morton. It disturbed him deeply to think that there were others nearby with the power to challenge him however little she was yet aware.

Jackson had recognized her immediately as the owner of the gift shop who had been the unwitting smuggler. The coincidence disturbed him deeply although he had striven to hide this from his merciless mentor. His hand traced the smooth surface of the obsidian knife in his pocket, feeling it grow in power.

"You look pale, Alex" a large elderly woman in a purple suit came up to him and he hid his revulsion, "just tired," he managed to find a wan look for the Mayoress.

"You must be exhausted with it all," she replied sympathetically and he nodded in reply before she dropped behind to answer her husband's call.

On reaching the sleek black Mercedes a boy, around four years old, rounded the corner on his own into the small space bordered by thick hedge on three sides that formed part of the promenade gardens. The blond hair caught the lamplight and his small glasses perched lob sided on his nose. The boy laughed, triumphant in his escape, hiding behind the only car that had been allowed to park in that area of the prom. Jackson smiled invitingly and the boy moved forward and took something from his outstretched hand and then his ears pricked as he heard his mother's voice from behind the hedge. Laughing again he put his hand to his mouth and ran to his mother.

Alone Jackson's dark eyes wandered up to the rooms over the Seven Rivers. The ringed hand perched on the driver's door suddenly dropped to his side as he glimpsed a pale thin face. A loud scream came from the other side of the hedge and his eyes shifted, when he glanced back the face had disappeared.

A scream of despair wracked the small area of the prom backing on to the gardens where Kyle lay dying, his throat swollen and his mouth blackened. Jackson slid noiselessly into the Mercedes and headed out of Pulton.

A first aider had taken the little boy across her knee and was pushing at his back praying the ambulance would arrive. A man in his fifties wearing a dark fleece came out of the gathering crowd. The young mother looked at him with unseeing eyes as he moved closer, tears ran down her face and her expression was horror struck. A dreadful keening sound emitted from her lips. The young first aider frantically tried to revive the boy without success. She looked up from her seat and caught the capable expression in the eyes of the middle-aged man nearby. Speaking softly in a Welsh accent he sat beside her and gently lifted the boy on to his own knee. He passed his hand over the child's mouth and produced a small black object. Kyle coughed and took a breath, his mother called his name with relief and the child was passed into her arms.

The Welshman looked up and strangely his expression seemed even more concerned. He lifted up his hand, "he swallowed a piece of coal," he said holding a small dark irregular rock in his hand. The small crowd clapped as the child looked out from his mother's shoulder, his glasses askew. The young first aider threw a puzzled look towards the man who had come to their rescue, there had been nothing in the airway when she had examined it. Then Kyle started to retch and she turned to help his mother.

"He'll be ok," the Welshman whispered softly to the still weeping woman as he moved round to the other side of the hedge. Carefully he examined the area where the Mercedes had been parked and then lifted the dark object to the light, it was not coal.

Chapter Twenty-Three

Kier found herself alone in the bookshop, her fingers pressed around a mug of coffee that rested upon the oak kitchen table. Evan had suggested that she and Gally stay in the upstairs rooms and her brother uncharacteristically gave little argument. The Welshman had been waiting for them both that afternoon and he introduced himself as if he had not seen her dozens of times wandering in and out of the bookshop. Kier, puzzled that he did not recognise her, but not wanting to make an issue, stood silent as Gally explained that Echin had asked them to stay there for a few days. He apologised for the inconvenience, suddenly a little embarrassed that they were foisting themselves on a complete stranger.

"Of course, I was expecting you," replied Evan. 'this is Echin's business. I only run it for him."

Kier was astonished but covered her surprise by thanking Evan for his hospitality. After they had eaten she noticed the dark circles under her brother's eyes, he looked exhausted. Gally seemed reluctant to leave her side so Kier headed to her bedroom telling them both that she was going to have an early night.

Once Gally had reassured himself that his sister was safely in bed, he made for his own bedroom falling asleep almost as soon as his head hit the pillow. Not only had the last two days been disturbing for both of them but they had also spent the majority of the previous night searching on the hills for Marianne. Kier also slept but she had awoken just after midnight to find that she and Gally were alone and that her brother was still deeply asleep.

She picked up her coffee and left the kitchen wandering past the Reference room. There was too much on her mind to allow herself to become lost in its contents including the fact that the only other person she had encountered there had turned out to be Echin Deem. Instead she meandered through the rest of the shop looking through the maze of small rooms and it occurred to her how little time she had spent in the rest of the building compared to the fascinating and unusual reference library.

In the evening, the place seemed to take on a more sombre aspect and she noticed that what had always seemed to her to be a disorganised melee of books was, in fact, a much more systematized collection. Books were grouped together by subject, rather than author and numbered rather than alphabetized.

As Kier came back into the corridor the cellar door opened and Evan threw off his fleece as he stepped into the hall. There was no flamboyant waistcoat, none of the sharp sarcasm she had heard him use so often, instead his face was furrowed with concern. He looked at Kier and signalled her to follow him, as he started upstairs. She found a shelf for her coffee mug and followed him into the large bay windowed room on the first floor that was obviously his bedroom. In contrast to the space below it was meticulously tidy and uncluttered. Evan placed a finger to his lips and walked towards the curtain. Kier placed herself behind the opposite curtain on the other side of the window.

There were two men on the prom looking along the row of shops. Kier immediately recognised one of them from the images Echin had shown her on the Chalycion stone, he had been the one who had appeared to help Jackson take Marianne. After a few seconds, the older one shook his head and they continued along the sea front heading north. Evan stood watching behind the curtain for several minutes and then, careful not to cross the window itself, he made his way out of the room with Kier following close behind.

Downstairs the kitchen was now full of voices and Kier picked out Echin's unmistakable tone but the most forceful voice was that of Siskin, his emotion raw, and the music in his American voice more marked than ever.

"I don't know who either of you are, I have never felt melody like yours before, a tsunami pulled by doves."

"The lute," Kier heard Tormaigh state simply.

Evan pushed open the door and they were welcomed into the small group around the table all of whom must have entered through the cellar for the front door remained locked and secure. Heads turned towards them as they entered the room and Evan's voice was edged with anxiety.

'Two mercenaries are scouting the area," he told them.

Siskin immediately nodded, "Cross and Banks, Jackson's men. I spotted them on my way in but I'm sure they didn't see me enter the building." Echin had instructed each of them to enter and leave through the cellar door and had given Siskin instructions to meet them in the bookshop that evening.

Evan nodded, "I took them up the coast before doubling back. I was so sure they hadn't followed me."

Siskin made room on the bench so that Kier could slide in beside him. He was dressed in dark clothes, his long hair pushed back into a wool hat and he looked every inch a soldier. Kier remembered Adam telling her that he had been in the American Special Forces.

"As you know Kier," he explained, "when the daughter of a friend disappeared from her home I was asked to help track down the kidnappers. I ended up joining an agency that specialises in human trafficking. We tracked a lot of activity to this area but then the kids seemed to disappear into thin air. Although we know Jackson is the main instigator, even now we don't have evidence to connect him directly with the horrors we encountered this morning. He seems to have enormous skills in optical illusion or something I don't understand. You Kier, were the only person to have seen him come out of that house and I imagine that fact had a lot to do with his somehow transferring the suggestion of self harm into your mind."

Kier looked at him steadily, "you knew?"

Siskin's tone softened as he told her gently, "I saw your face that morning and it was blank, unthinking. He's a formidable enemy. I was there this morning because we had news of a recent 'delivery' of children from India."

Tormaigh nodded.

"We need to visit this man I think."

"Good luck," Siskin replied. "He has a house on the hill overlooking Bankside just a little up the coast. It's a fortress and it's always been squeaky clean." Siskin gave them the details of Jackson's address and a look that Kier was unable to fathom passed between Tormaigh and Echin.

"There is a nephew I think?" Echin asked Siskin whose face assumed a veiled expression but then he sighed and it was with relief that he replied.

"I've come to ask for your help because of his nephew. When you gave me this address today I was shocked at the coincidence."

Kier was suddenly aware of the lines of strain and tiredness that furrowed his forehead and emphasised the rich brown of his eyes. She listened with sympathy and compassion as he told Klim's story.

"I came across Klim in my investigation, it's clear that Jackson has taken his inheritance as well as his mother's sanity. Then a few nights ago, I was able to help him escape from the two men who were outside tonight, Jackson's paid thugs. I offered him a place to stay and he took it but then a couple of days ago, he disappeared," he went on to explain, "I think he overheard me make a deal with Jackson to watch out for him and let his uncle know if and when he returned to my house. I had no qualms in agreeing to watch out for him but not in the way Jackson meant. Unfortunately, I never had the opportunity to tell Klim, he disappeared mid-week."

"Klim," Kier struggled to recall where she had heard the name and a light bulb flicked on in her memory.

"I think I may have seen him in my shop, let me see, must have been Wednesday this week." She gave an account of the pair in the Seven Rivers and how haunted the boy had looked, how he had been with the girl who she had seen so many times working in this shop.

"Gabrielle!" Evans interjected, "she phoned in sick the last few days. I haven't heard from her since Wednesday evening."

Siskin nodded and his voice was full of concern.

"Gabbie is Klim's girlfriend though he keeps the fact hidden to protect her," he looked at Echin as he spoke, "I found them both last night."

Evan placed his broad elbows on the table and leaned forward.

"Where is she man?" he demanded, "is she alright?"

Siskin directed his words to Echin and Tormaigh.

"She was horribly wounded."

Evan gasped in horror and Echin put his hand on his friend's shoulder.

Siskin continued, "it was a split second, irrational decision but my heart told me it was the right one. "He held Echin's eyes, looking for confirmation. Echin nodded gravely and Siskin continued,

"I don't think any normal doctor or hospital could have saved her, I allowed her to be taken by someone who has the same kind of alien melody that I hear when I am with the two of you."

He paused and his eyes searched the two men but it was Evan who spoke.

"Faer! Why has nobody told me of this!"

Echin looked over at his friend.

"There was little hope Evan, even in Tinobar, our place of healing."

A string of Welsh words tumbled out and Kier did not need to know their meaning to understand the horror that Evan was expressing at this news.

"It's only in the last hour that I've heard that she has remained on this side of the veil," Echin continued, "but her condition is still very fragile."

Evan returned to English speaking.

"What happened?"

Siskin gave his account of the events that had occurred following the call he had received early the previous morning on the shore road.

"Apart from Kier, Klim was the only one I had given that number to," he explained, "our reluctant good Samaritan may have saved his life. Unfortunately, from what Klim told me one of his friends was responsible for both his own and Gabbie's injuries."

"Where is Klim now?" asked Kier

Echin nodded to the door and it opened to reveal the pale and drawn face of the young man she had seen in the café a few days previously.

"Klim is a Reeder. Echin smiled. "He has been in the cellar. He followed Siskin's thought pattern until he was sure his friend trusted us and that he trusted his friend."

Klim, his lips a tight line and his face etched with pain said nothing. Siskin made a space between himself and Kier and he joined the group around the table. The American looked searchingly at the young man's face before he spoke.

"Klim, Gabbie is still alive."

The youth was unreadable, it was clear he had heard their conversation. He turned to Kier.

"Why would my uncle engineer a robbery at the Seven Rivers?" he demanded of her.

Kier looked towards Echin who nodded and then she told the story of the theft that had taken place and the way she had accidentally transported the obsidian stone.

"It was Luke," Klim told them quietly, "it was Luke who took it. Brassock bullied him into it. They chose him because they couldn't find me. He was my friend."

The lack of emotion in his voice troubled Kier.

Echin said quietly, "none of it was your fault Klim."

Klim's dark eyes looked over at Echin and whatever he found in the other man's face softened his expression.

"There is someone else you are trying to protect," Echin continued and Klim's eyes fell. The group remained silently waiting until he lifted them again.

"She's sick," he told them. "Swift. She'll be on her own and afraid. I don't know how to help her. I'm too far away to know how she's feeling." The words tumbled out in an unaccustomed request for help, whether he trusted them or not it seemed Klim understood that he could not help this other person without them.

'The Stozcist," said Tormaigh and Klim 's eyes sparked. "That's what she told us."

"She was used to take the stone from i's hiding place. They will have used drugs and fear to compel her," Tormaigh added in disgust.

Klim nodded, glad that Swift's story was vindicated and relieved by the two strangers who he could not read at all and yet seemed miraculously to know what had happened.

"A girl." Evan looked stunned as Klim told Swift's story and where she was now hidden.

"I'll have to take you," he said evasively, "and we should go soon."

Echin nodded his agreement.

"A Stozcist can't be left underground for long, and it has already been too long. One of us will come with you but there's also other, urgent work we must do."

He broke off and looked at Tormaigh who turned to the others.

"Faer has returned."

The words were barely said when a man entered with dancing blue eyes and blond closely cropped hair. Kier seemed somehow to recognise him though she had never seen him before and immediately she realised that he was linked to Echin and Tormaigh. There was that air of enigmatic confidence and something, she searched her mind for the right word...crystalline, she decided. It held them apart from everybody else, made it feel as if the surface was a mere glimpse of a vast array of complex materials hidden beneath.

"Faer," Evan stood up, "how is Gabrielle?"

The sculpted face, the jaw line so well defined, broke into an easy smile that lifted Kier's heart.

"She's safe," he told them.

Evan clapped his hand on his friend's shoulder in joy. Klim searched the newcomer's face and his expression softened a little not yet fully believing but convinced enough to allow himself some small relief. Faer looked at Siskin who bowed his head slightly in recognition, there was an exchange of silent and mutual thanks between them.

"The spear?" asked Faer turning to Evan, "did you see any sign at the festival?"

"Ah, I forgot!" Evan reached over the back of his chair searching his coat pocket.

"I have something to show you."

He brought out the small black rock that he had extracted from Kyle's body. The small group listened carefully as Evan recounted the incident that had occurred at the display. Tormaigh, his lips a tight line, handled the material briefly and then threw it back on to the table.

"Jetra. Made to look like a sweet no doubt."

His long face grimaced in disgust.

"The child would surely have died. This material expands immediately in response to human mucosa, seeping into the tissues. Only a Stozcist could return it to its original from and extract that poison from his body, the boy will never know how lucky he was."

Echin looked at them both and said sadly "It was a trap to draw out a Stozcist. They wanted the girl."

Evan stood up, he spoke with great weariness.

"And so again, no good deed goes unpunished! I have hidden away here these last ten years, watching my family from a distance, barely knowing them at all. That is why the mercenaries were here, they followed me. I have brought the enemy to our door."

Echin put his hand on his friend's shoulder.

'They were not looking for you Evan, they were looking for the girl. There was no choice for you. Men such as these would not even register the book shop's existence."

Siskin looked uneasy, "The same way Jackson hid the house in Roust?"

Echin shook his head.

"No one could see that house unless they were very unusual," he told them glancing at Kier. "Everyone can see the bookshop and it is open to any who seek guidance and sanctuary." He glanced at Evan, "however such men as you described would not willingly cross its threshold, nor even register its presence, unless particularly directed to do so. I do not think you need to fear tonight Evan, though my heart tells me that the enemy we seek is very near."

Kier felt anxiety gnaw in her abdomen.

"There's been mention of a spear by one of those caught in Roust," Siskin commented.

"The Perfidium," Faer explained, "an obsidian stone that has already begun to transform into a weapon with grave consequences. It was used to attack Gabbie. The only reason that the girl is still living is because who ever used the spear did not intend to kill. The spear itself, changed now from stone to dagger, was the driving force. Somehow the boy stopped himself from using it on you Klim when you were unconscious."

"Adam was right then," Kier found herself saying.

Siskin looked at her, "the man you live with?"

Kier coloured a little, "he's my PA and friend, he told me that Jackson had been obsessed with finding the spear when they knew each other in Scotland."

At Echin's look of puzzlement Kier repeated the story Adam had told her.

"Perhaps we could go and see Adam," he suggested.

"He'll be back in Manchester by now," she told the group, "at least I hope he is."

Kier left her fears unspoken and suddenly realised she had not charged her mobile. She explained where she was going and dashed upstairs to put her phone on charge only to realise that she had left the charger at the Seven Rivers. Anxiety pricked at her conscience and she was angry at her lack of concentration. She would ring him at the office, she decided, as soon as she could. There had been something unsettling about Adam that afternoon, only now did she acknowledge that whatever it was had burrowed into her consciousness leaving her feeling fearful and sad. Sighing she made her way back downstairs.

"There are three aspects to our search, each as urgent as the other," Echin explained, He took out the Chalycion stone, the pink striations were now almost white.

"Marianne is barely alive, her life hangs by a thread. Today we found where she had been held but we were too late, she had been removed. Tormaigh and myself will begin the search again very soon. If you are willing Siskin would you join with Faer to look for the girl?" Siskin nodded.

"Evan, with great care, please take Gally tomorrow and search for any residue of the obsidian stone in Pulton,"

"And me," asked Kier?

Echin looked at her in a way that melted her bones. She had great difficulty in registering what he said at first but when she realised he was suggesting she stay behind, she was defiant.

"I want to help look for the girl," she told him.

Siskin looked surprised but pleased and Klim nodded. Echin looked closely at each of them and nodded his assent. Eventually it was sorted and Kier was suddenly glad that Gally was still sleeping; he would never have agreed for them to be separated. The sun was piloting above the milky smooth water of the Bay as Kier slipped into her brother's bedroom. He was still deeply asleep and she kissed his forehead silently saying sorry for leaving without him.

Chapter Twenty-Four

Siskin pulled up as near to the cave as he could drive but there was still a hard walk uphill. He turned to Klim.

"Why don't you stay in the car and we'll go and get her?"

The musician had pulled his CR-V into a shrouded lay-by on one of the back roads to the crag. Klim's dark pain- filled eyes looked at Kier but his reply was simply to push open the door and tumble to the ground. He was already on his feet by the time they had jumped out to give assistance.

"She's dying," he said in a harsh whisper, stumbling through the trees and heading towards the cave, somehow finding the energy to stay ahead of both of them.

"Where's Faer?" Siskin said looking around for the other man who assured them he would meet them on this side of the crag. Kier shook her head and followed the confident strides of the man she had seen for the first time a few days previously and yet was sure she had known all her life. At one point, he reached for her hand to help her climb and she felt the callused tips of his fingers from long hours on the guitar.

The enigmatic figure of Faer appeared ahead of them on the barely discernible path. Kier knew that from a distance the crag appeared mostly rock face. In fact, it was accessorised by a substantial land mass to the back and sides reaching across the coast and also inland where a number of villages nestled against its broad back. She had learnt that many of the locals and tourists adopted the crag as their own and it was easy to understand why this was the case. It was full of twists and turns and views that rewarded in every direction. To the East the high peaks of the Dales, to the West the Cumbrian mountains and out to sea the horseshoe coast of the Bay.

Klim directed them through a wooded area to the right of which were well known paths popular with locals for dog walking. The crag was generally approached from the car park on the other side and it was therefore no surprise that anyone choosing not to be seen would have taken this back route that cut across left into the thicker woodland without the clear routes evident on the rest of the crag. Klim steered through the tall stems of beech trees in the netted light of the forest. Faer came to a halt in a small clearing within the trees and led them on a path that ended at a fence bordering on to farmland. The others followed him over the v-shaped ladder that took them across the fence into a field. It was just possible to make out an overgrown path heading upwards in the opposite direction to the one they had been taking.

"She's this way," he stuttered.

"There is another path Klim. We must first go this way."

Klim's eyes looked glazed with effort and pain but he followed Faer. He led them to a clearing in the middle of which was an old limekiln. Siskin explained to Kier, who had never seen one before, that the area was dotted with these small domed stone constructions left from the days when the limestone was burnt to manufacture lime.

The archway on this one was overgrown with ivy and inside was a small cave. They could just make out a chimney at the back, inside which were small boulders. Klim sank down allowing himself to drink some of the water that Siskin had taken from his pack. Kier and Siskin also rested for a moment drinking the water but Faer positioned himself outside the kiln.

In the early morning sunlight, his figure was silhouetted in the centre of the arch as he stood, back turned and legs planted firmly. There was an elemental quality about him and it crossed Kier's mind that he somehow fundamentally belonged to this landscape in a way that was far beyond her understanding. Klim quickly restless but looking exhausted, reached for some more water, rallying himself for the remainder of the climb. In a short time, he raised himself to join Faer, his whole-body tense with strain.

Faer turned as he approached.

"We need to split up. The cave is in a direct line from where we stand. The girl is in mortal danger, I need to follow another route. Klim will take you to where they were hiding. Find your way back on to the path and we will meet up outside the cave."

Without giving time for further discussion he entered the limekiln.

"What the..." exclaimed Siskin as their companion disappeared into the back wall of the kiln in a flash of silver. He entered the limekiln and examined the wall making room for Kier to see the small crystal on the surface that, even whilst they watched, winked out of sight. Kier put her hand to the wall and let out a small cry.

"What's the matter?" her companion asked concerned.

"I can feel her," Kier's dark eyes filled with pain, 'she's dying."

On impulse, she reached out to Siskin and held his hand. He immediately put his hand to his ear.

"You feel her too?" Kier asked with an expression of hope that she could share her strange episodes of being able to see and feel things differently from others.

"I feel her melody," he told her, "everyone has their own. Hers is dark and haunting and fading fast. They turned expecting to see Klim but the youth was well ahead of them heading back towards the original path.

"Come on Kier we have to be quick," he told her and together they jogged along the trail until they had almost caught up with Klim. Siskin suddenly turned, his expression alarmed.

"She's so mournful, come on," he shouted but Kier hardly heard as her whole being filled with a sense of the girl's failing body. It was as if the earth was absorbing her into its structure as life seeped from her physical being. Kier felt the cold creeping from the periphery of her body into the centre where one by one her vital organs were failing fast.

The two of them, experienced runners, moved faultlessly through the maze of footpaths at speed, unaware of the steep climb but Klim, injured as he was, remained ahead. As they neared the cave Kier could hear the same haunting melody that Siskin was following and that was transmitting from the dying girl, she was no longer in the cave. Suddenly a massive gulp of fresh breathable air filled her lungs and a scream of pain emitted simultaneously from her own lips and those of the girl.

"No," they both cried, moving even faster towards the source. They continued on until they came to a ledge. Siskin followed a narrow path and Kier saw a cave mouth and moved to enter. Her companion grabbed her hand however and pointed to a track that hugged the side of the mountain. Klim was nowhere in sight as they slowed to follow the difficult path that twisted upwards and eventually turned inland, ending in a grassy mound.

Faer was bent over a small bundle laid on the grass with Klim standing beside him watching anxiously. On the ground, unconscious, was a slight dark-haired girl, her distinctive features now fixed in extreme pallor beneath olive skin.

"Will she be alright?" Klim asked Faer.

Kier knelt down and reached out towards the fragile body, holding the small hand in her own. In her mind's eye, she saw a stunningly clear diamond. In the centre of the jewel a prism of light flickered feebly, translucent pastels of yellow, pink and blue that even as she watched turned to grey. She quickly found inside herself the place where she was most at peace. Since her early years, she had been able to picture herself beside an underground silver stream where she sought nourishment and freedom from everything she knew or thought she knew. In this place, she was free of every emotion with the exception of a deep abiding love that needed no justification for its own truth.

Slowly she felt a strength pass from her touch into Swift's body and she pictured the diamond becoming rich with a myriad of renewed colour. Faer stood watching with interest as a soft gasp came from the girl's lips and all three gathered closer, gratified to witness her dark eyes opening. The small hand squeezed the fine boned fingers that enclosed hers and a weak smiled played across her lips as she saw Kier. Klim picked up her other hand and Swift raised her fingers to his face, too weak to talk.

"I didn't know," he sobbed, "I didn't know."

Swift squeezed his fingers weakly and then her eyes began to drift again.

Faer stepped towards the girl and picked her up in his arms from which she had been absent only a short while.

"I need to take her to a place of healing."

"No!" Siskin's voice rung loudly and Klim turned to him in surprise, "She looks as if she's ok now. We can get her to Roust to be looked at."

Faer, maintaining his position, softened his expression.

"Time is still of the essence. Tinobar has healers that understand what it is for a Stozcist to remain underground for more than a few hours. Do you think you will find that in Roust?"

Siskin looked torn, he had let one young woman be taken by this man and despite reports that Gabbie was alive they had yet to see that this was the case. Faer looked at him, his cerulean eyes crystal clear.

"I am no kidnapper Eamon Keogh, you know that in your heart. Go with the others back to the bookshop: even with Kier's ministrations this child will not recover fully without Tinobar."

Siskin nodded, his eyes focused on the pale figure that Faer was holding.

"How are you going to take her?" Klim asked.

Faer smiled and sighed.

"I cannot take a Stozcist through stone, we will travel through water."

Klim looked dazed at his words but before Klim could react the Mourangil moved his hand across the top of Swift's body and she was immediately encased in what looked like a bubble. He walked a little way and his companions stood dumfounded as the grass parted in front of his feet and Faer turned towards them.

"She will be safe," he promised. Then he dropped, holding his precious burden, into the gap. The others leapt forward and as they did so they heard a faint splash long below them and even as they gaped with surprise the ground re-united and there was no telling that Faer had ever stood there. Each of them stood speechless until Kier turned to the two men, hoarse with emotion.

"Who are these people?

"If they are people at all?" Siskin replied.

Klim said nothing, biting his lip and Kier put an arm around his shoulder.

"I trust him," she said, "whoever he is, he will take care of her."

Siskin reached into his pack for some water and each of them sipped gratefully. Klim was clearly exhausted but the strain had lessened around his eyes and for some time they sat, letting the morning grow, exchanging stories. Klim was persuaded to tell the full story of Swift's rescue and his eyes filled with pride as they praised his courage. Kier spoke about discovering the house in Roust and the darkness grew in the young man 's eyes.

"We need to let the others know about the cottage at the back of the hunting lodge," she said thoughtfully, thinking of Echin who had gone to look for Marianne. "It may be that it's hidden in the same way as the house in Roust was changed so that it was invisible to most people."

"But you saw it?" Klim said to her, somehow picking the thought from her brain and realising how much the fact had disturbed her.

"Yes," she answered, but Klim said nothing more. Soon his eyes shut and his breath deepened in sleep. Siskin had wandered off and Kier found her eyelids heavy. A blade of grass tickled her cheek and a long- stalked yellow dandelion winked a greeting as she drifted into a dream of childhood summers.

Siskin's soft voice stirred her awake in what felt like only moments later.

"We need to start moving," he said, pointing to a group of walkers visible in the distance. Reluctantly Kier shook off sleep and saw that Klim was doing the same. As she took Siskin's hand to help her up she realised, to her surprise, that the morning had become afternoon.

The threesome dropped down into the woods feeling unhurried and at ease, each one lost in their own thoughts. Kier mulled over the fact that she had known how to halt the chaotic disturbance that had produced the trauma of Swift's physical state. She had instinctively understood how to help her just as she was certain that her actions, though critical, had not been enough to save her. She was sure that Faer was right, her needs would not be met by any normal clinician.

Kier realised that it had not been her first experience of this kind of healing, there had been other times when her unobtrusive touch had quietly relieved pain, but nothing as profound as her experience with Swift. It both disturbed and thrilled her. And Siskin, she thought, watching his lean, muscular figure manoeuvre through the forest, Tormaigh had called him a Lute. They seemed to be a small collection of oddities, somehow thrown together and Echin was the strangest and yet somehow the most familiar of them all.

She wondered if he had found Marianne. The other woman had been little out of her mind, even with all that had happened. Kier frowned as she recalled the events she had witnessed through the use of the Chalycion. Had it not been for the courage of the petite Canadian she would now have been imprisoned, even murdered. Kier's eyes filled with tears of anxiety as she thought of what Marianne may be suffering because of her.

Absently Kier rubbed her hand over her left shoulder where the fine hairs had pulled her skin into tiny goose bumps. A glance upwards revealed that the warm sunshine had been replaced by a barren sky fading quickly towards dusk. Like the others, she was dressed in vest and shorts, little protection against the stiff breeze that now stirred through the trees. They seemed to have wondered away from the main part of the forest but it was difficult to tell as they had travelled at such speed on the way up. Siskin, who was leading, turned to them, one hand over his ear, his eyes concerned.

"I hear the sound of scraping stone," he winced, "harsh and urgent. I think it's some kind of warning. We need to go back."

They had emerged into an enclosed area where the ground was bare rock and it appeared that only the most gnarled and misshapen trees had remained. Spidery wooden limbs formed a canopy over the eerie enclave. Klim's eyes were wide with unease and the strong angles of Siskin's face marked rigid in concentration. There were several paths leading out from the shadowed area but it was clear that none of them could identify the one that had led them to this sinister grove. Kier forced down the fear that had begun to engulf her, breathing in fetid air that did nothing to steady her quickening pulse. Siskin examined each path but was clearly reluctant to move far from Klim and herself and for this she was grateful. As he returned to stand beside them Klim felt threatened enough to lower his voice.

"To the left," he whispered.

Then, in the deep shades between rock and misshapen stump, there was movement. At Siskin's slight flick of the head she and Klim turned outwards so that now they formed a closed triangle, backs together. A sickly smell of rotting vegetation eddied around them and a flurry of leaves marked the ascent of small birds from the canopy above. On the ground, the scurrying exodus of small mammals and insects caused Kier to pick up her feet in horror and cry out as she saw a snake wind its way towards the bare ankle above her trainer. Siskin reached downwards, expertly herding the coiled reptile towards the shadows.

A sense of putrid emptiness oppressed them as if they were in a hollowed abscess that the mountain had excised. Kier found herself remembering every mistake, every regretted word and they hung on her spirit like ball and chain, weighing down her self-worth until it barely existed. Suddenly she realised the absurdity of her situation, after all she barely knew either of her companions. Clearly there was no need for her to be there at all and her eyes lighted on a path that had emerged through the shadows and that would surely lead her down off the crag. She looked at Siskin and it seemed to her that his face wore a look of suspicion and she lifted her foot to walk away replacing it again as Klim's voice came clear and cool as fresh water.

"They're trying to split us up," he said, 'they want you Kier." His eyes were filled with strain and he shook his head as if to dispel the images that had invaded his consciousness. Kier blinked away all thought of leaving and moved backwards, Siskin drew nearer, placing his body alongside her own. She heard a rasping voice reach through the noxious shadow.

"Come then and face the Roghuldjn."

Kier realised that a patch of mottled grey bark had broken away from the most distorted and convoluted of the trees. A hollow indent blinked open to reveal dark sacs in the centre of which a sickly green iris peered, cat-like, at each of them. Startled she saw that there were many more creatures unfurling themselves from behind withered branches, their camouflage so effective that it seemed that parts of the trees had split from the trunks. As they separated there was a flurry of green leaf above as if the branches sighed in relief.

The bodies of the creatures were long and sinuous, and they dropped to four legs with the predatory ease of a leopard. Kier was in no doubt that the powerful hind limbs would easily bring them leaping to where they now stood. The biggest of the creatures stalked across the small group, it's jaw jutted forward and from the savage mouth came a low growl.

"Fools, to bury a Stozcist!"

The voice now held the edge of anticipation and slowly each of the creatures peered closer until they completely circled the small group. The other two followed Siskin's lead and picked up branches to defend themselves. Siskin struck a light and the dry wood he was carrying leapt into flame. The creatures stepped backwards but then the leader hissed his breath towards the branch, extinguishing the flame. Siskin shouted, still waving the stick.

"Get back!"

Klim flung his heavy branch towards one of the Roghuldjn as it snapped at him. It was clear that these aberrant predators were playing with them, they were now completely surrounded. Directly in front of Kier the leader's malicious appraisal sent a sword blade of fear into her heart. He approached her, his jaw open in a savage grin. Kier glanced round in panic seeing that both Klim and Siskin were also inches from attack.

"Asin vi," she shouted, the words springing from deep inside her consciousness, "Asin vi Lioncera."

The Roghuldjn sprang backwards as the companions yelled their shock, scrambling uselessly as the ground fell from beneath their feet and they were enveloped in darkness.

Chapter Twenty-Five

Images of rippling water, liquid colour that fell with her into the deep earth. Without warning, her lungs heaved painfully as they expanded to gulp in air. Gasping, Kier had no idea where she was, just aware that her back rested against uneven stone. Her eyes remained half closed, unable yet to adjust to the light that filled the space in which she miraculously now sat. Slowly she forced open her eyes and saw that Klim and Siskin were on either side of her, looking as dazed and confused as she felt.

"Gabbie," murmured Klim hazily.

In a matter of seconds, they were surrounded by tiny fluttering creatures. It came to her that they were exactly like those she had seen carved into the chair in the reading room of the bookshop, alive and almost transparent. She was captured by their immense beauty and fragility as they focused tiny crystal eyes on hers. The minute butterfly wings beat so fast that they appeared almost still.

'Ortheria,' the name came to her as if snatched from the air and yet she knew it belonged to the tiny creature that was trying to lead her across a massive underground chamber. Lights flickered all over the solid vault of the ceiling that illuminated the whole space. Kier realised that she was feeling as much as seeing the spectacular colours produced by the various rock forms that winked and glittered from each wall.

Ortheria and a crowd of 'fossilia,' again the name seemed to manifest itself in her mind, fluttered around them. In the middle of the tiny gathering of creatures was a tray of fresh fruit and stone cups of water. The back wall of the arch altered to make an indented seat as Kier's legs started to wobble underneath her. Gratefully she sat down and allowed the water and fruit to saturate her parched body.

Siskin sat beside her and also drank the water. The liquid revived them both. Kier felt a surge of hope and a sense of wellbeing that somehow blotted out the dreadful attack they had experienced. Siskin looked enraptured by the tiny creatures and his eyes followed the fluttering crowd as they moved towards Kier.

"They're so full of music," he said, "I've never heard such vibrant chords before. Fossilia," he said the word out loud. "They're amazing aren't they, how do I know their name?"

"Ideation is the language of the universe," quoted Kier, "I read that in the bookshop once. I never understood it until now."

Siskin looked puzzled, "I suddenly feel as if I don't know anything anymore. Where are we?"

"I don't know." She replaced the remains of the fruit on a makeshift tray of what appeared to be tree roots that quickly disappeared amongst the fossilia.

"I think it was you who brought us here," Siskin said quietly.

"What," she looked at him, "how?"

"You said some strange words just as we were about to be ripped to shreds by those monsters."

"Roghuldjn," she shivered in memory.

"Why do you call them that?" he asked frowning.

"Didn't you hear that's what they called themselves?" She began to feel the same sensation of disbelief and abnormality that had occurred when she had read the inscription at the Mountain Inn.

Siskin shook his head, "No," he said gently, "I didn't."

Kier pulled her arms around her remembering how the strange words had leaped to her lips and had somehow delivered them from the malignant jaws of the Roghuldjn. It occurred to her that she should be feeling terrified by the unfamiliarity of everything but here she felt surrounded with reassurance.

The three companions watched in wonder as the little creatures wove in and out between them, elements of a spectacular dance of light and colour that bounced from surface to surface within the chamber. Klim absent-mindedly drank from the cup that hovered near his lips. Kier's eyes fell on one of the minerals that glittered on the wall behind, it was a deep green and seemed to grow in size. A few moments later a tall figure stood beside them and Kier recognised Tormaigh. Unmistakably he was Echin's companion but instead of looking out of place, here he seemed to fit perfectly. The Green black of his long hair was reflected by the constantly changing light patterns, his eyes deep pools of unfathomable depth. Kier impulsively flung her arms around his neck.

"I'm so glad you're here, where did you come from?" her muffled voice asked.

Tormaigh smiled a very human smile as she straightened herself up and she felt a gentle brush on her mind as she lifted her eyes to meet his. A glimpse of panoramic vistas of distant places crossed her vision as she did so.

"We are Mourangils. Thousands of us reside within the living rock, we hear the whispers of the planet and feel the motion that runs along its veins. This is Lioncera, the moving kingdom that may be summoned at need."

Kier looked around in amazement at the walls of shimmering minerals that glowed with energy.

"What of Marianne?" Kier asked, "did you find her?"

Tormaigh sighed.

"We have not found her, she is hidden, even from our sight." He smiled kindly as he spoke but her disappointment was keen and would have engulfed her were it not for the embrace of Lioncera. In this place, she recognised that

Tormaigh seemed almost regal, and she understood that he was a being far beyond her ability to comprehend.

"You have all had a lucky escape," he told them, "The Roghuldjn are a very old predator of mankind." Kier had the impression that the walls glittered fiercely.

Klim told them, "I've known the crag all my life, and there's never been any sightings or hint that they were there."

"The Roghuldjn can sleep for a hundred years and will stir only if a certain prey comes within their reach," Tormaigh replied. "You three appear to be that prey. As to how you came to be here you called and Lioncera responded, an event that has not happened in a hundred thousand years."

Kier was dumfounded and Siskin opened his mouth to question Tormaigh further but the tall figure moved towards the seat on which Kier had been sitting.

"Please."

He motioned for them to join him and then pointed towards the opposite wall of the chamber. Klim, more reluctantly, went with them and the small group watched as an outer layer of shimmering rock was stripped aside to reveal a richly coloured mural depicting an ancient scene. There were five figures standing inside a temple. Four of the figures were indiscernible, either because of the age of the primitive painting or because the early artist made it so. The fifth figure, in contrast, was vivid with detail. The artist had created a subtle aura around this individual. He appeared statue-like in a gown of stalactites and stalagmites. Where the edges should have appeared sharp, however, they disappeared into the underlying material and became intricate layers.

The effect was one of suggested contradiction; strength and fragility, motion and stillness. The face, to their surprise, was contemporary and not unfamiliar. The hair was old man's hair, worn long and thin to the shoulder. The result was that he appeared majestic in a common way, still as stone yet fluid, untouchable but vibrant and accessible. Kier blinked as the suggestion of movement at the edge of the mouth became more pronounced. All three stood in astonishment, as the figure then smiled and was no longer a painting but reality. He stepped into the middle of the chamber with a gentle tinkling sound. The three friends were speechless with awe. Tormaigh stepped forward and his whole being seemed to glow with pleasure as he greeted the old man. Together they turned and came towards the three visitors.

"This is the Tomer who listens to the whispers of the earth and knows its secrets," Tormaigh told them. "This is he who bears the burden of knowledge past imagining. He is beyond time, beyond space but not beyond love nor sorrow."

The ancient figure reached out to touch Siskin's forehead.

"A lute and seed," he said kindly. "To you is given the knowledge of the melody locked within each individual. You have the gift to find the notes of deep renovation should the time come."

For the first time since she had known him Kier saw a peace in Siskin's expression but he did not speak. As the Tomer approached Klim the youth's determined jaw relaxed in response to whatever it was he saw in the other's face. Klim's head bowed and the ancient figure spoke softly to him.

"You are a Reeder, another of the five seeds of the Myriar. You will know the minds of those about you, their thoughts will be to you as the wind on a reed. You must plant firmly or you will be swept away."

Klim looked up and his eyes seemed less pain filled though Kier thought he still seemed to hold the burdens of a much older man. When the Tomer turned to Kier, she felt a gentle probe of her mind, fresh and pure as spring water and she smiled in acknowledgement. At first, he did not speak but reached out to touch her right temple, it was the most magical thing she had ever experienced. It was as if the Tomer was part of her silver stream, her sanctuary, a place that washed and renewed and accepted. His eyes were as grey as a winter sky and deeply beautiful.

You are an Inscriptor," he told her, "your gift is to re-discover that which has been lost, to see beyond the barriers. His eyes continued to search hers, "and even more perhaps," he whispered before stepping backwards and speaking to the little group as a whole.

"Welcome to Lioncera. The walls of our kingdom are happy to receive you into this chamber, the first of the new age to enter its confines."

Kier thought that his voice was the sound that you would give to the voice inside your own mind if it was required to speak out loud; hard to grasp in memory but intimately familiar and trustworthy. The whole chamber seemed to glitter and give off a glow of warmth that enveloped them. The Fossilia fluttered around them so that they felt as if they were in the midst of a gentle rainfall of crystal and soft wings. Even though there were so few of them, the massive chamber felt crowded with an invisible audience, hushed in anticipation. Once again, the ancient figure began to speak, his voice becoming effortlessly amplified in the underground hall, his sea grey eyes calmly reassuring.

"I know that you seek knowledge and understanding of the events that have overtaken you and that will now determine your future. It is no accident that you have arrived here in this place and time, and from this moment I place on you a burden of protection for each other.

"Lioncera could only be summoned by one of the those who have been given gifts of great potential to entwine the past with the future and to influence the fate of your race."

Later Kier was to ask herself why she had not asked more but as Siskin reminded her it was enough to try to remember words that they could little understand in a place that they could never have imagined. The Tomer continued.

"This is a physical world but within that physicality lies many hidden folds. Within the fabric of this existence the threads of the physical are interwoven constantly with the esoteric. To us, the Mourangils of this planet, there are no physically immovable entities. We are Moura's indigenous race, reflecting aspects of this world above and below the surface. Moura is the name given to the planet itself and the earth is its surface. We can weave the threads of water and stone and wear them as you do clothes. Time does not have the same relationship with our physical self as it does with yours and this colours our way of seeing you. Often, we do not see one individual but generations of families and races of men. And yet it is to you as individuals that we now speak."

"You are not here by chance but by the choices you have made even before you came to be on earth. Now it is time to choose again. Mankind sits on the brink of a great evolutionary leap. There are five individuals, known to us as Seeds, who have been given gifts that have taken generations to mature and they can manoeuvre the physical world in a way that is different to the rest of your kind. Should you wish, you can move forward not only to grasp a glimpse of the future but to light the way for all those who follow. A way that would allow man to truly begin to know this planet upon which he resides.

"It is no accident that duality rides the currents of your beliefs and legends. As you have already experienced you are stalked by those who would end your race, believing that your species is neither capable nor deserving of any further development."

"Enemies?" asked Siskin, "who are they?"

"Devourils, "replied the Tomer, "those who have been created by the bound one, Belluvour."

The name reverberated in a tainted echo around the cavern and Kier sensed grief, prolonged and enduring.

"It has always been our task to listen to the rhythms of the earth, the pulses, the ebb and flow of its existence. It was our purpose to guide where we could, to work with those who sensed our presence and asked for help. Such was Candillium of the line of Ordovicia, in the early days of man."

Kier sensed a thrill pass through her body at hearing the name of this ancient place that had now become familiar to her.

"To Candillium the centrepiece of the planet's great gift, the Myriar, was given by Toomaaris, the youngest of our race. There are five outer points of the Myriar: the Stozcist, the Creta, the Inscriptor, the Lute and the Reeder. These were seeds of change implanted in those individuals who would lead the way for future generations of mankind. Candillium was to be the centre, the core that would allow her race to activate its power. Part of her gift was a lifespan that would have crossed three generations of her kind.

"Each of the seeds would have evolved over those years to become individuals of great power in their own right and together with the centrepiece, Candillium, they would allow man to leap forward into the next phase of existence.

"But Belluvour, filled with hatred for your race, shook Ordovicia to ash and stole Candillium."

Lioncera seemed to dim and Kier felt a stab at her heart as he went on.

"The seeds were saved by Candillium's foresight for she had sent each to different points of the planet just before Belluvour destroyed Ordovicia."

"What happened to her, to Candillium?" Kier asked.

The Tomer sighed.

"After the tragedy Toomaaris, Tormaigh and Faer; those who had worked closely with the Ordovician race, were chosen to follow Belluvour to Obason. There they found a place that reflected the rancid distortion of his mind. Such was the power of Belluvour that his brothers may have been lost to us for thousands of years had not Candillium intervened. Using the power of the Myriar she sank with Belluvour to the secret vaults of the planet and bound him. Even so Candillium lost her life and was hurled beyond the cycles of human existence."

The chamber dimmed once more as the ancient figure spoke and Kier felt suddenly that her heart might break with sorrow. Tormaigh's eyes were far away, in the distant past.

"It was a threefold tragic loss. Belluvour, Candillium and the Myriar," he told them.

Again, there was a hush in the cavern and Kier sensed that the memory of that moment was imprinted into every atom of the great cavern.

The Tomer continued, "the solid world shook and divided and the basin of Ordovicia travelled across the seas and became lodged in the West."

"What became of the Seeds?" it was Siskin who asked.

"They were scattered. The evolution that would have occurred in three generations has now spanned millennia. The gift is not genetically transmitted, it is passed on through unseen and as yet unacknowledged connections between generations. They have emerged periodically throughout human history but only one at a time. Now three of you stand in Lioncera, a Stozcist lies in Tinobar, and the Creta has been nurtured merely miles from this place. There can be no doubt that the Myriar is poised on the brink of its own creation."

The fossilia fluttered excitedly and it seemed to Kier they stood inside a glittering, majestic jewel that shone with changing colours, shades that she had never before seen. Overawed, the three humans were silent as the Tomer continued.

"It is not only to evolve the human race that the Myriar is needed, the poison has traced its way to the surface to tear the fabric of the planet. Belluvour draws to him those who allow greed, addiction, fear or simple jealousy to dominate their thinking. It is partly because of the bound one that men use resources without conscience or intelligence to bring about their own destruction.

"As more of mankind is drawn towards him the weaker the bonds that bind him have become. Many have been in his service through several lives for he sends them from the void, perverse distortions of the humans that they once were."

"Jackson," said the threesome in unison and with a sadness in his eyes the ancient figure nodded his agreement.

"And there are those of our kind who aligned with Belluvour when the continents divided. One in particular walks often in human form. When the Mourangils returned to Lioncera it was discovered that Nephragm was missing, a Mourangil who had worshipped Belluvour before any other. Unlike his powerful brother who hated the human race Nephragm, travelled among them and found that he adapted easily into the new species. At first Belluvour kept his purpose hidden and persuaded Nephragm, whose duties lay with the animals, to spend time with the new race, building knowledge of their habits and lives.

It was through him that Belluvour discovered that Toomaaris had been chosen to deliver the gift of the Myriar and that Candillium was to be the centrepiece. Nephragm, of them all, was the easiest human. He learnt charm, humour, charisma- all the attributes that made him attractive to mankind. He found amusement in copying different human forms and would shape himself to impersonate those that he had known. The forms were never sustained for they belonged only to the individuals who bore them but Nephragm would find he could create the forms in detail for long enough to create quiet mischief. An amusement Belluvour encouraged. When Belluvour was bound Nephragm turned in hatred against his brothers and what remained of the Ordovicians.

The kingdom of Lioncera was closed to him and he became a Devouril, persuading others to join him to bring down the race that had bound his beloved Belluvour. Instead of impersonating a human form, he took to stealing them, destroying the human being, implanting his own essence in the body. All through human history we have searched for him, but he does not dwell in the dark places of those he corrupts. Instead he is unobtrusive, appearing humble and likeable where he chooses to do so. Such is Nephragm, enemy of joy, manipulator of guilt, dark hearted and dreadful. He, most of all, prepares the path to return Belluvour to the surface. Such destruction would occur in this process that there would be little of the human race left on Moura."

Even in the illumined cavern with individuals of such stature Kier felt that some deep wound inside her had opened and would never close. She did not want to hear of such dark beings. The Tomer lifted his grey eyes towards her.

"There are also those who have worked tirelessly to protect you. Those of our kind who have walked the long strides of years with mankind and they have followed any sign of the Seeds emerging. Now is their time. Toomaaris, Faer and

Tormaigh have never lost their love for the first generations of your kind in Ordovicia and in particular for Candillium." He smiled at Tormaigh who nodded and then waited for the ancient voice to continue.

"No man or woman can leave Lioncera unchanged. Each of you must believe that you are equal to the task of resisting the reach of Nephragm should he pursue you, even to your door."

Kier firmly hoped that she would never have to feel equal to such a thing but she looked up at the Tomer and nodded. On either side of her, Klim and Siskin made a similar gesture. Kier sighed; there were so many questions she wanted to ask.

"Candillium, did the…" she struggled to remember the phrase he had used "did the centrepiece of the Myriar die when she used its power to bind Belluvour?"

The Tomer shook his head.

"She used the power that was her gift at that time, but the centrepiece and the source of its power is Candillium herself. Over the millennia, the core that she holds within has replenished, even as the Seeds planted so long ago, now appear to have come to fruition. The loss of any of the Seeds will reduce the impact of the Myriar, but Candillium is the centrepiece. Without her, the Myriar will have little significance for your race."

"How can she return? How is it possible?" asked Siskin.

"Purpose is a thing of many lives," the ancient figure told them cryptically. "Candillium was catapulted to other realms but it is hoped that she has elected to return. So powerful a being as she has become could not pass through the borders of flesh and spirit unnoticed by those who watch. There has been no sign and the time draws near. The events of today have shown us how near. There is however another alternative."

He paused, they remained silent, waiting for him to continue.

"Candillium may have elected to become fully human again. It is possible that she has willingly entered the cycles once more and is fully bound to the earth with no knowledge of her past. In this way Belluvour could not trace her arrival for she would have yet to discover it herself. Until she understands who she is, then none of us can help her, and she may walk beside us, and we would not recognise, even in Lioncera, the steps that once belonged to Candillium."

The Tomer bowed his head for a moment and then looked at each of them in turn.

"It may be that her whole life will pass and she will never find the kingdom of Ordovicia inside her. What I can say is that each of you will have a part in helping her to do so for you will be drawn to this individual, and each other, by the touch of the Myriar."

This then, thought Kier, was the source of the deep connection she felt for these people whom she hardly knew. Concentrating on understanding the words she had just heard she roused herself, just in time to see the statuesque figure stepping back into the painted picture. He smiled once and then his features became distant and the chamber visibly dimmed.

The fossilia seemed to anticipate the sense of loss that Kier felt as the old man disappeared from view. They crowded around the three companions and it felt as if their beauty and light were somehow absorbed into her skin. Tormaigh smiled as the fossilia finally departed.

"To those who can see, you will always bear the imprint of Lioncera. But now we must leave- time stretches outside these gates at a quicker pace."

"I'm not going back until I can see Gabbie and Swift with my own eyes," Klim told him stubbornly, his angular jaw set firmly. Tormaigh looked carefully at each of them. Siskin looked over at Kier and she nodded her agreement.

"We should stay together," Siskin said firmly.

Tormaigh sighed.

"Very well," he told them, "but you are needed on the outside. This is your time, we can guide but it is you and your kind who must go forward to act. But I will take you to Tinobar if you wish it, although in my heart it is not where I would have you be."

"Thank you," Kier told him.

Even as she spoke the words, an overwhelming sense of drowsiness encompassed her. Ortheria appeared by her shoulder, fluttering gently. The last thing she remembered before her eyes fully closed was Tormaigh disappearing into the mineral encrusted wall followed by a crowd of fossilia.

Chapter Twenty-Six

At first Kier was unaware that she had left the chamber. Fossilia crowded around her and she was lost in the magical crystal dance of their movement. Suddenly they were gone, replaced by whispering particles of light that moved in great swathes around her body so that her physical self felt part of the air itself. The sensation was one of weightlessness and wonderful freedom as she floated, invisibly wrapped in light, above the earth. Perception was transformed into a huge sea of different forms of energy and she allowed herself to be propelled overland towards the South West.

It was well past dawn when the three friends were deposited together at the edge of miles of moor and that rose above the countryside. Tormaigh led them along the path that graduated towards the brow of a hill. At the top, the path continued across the moor but Tormaigh veered left to follow a winding track down towards a shaded dell. At the bottom of the track he stopped and turned to them.

"Tinobar is a place of healing for those who are injured by the forces of Belluvour," his tone was admonitory, "it is not a hospital where visitors are invited.

The healers have bodies on earth but their focus is in Tinobar. Madeleine, who holds the keys to Tinobar, is thought to have the mind of a three-year-old but she works here tirelessly in spirit form along with many other assistants. Their purpose is to help those who have been deeply assaulted, where the inner light of being has been almost extinguished by dreadful forces. In most cases it is not the physical body that is treated. However, both your friends have sustained physical injuries that can only be cured by the ministrations of these spirit healers. Be warned, all those who work here fiercely guard Tinobar and they agree to your coming only reluctantly because I have asked them to allow it. Do not touch your friends or do anything you are not asked to do."

The trio were apprehensive as Tormaigh moved to one side and beckoned them through a stone arch that appeared to occur naturally from the surrounding rock. Kier felt her spine tingle as she passed beneath the arch into an enclosed space where wildflowers scampered across the grass and trailing flowers folded from above like curtain fabric. Amidst strings of daisies the land parted to receive a fresh stream that started from a tinkling waterfall in the corner of this idyll.

"Oh," Kier said out loud in wonder only to find herself facing the figure of a big square featured woman whose no nonsense eyes looked her up and down with disdain. The woman was insubstantial; Kier knew that if she were to reach out that she would not connect with flesh. Her presence was strong however as she stood, hand on hips, looking over the three of them. On her 'spirit body' she wore a cloth hat that fitted tightly around her head and a smock, tied with a rope that was a collection of apparent charms.

The fairy tale dell dimmed into the background and Kier understood that she was operating on more than one plane of vision. Physically the picture book place still existed and she realised that this physical place was part of the healing for the tortured souls who squirmed restlessly or even worse, were listlessly unaware. Tinobar was not just a place to which healers brought patients, every facet of the space had its own kind of energy that fed and nurtured the spirits within.

"I am Madeleine," said the dour woman without smiling and she bent towards her belt and extracted a key that gleamed yellow. Immediately a golden fence appeared around the dell at the centre of which, where they stood, was a massive jewel encrusted gate. Madeleine placed her key in the lock and led them through into Tinobar.

It felt to Kier like moving from the city to the country, the sky seemed wiped clean. As Madeleine led them further in however it was evident that Tinobar was no fairy tale. The wounded were everywhere, some high above her, some floating within the stream. Each individual essence gave an aura of a physical self but Kier knew instinctively that this gave little clue to the way they would present as physical beings.

Siskin and Klim had their hands either side of their heads as the tortured cries reached them. Kier felt a sense of profound despair emanating from a branch beside her. As she came closer she had the impression of a man, his face distorted with fear, his mind splattered with terrible memories. As they walked Madeleine's deft hands moved from her belt to each individual, administering and checking.

The more Kier concentrated on each separate being the more she became aware of other helpers, dressed similarly to Madeleine. Their expressions were focused upon their duties and each individual being was accompanied by at least one carer; the whole place, she observed, was as busy as a general hospital.

Eventually Kier realised they had reached the waterfall at the back of the dell. On either side were grass cots and in each one the undoubtedly corporeal forms of Gabbie and Swift lay sleeping. Klim dashed to Gabbie's side and then quickly moved to check on Swift. They appeared to Kier like two broken dolls and her heart filled with fear for them. Madeleine's whole aspect changed as she addressed them, her eyes softened and her voice was gentle.

She turned, a look of respect and wonder on her face.

"You are all so connected, even in the short time you have been here these two have been nurtured by your presence."

Madeline examined the two girls carefully.

"I charge you all with each other's wellbeing, they are ready to leave." Kier noticed the puzzlement in the healer's expression as she spoke and then the visual appearance of Madeleine and Tinobar disintegrated leaving them alone with Gabbie and Swift still sleeping.

They had arrived at dawn and it was now dusk and Kier glimpsed the moon, full and white, giving leave to the setting sun. Then Tormaigh was with them.

"We must hurry," he told them, reaching towards the two girls, within seconds they had disappeared. Kier felt the dusk claim her and she was folded in the air giving herself up to the return journey.

Chapter Twenty-Seven

It seemed a lifetime since she had stood in the window of Seven Rivers looking out at the lights on the prom beyond which stretched the dark line of the sea. Now her view was further up the coast as she sat upstairs in the bookshop and Kier struggled against an almost overwhelming tide of despair. All that she had seen, truly wondrous experiences, could not compensate for the loss of her brother. Over and over again she berated herself for not waking him, for not doing as he wished and staying together. All the childhood scenes of Gally's never ending patience and protection for his younger sister ran riot in her mind and threatened to incapacitate her entirely.

Siskin knocked softly and entered the dark room where she sat in an armchair, staring, seeing only the inner turmoil of her own thoughts. He spoke softly, "his melody is strong and true Kier, it seems to me that what Evan told us was the use of another illusion. I believe your brother to be alive."

Kier felt the tears wet on her cheek and she lifted her hand to cover that of Siskins whose fingers overlapped the armchair. Words seemed impossible to make. They had arrived back from Tinobar full of joy that both Swift and Gabbie were now well and sleeping naturally in rooms on the third floor. One look at Evan's sombre face however was enough to make her realise that something dreadful had occurred in their absence.

As Kier had looked around desperately for her brother Tormaigh led her to the kitchen where the story of what had happened the previous day unfolded. The Welshman had explained how he and Gally had tried to fulfil the task they had been given to find any further sign of the obsidian spear. Using Evan's unique talent as a Stozcist, Gally went with him to check that they were not watched, and to make his companion's work less obvious.

Evan had picked up the trace opposite the Seven Rivers. He had looked up at Gally and nodded his certainty that the 'Perfidium' had been carried by the same individual who had given Kyle the foul poison the evening before. Gally's eyes combed the sea front as Evan moved up and down the area, concentrating until he felt he could definitely confirm the stone's stage of redevelopment.

Then it had happened without warning, Gally had burst into flame in front of his eyes. Evan cried out and jumped back, removing his jacket to smother the flames but by the time he did so Kier's brother had vanished, nothing at all remaining. Evan had looked around him in shock, the area was not busy but there was the usual amount of people nearby, an old couple were watching him in alarm but no one seemed to have seen what happened. One thin man with glasses helped him as he lost his balance, steering him to the same seat that he had used the previous evening to save the small boy.

The man had wanted to take him to his flat across the street but Evan had refused, needing desperately to get back to the shop. Then Echin was there, heading down the prom. Evan turned to the thin man to say thank you but he had disappeared. Grief stricken he relayed to his friend details of what had occurred and Echin, his eyes unreadable, put his arm around the Welshman guided him back to the bookshop. Evan could not remember any details of the short journey, just an impression that he had entered a tunnel and arrived out the other side.

Tormaigh was insistent that they stay together in the bookshop that evening and everyone was too numb to object. The strange trio had departed almost as soon as they had returned from Tinobar and had not yet arrived back. Kier felt as if her heart could never again be whole, she longed for her brother's presence as she had done so many times as a little girl, his wonderful brand of good humour somehow making everything ok. Now it seemed that nothing would ever be ok again.

*

A solitary ash tree stood defiantly on the exposed ridge, just as it had done for over a hundred years. Its leaves folded around the equally solitary figure of Echinod Deem. Together they became an exquisite silhouette against metres of white limestone laced in moonlight Down below, the Inn of the Three Mountains nestled in the river valley; a single light shone in the corner bedroom. Echin watched as the light was extinguished and then a little later a dark figure came out of the back of the building.

The figure defined itself into the body of a young man as it passed through the gate and out on to the road. In a few seconds, the figure was lost to sight once again as it crossed the lane and started up the path that would take him to the top of the ridge.

Josh Allithwaite had never felt the need to share his differences from his fellow man. For one thing, he could sense Echin's presence and make him aware that he knew of his arrival without the use of a mobile and this was handy since there was never a signal on the mountains. For another he could paint the inside of someone better than the outside. No matter how an individual looked on the surface Josh saw the hidden being. He recalled many times when he would rather not have done so. Tonight, as the cold air evaporated on his warm breath, his limbs pulsing, the anguish of his mind was eased in the joy of movement. The relief was intense as he ran easily up the path he had known all his life to greet the man who was friend, brother and hero.

At the top Echin stepped out and came towards the young man. Josh reached out his hand allowing his companion to pull him up the last few feet. Wordlessly they headed back to the shelter of the ash tree.

"You should come down Echin, Dad would be glad to see you."

His friend smiled, his conversation with Matthew earlier that week had gone some way to improving the landlord's acceptance of his presence. However, Echin remembered Mathew's many silent protests at the strangeness of his guest when the huge publican had taken himself off fishing during the short visits when he arrived to speak with Marianne. Only Matthew's deep love for his wife had allowed him to tolerate his periodic arrivals prior to her disappearance and now his confusion and grief were too raw to deal with Echin's return that evening.

'She's still alive Josh, don't give up hope, Marianne has her own resources."

Josh's head went down and he sighed deeply.

"It was terrible when he went to see the body, it could have so easily have been her. But dad knew straight away. The police are still checking, all lies and nonsense."

Echin gave a solemn nod.

"Josh, I want you to think back to just before Gally arrived, say a week. Did anything seem different, anyone showing particular interest in Whistmorden?"

Josh stood up restlessly, somehow avoiding the natural gaps in the limestone.

"Well you know about Beeston and that creep of a business manager trying to say that our land belongs to him?"

Echin stood up beside him.

"Someone else Josh. I think there would have been another visitor to the Inn, he or she would not have been able to eat or drink."

Josh shook his head and then something seemed to occur to him.

"I don't know…. there was one evening about a month ago, I was sketching in the bar and this guy came in, a little older than me." Josh shivered with the memory and then his face went blank.

"Go on Josh"

"Eh- what was I saying?

"This man, you drew him?"

"Yes, I drew him. Bit cold up here, let's go down to the kitchen."

Echin looked at his young friend carefully and Josh started to become uncomfortable under the scrutiny. He turned his face away and began to walk back to the edge.

"Josh."

It was a tone Echin had never used with him before- a command that turned Josh back to find he was more uncomfortable than ever as the Mourangil locked into his eyes and suddenly all he could see was an intense blue light. It was as if he was being pulled down underwater, he couldn't breathe. And then he heard himself gasp and was back standing on top of the ridge with Echin again. The blue light had disappeared and with it a vague sense of compulsion.

Echin was looking disturbed.

"Tell me now about your drawing."

The force of command had gone but there was still something compelling in Echin's voice. Josh suddenly realised that this was the first time he had spoken about the incident. Only his mother and the man standing with him knew of his strange gift but he had not told Marianne about the drawing. It came to him suddenly that he had not been able to tell her.

"Well as I said he came in alone and took the window seat on the far side of the room. It was late Sunday afternoon after dinner but before the evening regulars. I was sitting sketching beside the bar, I'd just finished drawing one part of the room and he caught my eye. Mainly because he'd bought a pint and half an hour later it hadn't been drunk. He was reading the paper, and he had one of those faces that people take to. Not too fat or thin, smiled easily, seemed kind of diffident and polite. Nothing out of the ordinary but I was curious to sketch him.

"Almost as soon as I'd started I wanted to stop but couldn't. What came out of my pencil was the most alien thing I've ever drawn." He shook his head in revulsion.

"As I sketched the flesh seemed to fall away from his face and what I drew was a smouldering black coal-like mineral."

Josh's eyes widened as he recalled his drawing.

"The rock was organic with red tinted vessels running through it, his face bore a human outline but there was no humanity in it."

"Nephragm." Echin 's face was a mask, his eyes dark

"You know him?"

"I know him."

Josh heard the urgency of Echin's next question.

"Did he see?"

The young artist shook his head. It had taken all his years of concealment not to cry out or react.

"No, not then, I could see the creature that I drew squirmed beneath. I didn't dare try any link and I was terrified he would realise what I was doing. You know it only takes a quick look for me once I have a pencil. I didn't have to keep looking over at him, by that time I could see every movement from the inside. "

Echin was as tense as Josh had ever seen him and he concentrated on remembering the incident.

"Later I think he realised something because he came over. By that time, I'd slid the paper underneath the last sketch because mum was working in the bar." His voice broke a little but then he recovered himself

"He said something about the Inn being very unusual and left."

"And where is the sketch now?" his friend asked.

"Burnt"

Echin looked thoughtful as Josh continued.

"Couldn't talk about it. Didn't dare keep it. I meant to call you or speak to my mother but somehow I never did."

"He manipulated your mind," Echin told him.

Josh looked alarmed.

"Hypnosis?"

"Kind of, a very old malicious form."

"So, he sussed me?"

Echin 's expression was grim, "had you not been in the Inn with its protection and Marianne had not been nearby wearing the Chalycion, he would have known you as a Creta, one with the gift of vision beyond even his own. At that point, I believe he would have undoubtedly destroyed you."

Josh took a deep breath and the moonlight shone on the waxen sheen of his face.

"Why? What is this thing?"

"He's Devouril Josh," Echin said, his face pained. "They do not commit to human forms as we do for that would take respect and understanding and they have long ago lost that capability. The flesh he wore was real enough but its owner will have been murdered. Nephragm has long practice of maintaining physical life with his own presence but this cannot be for more than a limited time. Weeks only."

The young man whistled and Echin reached out to hold him as his foot slipped over the edge of the ridge.

"I don't think he realised what'd you'd done but whatever he saw in your expression bothered him enough to stop you speaking about that night. Has he been back since?"

"Not as far as I know."

Echin let out a rare sigh. His arm folded around Josh whose sense of dread was lessened but not removed. Echin looked sadly at the young man.

"The Inn is your greatest protection. Stay there as much as you are able. And keep Matthew there with you"

Josh shook his head.

"Some chance! Anyway, it didn't help mum." There was bitterness in his words and Echin saw that strain had pressed its weight to an almost unbearable limit in the young Creta.

"The creature that attacked your mother was of a different ilk though steeped in the same evil."

Echin reached into his pocket and Josh's artist eyes saw a prism of coloured light in the small stone that Echin was holding and immediately recognised his mother's pendant. His eyes filled with tears as he gratefully took it and fastened the silver chain around his neck.

Chapter Twenty-Eight

Gabbie sat up straight. Her hand searched her lower back and felt the smooth surface of a healed scar. Luke's face as he attacked her leapt into her mind, glazed angry eyes with oversized pupils, the cruel weapon hidden in his pocket. A mournful scream echoed in the large room and it took her some moments to realize that the sound had come from her own lips. Someone rushed in to the room, the last person she expected to see. The Welshman had lost his permanent look of disapproval, he wore a white shirt and a waistcoat of blue silk. He smiled at her and held her hand.

"Gabrielle," his voice was soft and welcoming. It occurred to her that she was upstairs in the bookshop, the slightly open window brought the rhythmic sound of waves hitting the shore. Questions floundered in her head.

"How long have I been here, how did I get here?" she demanded noticing the closeness of a chair to her bed, someone had been sat with her.

"You've been here since yesterday, Monday," Evan told her.

"How long is it since…"

"Five days," Evan answered "five days since you were stabbed."

"But how did you know?"

She was utterly confused. How could it be that the knife wound had healed so quickly? She recalled how she had felt; as if she were the last dot on a screen before it shut down. She knew she had been near death and her insides lurched. How on earth had she come to be in the bookshop? And how did Evan Gwynn seem to know all about it? To her great surprise she found tears running down her cheeks and she pressed her face against the broad chest of her employer.

"My poor child," he said, "you'll be fine now.'

"Klim," she said as she moved herself backwards, "I have to go and warn him."

She went to get out of bed but Evan did not move from his sitting position on the covers.

"You can't go anywhere," he told her firmly.

"Please," she was pulling at the bed covers, "I have to. Oh my god, Swift!

"Calm down Gabbie, they're all safe." Evan had adopted the tone of finality she had heard so often in her employment but she looked at him fiercely.

"How can you know? You're just saying that to make me quiet!"

He laughed.

"And that would be an achievement!"

Free of makeup, the translucent appearance of her skin reminded Evan how gravely ill she had been. He smiled gently.

"But I do know, they really are safe." he told her, his voice soft. "They're here!"

The door opened to reveal Klim hand in hand with Swift. Gabbie failed to notice Klim's jacket on the back of the chair next to her bed where he had spent the night. Nor did she realise he had given Swift his hand to help her walk to Gabbie's room. The joy on Klim's face as he saw Gabbie finally awake was short lived as he noticed that her return smile failed to reach her eyes. Evan stood up and others entered the room, including to Gabbie's surprise, the beautiful woman they had seen in the Seven Rivers café the week before and who had given them a meal voucher. Automatically Gabbie tried to straighten her hair and then she saw that Swift was pale and shaky. Kindly she patted the bed for her to sit down and the other girl gratefully slid beside her.

"I don't think any of us feel much like sleep so why don't I help you two get ready and then we can all go down and have something to eat," suggested Kier.

Gabbie looked at Swift and the older woman explained that she had only woken an hour ago and she had also been critically ill. Gabbie suddenly realised that everyone was still in their night clothes apart from Klim and Evan. Swift and she herself were wearing too long t-shirts that she suspected belonged to Kier.

'What time is it?" she asked.

"It's 5.30 am. Come on, let's have a look through my things and see what will fit."

When everyone else had left Gabbie looked at the other two women, her eyes lost.

"I remember so little," she said hesitatingly. "I shouldn't have left you Swift."

Swift squeezed her hand.

"I thought I was suffocating, I couldn't breathe," the other girl told them and she trembled with the memory Kier put her arms around them both.

"Let's just be glad that you're both here with us. Maybe talk about it all later when we're looking back and the world has turned to normal again."

"I don't think I will ever feel normal again," Gabbie commented sadly.

Kier silently agreed and then suddenly looked alarmed.

"Oh my god, I forgot Adam," the thought accosted her, "he'll be out of his mind with worry."

"There's no signal here and it seems to have some effect on the battery. Stone dead," Gabbie told her.

Puzzled Kier nodded.

"I'll try him later. Can't I even charge my phone here?"

Gabbie shook her head. "No guarantee, sometimes it charges, sometimes it doesn't. There's a landline downstairs and Evan has the internet. Maybe you could email him."

Kier looked puzzled and shook her head.

"How can the Internet work and mobiles not?"

Gabbie threw her hands up in the air.

"I don't even ask anymore! This place makes its own rules."

It fell to Kier to explain to the two young women that they had both been saved in Tinobar, an 'otherworldly' healing place to which they had been taken. To her surprise neither Swift nor Gabbie looked sceptical or questioned her. She wondered if they had discovered some private memories of the experience. Or perhaps they had yet to process all that had happened to them in the last few days.

Gabbie found her strength quickly and Kier gave her some jeans that she could roll up and a blue crop- top that was more like a T shirt on the young woman.

"I'll be fine," she told Kier, as the soft brown eyes looked carefully at hers.

Kier nodded and left to find some leggings that she thought might fit Swift.

*

Evan was three floors below in the cellar, taking refuge in the routine of sorting books, when Gabbie entered.

"That's my job," she said as she moved down the steps. She was surprised and gladdened by a look of joy on Evan's face as he put down the books and came towards her. He held both her hands in his.

"You're up! I'm so glad to see you so well my little Gabrielle! And your friend?"

"I think we'll both be ok," she told him," I thought my legs would be wobbly. But look, they work!" She pointed to the steps she had just descended.

"If you're all up we should go get some breakfast." Evan turned towards the cellar steps.

"Evan."

Gabbie's voice was hesitant, partly because she had never spoken in this way to her employer and also because of the question she was trying to form. Evan sat back down on the chair he had vacated and motioned her to a table nearby on which she perched herself. Her hair was pinned back in a clip and all the tough bravado of her everyday life had mellowed to a hidden steel. Evan waited for her to continue with uncharacteristic patience and Gabbie suddenly realised how much affection she had for the old man.

"I don't belong here like the others, I'm just ordinary and I want to see my dad." Her thoughts flew to Klim and Swift holding hands in the doorway, how they seemed to fit with each other somehow.

"He'll be back in the next couple of hours," she continued, "he'll already be freaking out that we've not been in touch. I left him a message that my phone was broken but he'll be wanting me there."

Evan looked at her and thought of his own daughter; how much he missed her.

"I have never thought of you as ordinary in any way Gabrielle."

She smiled her thanks but shook her head.

"You know what I mean Evan. I can come back later but I'm going to head home"

"Have you spoken to Klim?"

The blonde head moved from side to side and her eyes would not make contact with his own.

"You want me to tell him, is that right?"

Her beautiful blue eyes lifted towards him as she nodded. "He's safer here. He'll only want to come with me."

"How about we go up and have breakfast and then I promise I'll drive you home when I know your dad's back? That way I'll know you're safe and I won't spend the rest of my day worrying about you?"

Gabbie came towards him and hugged his middle.

"Deal" she agreed.

The kitchen had never been so busy since Evan had taken over the shop but he had kept the freezer well stocked with food as Echin had asked. He had placed himself by the hob cooking sausages and bacon, scrambled eggs and toast for any that wanted them. Gabbie acted as unofficial waitress passing out the meals. Kier and Swift had little appetite but the others ate hungrily and finally everyone was fed and the dishes cleared. Swift had placed herself between Klim and Kier. Although she looked smaller than ever her voice was firm and strong.

"Where are these people you have all been speaking about? Echin did you say?" She looked at Kier, "and two others?"

"Faer and Tormaigh," supplied Siskin.

"Yes. Where are they?"

The group hunched around the table, eyes fixed on Evan as he turned from the coffee maker.

"I don't know where they are," he told them, shrugging his shoulders, "I wish they were back here to answer your questions themselves!"

"But who are they Evan, really?" It was Gabbie that asked and the Welshman sighed, drawing up a chair.

"Klim said that Faer took Gabbie and me through solid stone," Swift told them and Gabbie suppressed the stab of jealousy for she had yet to speak to Klim on her own.

'That doesn't sound normal," she commented, mainly to cover her confusion.

Evan smiled.

"We are graced by the presence of Mourangils. They were here before the dinosaurs, before man, before anything we really know about. And when I say 'they' I mean those same exact people."

"No way," Gabbie was shaking her head.

Evan laughed and he drew himself up, his welsh lilt became more pronounced and musical.

"The Mourangils call the planet Moura and they reside often in mineral and rock. They can also travel the oceans faster than our planes travel the air and if they wish the clouds will carry them. Each continent has its own set of Mourangils. They are not limited by territory but link together to balance physical existence so that creatures such as ourselves may reach our potential on Moura."

Evan wondered what experiences his companions had already had that they accepted his words so readily. He continued in his bardic tone.

"Echinod Deem has walked in human form for more years than we can count and he understands our needs, our weaknesses and our strengths in a way that transcends his nature."

Evan's hands swept around the room in a dramatic gesture.

"And he has owned this site where you now sit for as long as man has inhabited it. Down through the ages it has changed its purpose from church, shelter, alms-house, hospital and school amongst many others. Here he and his brothers return to fight against the enemy that is within."

"Within?" said Gabbie, "how within?"

"Belluvour, the bound one, feeds from our corruption and rattles the secret vaults."

'The secret vaults?" quizzed Gabbie.

Evan stood up and in the rich baritone of his performance voice he recited:

"Solitary is the beast for he swallows all those who come to
him.

Terrible is his maw.

In the secret vaults, does he rage against his prison

Cursing the light that binds his purpose.

But still men feed him and he grows strong,

Regurgitating the perversion of their souls

To serve his will."

"Nice," Gabbie shivered.

"It's so unbelievable," said Siskin and yet we've always
been obsessed with good and evil, angels and devils."

"Exactly. Echin is forever saying we already know far more
than we think," Evan replied.

Kier did not disbelieve Evan's words even as, she thought,
they removed any hope she might have had that Echin could
ever share the force of emotion that he had engendered in
her.

"But how is it that a place as ordinary as Pulton should hold
so many secrets?" she asked.

"Originally this land mass was on the other side of the
globe and Pulton was a few miles from Ordovicia where a
young Mourangil would come to practice the art of being
human."

"Really?" she replied, her voice small, "please go on Evan."

"That's about as much as I know of their history," he told
them, and it took the best part of my lifetime to find it out."

Evan's bardic communications were clearly at an end as he
picked up a tea towel from the back of one of the chairs and
turned away from the group. Slowly each of them left the
kitchen and Gabbie slipped upstairs to get her bag, returning
a few minutes later. Evan nodded and picked up his car keys
from the rack determined to see her safely home.

Chapter Twenty-Nine.

Kier awoke to the sound of thunder. She had lay on her bed after breakfast and sunk into a deep sleep. Getting up she made her way to the window that looked out over the prom and it seemed to her she had slept through summer and winter had arrived. Black clouds shrouded the Bay and the water was turbulent below. Families who had been playing on the beach were packing up hastily and she realised with surprise that she had slept only an hour. In that time, the promise of a beautiful summer's day had been replaced by a biting shower of rain and resounding angry skies. Another thunderclap reverberated around the room and Kier went to her door to see Klim heading upstairs to an attic room he had discovered.

"Wow," she said out loud as she followed him into the room where there was a wall-to-wall couch, music centre and TV screen.

"Not what I'd expected either, "Siskin said, unplugging an iPod, "Echin's attempt to keep us out of mischief I suspect. No mobiles but plenty of multi-media."

"Where's Gabbie?" asked Klim and Swift looked up from a computer game.

"She's gone home," Kier told him, "Evan took her."

Swift shifted awkwardly in her seat as Klim's mouth tightened into a tight line. He looked anxious and Siskin voiced the restlessness they were all feeling.

"I have things to do. My target is still Jackson, until we deal with him no one will really be safe."

"I need to contact Adam and enlist his help in tracing Gally if I can," Kier told them, her voice breaking slightly, "Why don't we arrange to meet back here tonight, give us all a chance to..."

Kier's suggestion was cut short by Evan's appearance at the open door; he seemed astonished by the sitting room.

"I am beyond being surprised in this house," he told them, shaking his head. "The rugby will look great on that screen," he said appreciatively.

"How is it you've never been in here before Evan?" asked Swift.

"Because it didn't exist," he told her simply, shrugging his shoulders.

"Or it existed and you didn't see it," suggested Klim intuitively. The house had filled his mind with glimpses of hidden pockets of thought ever since he had arrived.

"Maybe," Evan nodded thoughtfully. He was holding a towel to his head for he had been soaked in the short time it had taken him to walk from the car to the house.

"It's wild out there," he told them rubbing his thick hair and drying the trickles of water that ran down his face. "You'd best turn on the news."

Siskin picked up the remote and quickly navigated to a news channel. The group was shocked to see a number of earthquakes reported simultaneously around the globe, in places where they had not occurred at any serious level for millennia. They watched in horror at the accompanying tsunami in parts of Australia. Kier's ears pricked up at the reporting of a tremor in the Northern Dales though this had been considered as being below any serious level of concern,

"I think we have found the reason why our friends have not returned," Evan told them.

At that moment, a thud hit the sky-light window shortly followed by the deafening screeches from a mass of herring gulls as the pane filled with the frantic flapping of white wings. Evan threw down the towel and headed downstairs to be quickly followed by the rest of the group. He ran to his own room where the massive window revealed sweeping clouds of birds splashed across the sky. Flocks of waders gathered together and formed great swathes of grey dots, buffeted into changing patterns, twisting and turning, small patches breaking off and reforming as they headed inland. The sound that started as a hum on the other side of the Bay became a cacophony of beating wings and piecing cries as they reached Pulton.

Evan and Swift cried out in unison and the small group huddled around them.

"Something's pushing it apart," Swift screamed, "underneath."

"It's out in the Bay," Evan said, struggling to calm himself as Swift buried her head in her hands, "se está desgarrando! The crust is being torn apart!"

Kier looked out of the window to see a terrifying upsurge in water on the other side of the Bay. As if in slow motion an increasing wall of broiling dark water heading directly towards them. She reached out her hand to Klim who took it and in turn found Swift.

"We need to be under the lintel," shouted Siskin.

"Stay as you are," yelled Evan, "the building will hold."

Evan took Kier's other hand and the small group held together as a loud boom overwhelmed their senses. She felt Klim beside her pouring strength into his fingers to keep her upright. Locked in the circle Kier was stunned to realise the room remained barely touched even as screams slammed against the window and the exposed edge of the small town was swallowed in sea water. The battered wood of a fishing boat flew past the window and the glass was doused in debris filled sludge but somehow remained intact.

Around them they heard the sickening rumble of falling masonry and the splintered cry of shattering glass. It was a matter of seconds that seemed the longest age as suddenly nothing was solid. The room shuddered but their small circle seemed somehow remote. Any minute Kier expected the floor to shatter underneath them but Evan held them together. Siskin was the first to break the circle as the earth stopped shaking.

"We need to get below," he told them, "there could be an aftershock." He stood at the door as they filed out to discover that the shop had, in the main, been little damaged apart from a general disarray of furniture. On the bottom floor books had spilled off the shelves but the walls had held firm. Klim was heading for the front door.

"No" said Evan firmly, "stay inside" but Klim, who could hear only the shouts of the people on the street, had already opened the door to reveal utter chaos outside. One of the larger boats had lodged against the rubble that had been the lifeboat station. The road was split and filling with tidal water. Parts of surrounding buildings littered the prom and there were screams of distress in every direction. Kier's thoughts flew to Gina and the busy café, the families that would surely have been inside at this time of day.

The whirring of a helicopter drowned out every other sound as it landed feet away on part of the road that was still solid. Together Siskin and Klim slammed the door shut as they saw Brassock's savage face, still grazed from his recent fight, in the doorway of the helicopter. Siskin turned, ushering the others down the hallway just as the cellar door opened.

Echin calmly entered the hall. "In here," he told them, ushering them into the reference room.

It was only hearing the gasps of incredulity from Evan and the others, that Kier realised that this room had been previously visible only to herself. Echin's glance towards her reminded her that he had been the silent companion with whom she had shared the room a few days previously. Was it really only a few days she thought and then was astonished to find that the book shelves seemed to have been absorbed into the walls to make room for the group. Now their outline appeared like wallpaper. The unusual furniture had also disappeared into the floor where it looked like artwork set in stone.

Kier said nothing, watching the hall from where she stood, her back against the wall of the reference room, her body just inside the fine line that separated the mysterious space from the rest of the building.

"If you stay in here," Echin told them, "they cannot see you."

He left them just before splinters of wood exploded into the narrow hallway to the drill of a sub machine gun. Brassock kicked open the remaining door and his eyes quickly searched the stairway and narrow hallway. He ushered in two mercenaries, both armed. One headed to the stairs and the other towards the many small rooms where shelves of books were now scattered on the floor. Kier's audible intake of breath made Brassock turn in her direction and she placed her hand across her mouth as the brutish figure turned back and Alex Jackson entered the hall.

The arrogant strides sounded clearly on the floorboards as his cold dark eyes took in the untidy conglomeration of books and the shattered equipment that filled the workspace behind the counter. He was inches from her as Brassock reached the kitchen door and for a moment she thought he had broken down whatever illusion Echin had employed to keep the place invisible. His hand reached up towards her face but his fingers brushed along a solid wall that Kier could not see. The physical likeness to Klim was unmistakable but that was where all similarity ended. Klim's soulful eyes spoke of selflessness and courage; those of his uncle told of cultivated greed and self-worship.

As his employer approached, Brassock flung the kitchen door open to reveal Echin's hooded figure calmly reading at the table. He looked up with mild surprise to meet the probing dark eyes of Alex Jackson. At the same time, the other men returned from upstairs shaking their heads. Brassock nodded Cross to take up position at the front door and Hardy to check the cellar; he then followed Jackson into what appeared to be the only occupied room.

Echin looked calmly at the two men who had entered the kitchen and did not react when Brassock came towards him and pushed the muzzle of the gun towards his face.

"You need to stand when Mr Jackson enters the room, book man."

Still the figure in the hooded green sweatshirt did not move and when Brassock approached to heave him from the chair the ex- wrestler found himself falling over his own feet, unable to stay upright, his head hitting the corner of the table as he toppled to the floor where his moans were ended by Jackson's boot in a vicious kick. Cross came closer but his employer signalled him back to the door. Hardy banged the cellar door closed as he re-entered the narrow corridor.

"Nothing below," he reported.

Jackson's eyes never left the face of the man opposite who seemed once again engrossed in his book. The mental effort to probe the other man's mind produced sweat on Jackson's forehead and a hint of fear and uncertainty in his eyes as his attempts became increasingly futile. His arrogant voice flung his words across the room at the unmoving figure that remained seated at the table.

"You have something of mine," he accused.

Echin lifted his head and looked coldly at the unwelcome visitor. He put his hand into his pocket and the jetra stone sat in the centre of his palm, a black nodule of poison. Jackson's eyes widened and he took a step back; clearly the jetra was not the item he sought. A tilt of Echin's wrist threw the stone into the middle of the table. He looked up from the table and stood up, the hood of his sweatshirt falling away as he did so.

Jackson paled as the first glimmer of recognition filtered his consciousness. His foot took an involuntary step backwards but he steadied himself, his expression a mixture of loathing and fear.

"You," he spat out the word as if it would choke him. Then Alex Jackson previously Alec Klimzcak lurched his mind forward in attack only to see, in those final moments of awareness, that the savagery that he had directed outwards rebounded back towards him and thought was no longer his to own.

The kitchen door banged shut and outside the two mercenaries rushed towards it, their kicks and shoves having no effect. Then just as Cross lifted his gun the door swung open again to reveal Jackson's unmoving figure. He did not turn as the two men entered but stared blankly at the wall opposite. Brassock lay unconscious on the floor but there was no sign of the hooded reader, and no exit apart from the one by which they had been standing the whole time. The two mercenaries searched the kitchen examining every cupboard and wall remaining unaware of the glint of blue mineral rock ingrained into the stone.

"We need to get them out," said Cross, his eyes still searching in a bewildered scan of the kitchen as Hardy steered the dazed Jackson out into the waiting helicopter.

"Get back in here," Cross shouted to Hardy underneath the cacophony of the helicopter blades once Jackson had been deposited beside the pilot who was in his forties and looked terrified. Eventually they heaved the unconscious Brassock alongside their employer. It was only a matter of minutes before the helicopter whirred upwards and the attackers made their departure.

Siskin had held to his instructions reluctantly as the malicious group forced their way into the house. He had moved to the edge of the doorway in front of Kier when Jackson entered the kitchen. There he had stood rigid, ready to spring into attack if needed as they witnessed the exchange in the kitchen. The whole group had moved forward when the kitchen door slammed shut but Siskin stood firmly, signalling quiet as the attackers re-entered the room and then left the building.

Klim's eyes followed his uncle's vacant gaze as he was dragged towards the helicopter knowing that finally the malevolent influence could no longer hurt him or those that he cared for. Slowly the small group in the reference room filed out into the corridor and made their way towards the kitchen. Kier followed behind the others and then turned as she heard a whimpering from the street. The front door was hardly standing and she stepped over the rim on to the pavement.

Six feet away the earth had cracked producing rubble strewn devastation and deep strips of sea water that loomed like a giant octopus stretched around the building, now the only building Kier realised. Her eyes stared in shock at the remains of the levelled properties that had previously been a row of shops. Tears stung her cheeks as she saw the bodies of families, some with limbs sundered and she held her face in her hands. Then her breath caught as she saw a pain filled face trying to lift a heavy rock from his body as the water lapped around him.

"Adam! Hold on, I'm coming," she cried, running out onto to what she thought was the remaining solid road only to find the earth disappearing into a crevice that opened up beneath her. Unable to stop herself falling she was swallowed by the foul dark air that issued from the gap in the road and then all thought vanished as she plunged into total blackness.

It may have been moments or hours before consciousness reasserted itself. The air was stale and evil smelling and Kier's breath was shallow. Trying to suppress the rising panic she felt the walls that encased her body with only inches to spare. She was entombed. The scream began to rise inside her but she fought to suppress it, knowing that already there was little remaining air. She was assailed with a desperate need to stretch her limbs and they twitched helplessly in the enclosed space.

Deliberately she made herself slow her breathing and stretched her fingers towards the front pocket of her jeans where the key to the flat was attached to a small LED torch. Bringing it to her chest like a precious jewel Kier shone the light, merely for light's sake in that terrible dark place. Comforted by the sight of her own two hands she silently called to Gally, desperately hoping that he was still alive as she tried to ward off the despair that was now creeping invisibly into the earthen coffin. Her thoughts flew to her parents far away and all anger left her in the immense desire to be with them again. Every act that had left a bad taste on her conscience, however small, seemed to crawl like worms into the confined space and choke her with remorse.

Kier thought of others that she loved and might never see again. Adam, the first time she had seen him, small and wrecked by abuse, and surprisingly Echinod Deem. The oceanic depths of his eyes held her thoughts, made her feel as if she had known him for all of her living and not just these last few days that had shifted the axis of her sense of reality. It was a few seconds before she realised that the rasping sound was that of her own laboured breathing. It was too much effort even to maintain the gentle pressure on the key fob so that her fingers slipped to her side and the fragile light was extinguished. "No" she whispered, "I have so much I need to do."

Chapter Thirty

Gabbie's eyes flickered, her mind filled with memories of bonfire night before her mother had left. Red toffee apples, six-foot flames, her mother lighting a sparkler and placing it in her small gloved hand as they stood together in the part of the railway ground that had effectively become a home for engines that had come to the end of their working lives. It was the place her Dad took her to watch the steam engines when they came in to be refurbished and where every bonfire night there was a fundraising evening to help restore the old station. There was the rumble of engines passing close by and Gabbie would wave excitedly at the passengers whose faces were vivid in the firelight.

The noisy vibration continued even though her eyes were fully open and Gabbie sat up on the orange couch where she had fallen asleep waiting for her father to arrive home. Tears ran down her cheeks as she looked around the room that she had hastily tried to return to normal. The house had been ransacked, their small possessions rifled through and thrown everywhere. Frantically she had gathered up the scattered clothes and broken pictures trying to return everything to normality as much as she could before her father arrived.

They had so few things that once she had swept the broken glass and returned the clothes and papers to where they needed to be, the cottage began to look like home again. Then she had sunk back down upon the sofa and tried to phone her dad but he hadn't answered. Exhausted, she had slept and now it was mid-afternoon on a summer's day that was more like January.

The mobile beside her suddenly sprung to life and played a familiar dance track that she could no longer name.

"Dad," she cried out seeing the number and pressing the receive button.

He was as distressed as her.

"Gabbie! Thank god, I finally got you! Are you alright? Where are you?"

"I'm at home, of course I'm ok. Where are you?" she asked, him holding the phone in both hands like a rope.

"I'm sorry sweetheart, the borders have all been shut with the uproar."

"What uproar?" she asked

"Gabbie don't you watch the news! Vesuvius, the volcano, it's erupted, I'm stuck in Italy unable to get to Naples."

"But you're ok dad?" she asked him anxiously.

"I'm fine. I'll get back as soon as they open the ports again, I'm more worried about you. What happened in Pulton?"

"Pulton! When?"

"Just today, it's on the telly." Gabbie went over to the TV and switched it on to the news as her dad continued.

"They showed the road outside the bookshop ripped apart. It's the only building still standing."

Gabbie's eyes widened in horror as she saw the devastation that had wiped out the buildings along the prom. The bookshop, lonely and windswept, stood surrounded by rubble. There were pictures of survivors and Gabbie recognised Mrs Porpett who somehow seemed as proper as ever, her blouse and skirt looking barely rumpled. Only her eyes, teary and bewildered, gave a clue to how lost she was feeling.

Others had lost their lives and Gabbie's eyes filled with tears as the camera revealed scenes of people in body bags being taken away in mortuary cars. Her thoughts immediately flew to Klim and the others.

"Gabbie are you still there?" her dad's voice penetrated through the shock.

"I'm here dad," she told him, her voice shaky, swallowed by the sound of engines starting.

"They're starting to move," her dad was shouting over the noise. "I'll ring you in a bit, keep your phone on. I love you."

"Ok Dad, I love you too," she said and then, as she ended the call, she found herself sobbing freely and wishing that she had not lied to Evan, signalling to him that her father was already home when they arrived back at the cottage that morning.

There was little credit on her phone but she used the last of it to leave a message on the bookshop Ansa phone asking Evan to ring her so that she would know everyone was ok. She also told him that her dad was unable to get back and that someone had been inside the house. She glanced at her watch- the next bus was in twenty minutes but they probably weren't running anyway and she found herself reluctant to leave the tiny cottage.

There had been many times since her mother left that she had felt lonely, but this was different. It was her own actions that meant she was curled up on the couch, instead of being with the others. Despite her words to Evan she had never before felt that she belonged so much with any group of people. She had put herself outside the protection that had been offered and she was frightened. Her heart ached as she realised that she had not even said goodbye to Klim who had been the focus of her existence for so many of her young years.

A sound in the street outside made her sit upright, her ears straining to hear. She switched off the television and every nerve tingled with fear as she caught the distinct sound of someone carefully lifting the latch on the back gate. Immediately she was out of the front door and running along the maze of streets that formed the estate on the edge of Bankside.

Gabbie ran through the long passageways between the back-to-back houses realising that she would be more at risk running in the open than finding somewhere to hide. The pavements were empty as Danny's red front door came into view as she rounded the next corner. The old coal hole was still there opposite the front door as it was in many of the small houses. It was a space about four-foot-high that sloped down inside and it was where Danny kept her push bike. Her mum was always telling her off for not locking it properly and Gabbie pushed at it gently, sighing with relief as it opened to her touch. She crept inside the dark space and squeezed herself in alongside the bike. After five minutes of huddling in the dark with a pedal pushed against her midriff Gabbie began to think she had panicked needlessly and was just about to untangle herself when she heard footsteps echo from the narrow ginnel from which she had just emerged.

They became quiet as they approached the coal house and Gabbie, holding her breath, frantically felt around for something she could use as a weapon, her small fist rounding on a large spanner.

The loud knocking on Danny's front took her by surprise and she stifled a gasp. Gabbie, who knew the teenager well, could hear the apprehension in the voice of the small brunette as she greeted whoever was standing there.

An angry voice demanded, "where is he?"

There was a shuffling and Gabbie heard Luke's voice not more than a foot away from her.

"What?" he asked sullenly.

"You're wanted. Someone's been in the girl's house, her old man must be back."

Gabbie heard the quiver in Luke's voice as he whispered.

"He'll call the police."

"It won't matter who he calls," the other voice replied harshly, "out."

Gabbie heard the sound of a slight scuffle and imagined Luke being pulled out of the house for she could hear him muttering under his breath, right beside the door of the coal hole. A few moments later there were two pairs of footsteps moving quickly through the narrow passage back towards her home. Then Danny's light footsteps were out on the pavement and Gabbie thought of calling out but then decided she couldn't take a chance. Instead she made herself wait until the front door closed once more and the grey emptiness of the street returned, before carefully lifting the latch and creeping out from her hiding place.

Dusk fell far too early for August that evening but Gabbie welcomed the shadows as she made her way back towards the house, pulling up the hood of her blue sweatshirt, trying not to be seen. There were cars pulling up in the communal car park and it was clear that much of the small community were returned from Pulton. She found a space behind a massive tub that was partially fenced off from the rest of the area and listened to their chatter. She recognised many of the voices, mostly mothers of people she had known from school as they unpacked flasks and empty Tupperware tubs. It sounded as if they had gone to help after the earthquake and were obviously shocked at the localised devastation.

"No one knows where the owner of the book shop is," Anna Posslethwaite said in hushed tones.

"Did you find her?" it was Danny's voice, she had come out at the sound of cars

"No love," said a male voice that Gabbie recognised as Danny's father, a good man who worked on the station.

"Maybe it's a good thing she hasn't been seen for a week," said another woman, "she may be away somewhere with her dad." It was Karen Dewhurst who lived in the house next door.

"She never said anything about going away," said Danny, her voice tight with concern.

"Never mind love," her dad told her, "I told the police we didn't know if she was at work and they said even if she was then she was in the one place that's still standing on that row of shops."

"Weird that," said Anna.

"I've seen weirder," replied Danny's dad.

Gabbie felt tears run down her cheek at the realisation that they were speaking about her. Suddenly another tremor shook the ground underneath them and Gabbie realised that she could be easily pinned under the massive weight of the tub. There was a moment when she could feel everyone, including her, holding their breath, waiting to see if it would progress to the kind of event that had occurred in Pulton. The vibration stopped but there was an eeriness in the shadowy skies.

"I think we all best get indoors", Karen suggested in hushed tones, "and for myself I'm going to do some praying."

The small gathering dispersed but Gabbie stayed in her hiding place behind the fenced off tub of grit at the back of the car park. She toyed with the idea of heading back to see Danny but that would be impossible without being noticed and that's something she couldn't yet do. Instead she decided she would wait until everyone was safely indoors and busy and then she would make her way back to the cottage.

*

"Gaabee," the noise was insistent and seemed to be coming from the clock radio that read 5:05. The central heating was switched off but Gabbie was certain she could hear the rhythm of three long beats followed by three short beats alternating. She recognised the Morse code they had learnt on the "join the army day" and knew that this meant SOS.

Her eyes flew back to the display on the clock 5:05 but the red digits also looked like SOS.

Locked in her bedroom, tucked under the duvet she had fallen into an exhausted sleep. Outside the sky was already fully dark and yet in mid-August there should, at teatime, been hours of daylight left in the day. Gabbie reached for her phone, the time shown was eight pm. Still early for the darkness outside and Gabbie felt completely disorientated. It was the first time the clock had been wrong but that wasn't surprising given the tremors they'd experienced. There were no missed calls and her credit was gone. Whoever had ransacked the place had taken the money from her "rainy day jar"- a dated Ovaltine container that she had used since primary school.

"Gaabeee," there was no mistaking the sound this time. The radio was permanently set to alarm only so there should have been nothing coming from the speaker.

"Gaabeee" it sounded again.

"What! "she called out "who wants me! "

"Straals," came the answer back.

"I've lost it, I've really lost it," she said out loud talking to herself, covering her ears to the sound of the clock radio and trying not to notice that the time hadn't moved on the display.

"Must leave now," came the tinny voice.

"Why?" she replied.

"Go." The piping sounds got louder, the SOS flashed on the display and Gabbie dived out of bed, backtracking to pick up her phone and jacket before leaving the house. Once outside she tucked her long blond hair carefully under her hood, secure that she would be difficult to recognise.

"Cracked," she told herself, "I've really lost it!"

Automatically she turned in the direction of the back shore but had only taken a few steps to the other side of the road when a tremor struck ripping a massive crevice in the road and shaking the estate of little cottages, so that in seconds her own small home was reduced to a pile of rubble. Gabbie could hear Karen and her family screaming and running towards the front door on the other side of the house– she moved to go back and help but it was impossible, the gap in the road was too severe. The sound of glass breaking and the ground rumbling was terrifying and Gabbie stood there in shock until she noticed a figure standing at the side of her. At least she thought it was at the side but when she looked again it had moved in the direction she had intended to go.

The woman looked in her forties, pale blond hair and a gentle, kind face, her arms beckoned Gabbie to follow. There was a luminous quality about the slight figure who wore a pale blue dress and sandals. Gabbie went towards her only to find that she seemed much further ahead than it appeared at first but when she turned and smiled Gabbie continued to follow.

It seemed no time at all before she felt the fresh spray of cold water upon her cheek as the tide splashed high against the rock upon which she was climbing. To reach the sea from her house was a good hour's walk and yet following the pale figure it had seemed little more than ten minutes. The woman disappeared several times and Gabbie kept checking the small caves along the way in case she had become trapped. At one point her foot slipped into the water as she scrambled in the dark across treacherous rocks, the sea turbulent and unpredictable.

There was little visibility for the moon was shrouded in wispy threads that enhanced the eerie atmosphere of an evening that had taken on a dream like quality. Doggedly she continued, using all her familiarity with a route that she and Klim had taken into Pulton on many occasions. On another level, she knew her dad would be furious with her for setting out in the dark after a stranger and yet perhaps he would understand that there was a familiarity about the female figure that drew her onwards, something she couldn't quite place.

A tall barbed wire fence cut across the meagre path she had been following. When the tide was out it was possible to walk around it on to the shore but right now the only way forward was to go up on to the road across about a mile of field. She remembered that the field was full of ditches, some of them particularly deep. As she made her way uphill keeping close to the fence she heard a splash ahead of her to the right. She followed the sound, moving quickly as the moon began to assert itself and its light shone on the log like form of an otter as it disappeared into one of the channels.

Gabbie caught her breath as the woman's petite figure stood directly in front of her on the other side of the small channel. It was at this point that she noticed that the sandals that she wore were completely clean, as were the rest of her clothes.

"Are you a ghost?" she confronted the woman, feeling strangely unafraid and just comforted by her presence.

The cornflower blue eyes smiled and the woman shook her head pointing towards the road and a vehicle that had parked in a little used overflow car park. Gabbie squinted to see better as she crept nearer and then her heart leapt as she recognised Klim's face, etched with worry.

Running she cleared the small fence in a bound and flung her arms around his neck even before he had a chance to realise she was there. The young couple held each other, Gabbie sobbing with relief as she felt the warmth of his strong arms around her, enveloped in the fierceness of an embrace that left her in no doubt that they belonged to each other first and last. Over his shoulder, she looked back over the fields but the woman who had guided her to Klim had disappeared.

"All I can say is you make beautiful music together." Siskin had come around from the driver's side of the jeep where he had been changing a tyre. The flat, probably caused by the earthquake debris, had taken them off the road on their way to Bankside.

"He was going to walk," Siskin told Gabbie, "so I volunteered to bring him."

Gabbie scampered over to the ex- soldier and hugged him.

'Thank you, thank you so much" she said, her eyes filling with tears, "I'm so glad to see you."

Klim, who knew his girl, shook his head. "Noggin," he said smiling, "complete noggin!" It was the happiest Siskin had ever seen him.

Chapter Thirty-One

Tendrils of fog shadowed the vehicle as Siskin drove along the lonely roads. Gabbie shivered, she had no idea where they were. During the journey, her phone rang and she was overjoyed to hear that her dad was on his way home from Italy, swallowing her disappointment when he said that it would take another few days to arrive. He was panicked by the news of the second earthquake and Gabbie heard the croak in his voice. Gently she explained that their small home had been virtually demolished but her father was only interested in the fact that she was safe.

"None of it matters sweetheart," he told her hoarsely, "only that you're ok. Where are you?" he asked.

"A few of us are being taken to a hotel," she told him feeling that she was stretching the truth only just a little.

"I'm not coming back to Europe after this trip Gabbie, I'll find something at home."

Gabbie smiled and held the phone closer.

"That would be great dad. Look my battery's nearly gone and the charger was in the house, don't worry if it goes, I'll see you soon."

The charge completely went as the call ended. Suddenly she felt, after all, as if she had been underneath the roof as it fell in and destroyed the little railway cottage. She thought of Karen and her family and the others who had gone looking for her. Klim pulled his arm tight around her. Carefully she placed her mobile in her pocket and nestled into his shoulder letting the tears trickle silently down her face.

The journey seemed all too brief as Gabbie pulled herself away from the warmth of Klim's arms and Siskin drove into the forecourt of an old stone pub where a sign "Inn of the Three Mountains" was barely visible in the mist. The windows, unusually for a pub, had all the curtains drawn and all outside lights extinguished, except for the one that hung over the entrance. There was a notice on the huge oak doorway that advised that the Inn was closed for seven days.

She turned back to the others who simply ignored the sign and carried on round to the side door. To her surprise, it opened as they approached and Swift ran out to meet them. It was to Gabbie that she ran, flinging her arms around her neck.

"I'm so glad you're here," she told her and Gabbie hugged her in return, pleased but also masking her surprise at the warmth of the other girl's greeting. Hand in hand they entered the kitchen followed by the two men and Swift locked the door behind them.

The massive figure behind the ornate bar twitched his moustache as they entered and Gabbie puzzled, realised that the lounge was full at what the old railway clock on the wall told her was two o'clock in the morning. Evan was there in a bright purple waistcoat and with a huge grin he swept her up in his arms. She found herself so glad to see him, as if had been weeks and not yesterday morning.

He introduced the others and she saw Echin sitting between two men that Evan referred to as Faer and Tormaigh. Faer, she instantly realised was the man she had seen in the park when Klim had gone missing. These then were the Mourangils about whom she had heard so much. It came to Gabbie that they were like something out of a story, knights or kings, different and above the rest of them somehow. The door to the entrance hall opened and a young man entered. He was slim and graceful with a bone structure any girl would have envied.

"This is Josh," Evan told them and then with a nod of his head towards the bar, "Matthew's son."

Gabbie hid her astonishment, this fine boned, lean muscled man in his twenties bore absolutely no likeness to the giant behind the bar. Josh came over and smiled and Gabbie found herself smiling warmly back and caught Klim's dark eyes watching carefully. Josh turned to shake hands with Klim, Gabbie thought they looked as different as night and day. The enormous hearth was home to a log fire that immediately drew her towards it and she was more than happy to curl up on one of the benches followed by Swift who came and sat beside her.

Josh left the room and returned shortly with a pan of hot soup that he placed on a side table for everyone to help themselves. Before Gabbie moved however Josh stood in front of her, his eyes an unusual cornflower blue that reminded her of someone.

"Special service for you," he grinned softly handing her a tray with a dish of fragrant chicken soup and hot buttered bread. Gabbie uncurled herself and gratefully accepted the soup, ignoring Klim's glacial stare as he placed himself on the bench opposite. It was only as she finished the delicious meal that Gabbie realised she had not eaten since breakfast the previous morning in Evan's kitchen,

"Where's Kier?" she asked, expecting to be told when she would see her.

There was a silence and then, "taken," said Tormaigh simply.

Everyone was now sat around the biggest table apart from herself, Swift and Klim who occupied the benches by the fire. Gabbie put her tray on the floor as she stood up, coming nearer to the table.

"What do you mean?" she asked, the state of alarm that had filled most of the day before now returned to her in a gut wrenching fear.

"Not long after you left yesterday," Evan told her, "the earthquake struck."

Gabbie frowned, "but I saw the bookshop on the telly, it was untouched."

Evan, who was nearest, reached out and touched her arm.

"Kier ran out into the road. The ground just opened up beneath her."

"No!" Gabbie was surprised the shrill sound was her own voice as she put both hands to her temples, fearing to hear any more.

"We think she saw her friend in the rubble, she called out that she was coming to help," added Klim.

"Why didn't you tell me before?" Distressed, Gabbie turned to Klim and Siskin, it was the older man who replied.

"We just didn't have the heart," he told her, "we knew you'd know soon enough."

Gabbie stared wordlessly at the musician and Josh found a wooden chair for her to sit nearer to the table. He found two more for Klim and Swift as he signalled them to join the group. Then Gabbie found her voice again.

"I don't understand," she looked at Tormaigh, "you said taken – you mean she might be alive?"

Echin spoke softly and his voice soothed her without having the patronising edge of adults that made her so angry, or at least used to make her so angry. It all seemed unimportant now.

"I think Kier was tricked out of the bookshop."

Gabbie looked at Klim remembering the stories of his uncle's ability to create illusions.

"It wasn't my uncle this time," he told her, "he'd already tried to attack us before the earthquake happened. He was a mindless wreck when Kier left the shop."

He looked towards Echin whose face was grim as he explained.

"Your uncle's own evil made him vulnerable, the harm that he wished to inflict was turned inwards on himself. The earthquake and Kier's loss was due to Nephragm."

Klim and Siskin gasped, remembering the words the Tomer had uttered in Lioncera. The others looked at them puzzled, apart from Evan who buried his head in his hands.

"Ach! In Pulton, in our own time."

"Who is he?" asked Swift.

Faer looked at her carefully before answering. "Despair, rejection, delusion. A dreadful enemy of your race, a Devouril,"

Tormaigh sighed as he looked at the blank and frightened faces around him. In his unusual accent, his dark skin glistening in the reflected firelight and his green eyes unfathomable, he told the tale of Candillium and Toomaaris in Ordovicia. Even Matthew seemed captivated and Gabbie's eyes filled with tears as he described Candillium's last days on Moura.

Echin took out a piece of paper upon which Josh had sketched.

"Nephragm was here in the Inn not five weeks ago, and because of Josh's gift we can see what he looks like now. Once a Creta such as Josh links a being to his drawing the link is retained, even if the form should shift as it has done in the case of Nephragm. I am sorry but whoever owned this original form will now be destroyed and Nephragm will have taken it because of his link to one of you."

He passed around the photograph and each person reached out apprehensively and then shook their head, having no knowledge of the face that stared at them from the sketch paper until finally Evan cried out in surprise.

This is the thin man who came to help me when Gally was consumed. I do not know his name." His grey eyes clouded at the memory.

Echin looked grim. "I suspect Kier's attachment to whoever this person once was enabled Nephragm to draw her from safety." Echin produced a canvas, placing it on the table.

"What Josh saw on the surface is one thing, the reality of him he painted from memory at my request."

There were gasps of horror and Gabbie saw Matthew's mouth tighten and his eyes harden in disbelief. Then the canvas was tilted towards her and both she and Swift cried out at the alien creature that Josh had depicted. The coal black body comprised powerful animal limbs folded tight and mapped with blue lines. The shoulders hunched in vulture like peaks either side of a long neck and two of the vessels on either side of the head dilated into eyes that were lidless voids.

Faer, looking at the painting, told them, "only one with Josh's extraordinary gift could see such a thing, even we have not seen Nephragm in his current true physicality."

"But does he not move around the earth the same way that you do? Through water, air and stone?" Evan asked.

"Nephragm has endured because he becomes invisible in plain sight within the human race. He has the power to move in the elements but the Straals can pick up his imprint."

'Straals," Gabbie repeated, "I know that word." The group waited for her to continue and then she remembered. 'The radio," she said excitedly, "it told me to leave just before the earthquake happened, I thought I was going crazy."

"Mechostraals," Faer told her," they can only make sound when they are collected together for an unusually serious purpose, you must be highly prized Gabrielle."

Gabbie was filled with a sense of awe and it was a moment or two before she tuned into the conversation once more.

"The Devourils are unable to reside in normal mineral rock, only very specific stones will bear them," Faer explained, "such a stone is the Perfidium."

"What does it look like?" asked Swift.

"It is a piece of obsidian fashioned into a spear. Throughout human history it has been used to direct and amplify Belluvour's desire to destroy mankind. After the great wars of the twentieth century we managed to place it beyond reach, so we thought, until Jackson discovered a Stozcist, one of only two humans in the world who could take the stone from its hiding place."

Swift gasped, looking stunned.

"No!" she cried and immediately. Gabbie took her hand. "It wasn't your fault," she said loudly, her expression challenging anyone to disagree as she turned to the others.

"No blame is attached to you," Echin told her gently.

Swift looked around hesitantly and then told the story of the night in Caral.

"It was like a dream," she cried," I didn't even know where I was. It was a long drive from Lima. There in the middle of the desert was the strangest sight in the moonlight- old pyramids and buildings that had once been a city, old, old stone." Swift's eyes were distant with memory.

"I knew immediately we arrived where the stone was hidden. I did not think any evil of it." Swift looked around and Gabbie squeezed her hand.

"I saw it in my mind's eye deep below the earth, wrapped in a shining white cloth."

"Crysaline," explained Tormaigh- it is a crystal that can only be touched by a Mourangil or Stozcist.

"I willed myself beneath the stone," she looked at Klim whose expression told her nothing. "Then I was there inside it, as long as I kept moving, the molecules inside the stone made room for me. At least that's how I thought of it."

Encouraged by Faer's nod of approval she continued.

"I found the stone wrapped in the white cloth like crystal you call crysaline. It did not feel hard or sharp to my touch but soft like Alpaca and it was only when I unwrapped this covering that I realised the darkness of the stone it had hidden. I tried to leave without it but the stone forced its way into my hand. It was as if the whole place screamed at me and I fled from the altar, releasing it as soon as I could."

"I am

added, tears streaming down her face.

Echin spoke softly, "Jackson stands upon lifetimes of evil but in the end, he has brought you to us and for that we are truly thankful."

Swift's dark eyes looked grateful.

"We now know," explained Echin, "that you were observed that night by the caretaker Josef."

"Swift looked up, surprised.

"He managed to exchange the stone Jackson wanted so badly, for plain rock," Echin continued. "Then somehow it got shipped with the crystals that Kier had bought for the gift shop"

"We were able to remove much of the power of the Perfidium by altering its shape," Faer told them, "but the more it is used to corrupt and maim, the quicker it will return to its original form. Jackson took the opportunity to goad a young man into theft, the evil that the same individual has now perpetrated has almost re-formed the spear."

He looked towards Gabbie and Klim.

"Luke," they said in unison and Faer nodded.

"When the spear is complete he will use it on Whistmorden."

"Why?" asked Siskin. "Why Whistmorden?"

Echin recited the words that Kier had so easily translated:

"Beneath the grooved and weeping stone of Whistmorden
lies abandoned Obason, the tainted land."

"What will the spear do?" asked Klim.

Echin looked at each of them in turn before replying.

"The bonds that Candillium created to hold Belluvour grow weak. As a result, he is able to amplify the power of Nephragm enabling the changes on Whistmorden. There is an area underneath the surface where we cannot enter and where it is certain that preparation has been made to receive the Perfidium once it is re-made."

"Receive?" queried Swift, "do you mean the rock has been altered to welcome this thing?"

Echin nodded.

"Nephragm has altered the mineral composition of Whistmorden so that it will act as host to the Perfidium. Should the fully formed obsidian blade make contact it will behave as a virus to bring a permanent alteration to the fabric of the planet surface. Slowly the planet would alter as the virus spreads so that the earth would favour the darker stones that will hold the Devourils. Not only this but eventually the changes would mean that the environment would cease to support human existence."

There was a gasp of horror around the room.

"What can we do against this thing?" asked Klim getting to his feet. Siskin and Josh came to stand beside him and echoed his question.

"It is your time," Echin told them both, "you are seeds of the Myriar, there is much you can do."

"No!"

Matthew's huge frame made the table shake as he moved his chair backwards, pushing against the oak.

"Not my son. He is not part of this fairy tale!"

Pain seemed to ravage his features as he directed his words to Echin.

"I allowed you to come here, all of you, for Marianne's sake and because you were in trouble but I cannot be part of this nonsense and nor will Josh."

He looked at his son who would not meet his father's eyes and Matthew stood up and turned, preparing to leave the room. As he did so Gabbie's eye caught a picture at the back of the bar, it was Matthew with a smiling woman with blonde hair, later she heard he had brought it down from their bedroom since his wife had gone missing.

"But that's her!" she said amazed, "that's the woman who helped me." To everyone's astonishment she ran over to the photograph and lifted it down from its pride of place behind the bar. Matthew was too stunned to disapprove as Gabbie scrutinised the face of the woman, holding the picture tightly in both hands.

"It's her," she announced firmly, "this is the woman that came down the shore road with me last night."

Gabbie told her story in her straight forward way and there could be no doubt in anyone's mind that Marianne had guided her away from the earthquake into the car park where Klim and Siskin were changing the tyre on the CR-V. Matthew and Josh came closer and seemed to drink in every word that she said.

"But where is she now? Where did she go?" Josh asked her, his face filled with hope.

Echin stood up and spoke gently but firmly.

"Marianne has long been able to divide her body from what you would call her spirit. The energy that is Marianne was able to travel for a short time and I suspect that, for a period, Nephragm lost the seal that has been placed around her since her capture. It may be that he was transporting her body to a different place – during this time Marianne may have been able to make herself visible to Gabbie.

Matthew shook his head, not understanding.

"But in that case, she would have come home," he said.

"You would have been unable to see her," said Faer, "and Gabbie's need was great."

"But then how did I see her?" asked Gabbie feeling intensely uncomfortable as she began to realise that the woman who had helped her was Josh's mother and Matthew's wife.

"Why did the straals save you from the earthquake? The answer is not yet clear," replied Echin.

"Matthew, yours is the closest dwelling to Whistmorden and has protection against the Devourils. I have no doubt that the plan was to remove you using Beeston and then destroy the building to begin a more aggressive attack on the area. However," Echin shared a glimmer of a smile with the big man, "you were more stubborn than he had bargained for and apparently unaffected by Jackson's attempts to influence your mind. A rare quality."

Matthew walked towards the door where he turned.

"Marianne said once that my stubbornness would both save and slay me. You have told me, Echinod Deem, that you believe my wife and the two friends that you have lost are most likely together and yet you ask her husband and son to remain behind when you leave to find them tomorrow."

Echin nodded, "I do ask it Matthew, for the reasons I have given, Nephragm would use your attachment and Marianne would be put at even more risk."

The big man looked at him levelly, and then at the others.

"I suggest then that you all get some sleep," he said simply, turning back towards the door.

Gabbie was torn, one part of her was filled with questions waiting to be answered and the other exhausted and wanting to process what she had learnt already. Matthew's firm voice however had its effect on the group and one by one they made their way upstairs.

Chapter Thirty-Two

The summer wind wheezed through the eerie landscape like a creature in pain and Kier could see a slight lifting of the gloom as dawn brokered its way across Whistmorden.

"Asin vie Lioncera," she whispered again and again in her head but there was nothing but nowhere. 'Nowhere,' is what she had come to call the desperate place that was antithesis to the kingdom that had saved her from the Roghuldjn. She was encased in a world where she could neither move, nor breathe, suspended in crystal, or some mockery of crystal that had been made to hold them.

She had no doubt that her own reflection would mirror what she could see in her brother's face. The same frozen expression, tortured eyes looking outwards, immobile and yet fully alert, somehow able to see, hear and smell but unable to take comfort in the escape of sleep. The tortuous situation seemed even more cruel for Gally, horror etched on his face in this place where once his young dreams had soared above the white limestone. Next to him Marianne's tormented gaze was fixed in agony and the blood that had been seeping from her abdomen splashed in streaks of red across the crystal tomb.

The limestone pavement under which they had been carefully positioned formed a domed ceiling above them, opaque in the world outside and yet transparent inside the hollowed-out hall of invisible inanimation. In physical terms, the bodies of three prisoners were caught so that time, the precious enemy, moved on normally somewhere but not here, not for them. Inside these immobile bodies, in the inched minutes, she found herself thinking of Echinod Deem, calling to him in her mind, trying to seek him out.

"Ah, my dear," came the voice, the Edinburgh accent so true and its speaker so false. Adam, whom she had trusted with everything, to whom she had given shelter and friendship, Adam had betrayed her. He walked round to face her, occluding her view of Gally.

"You make beautiful specimens, all three. But I won't be allowed to keep you I'm afraid, my brother will insist." He sighed, "I may even weep for you my beautiful one," he told her cheerfully.

Kier was still trying to process the fact that Adam, her closest friend, was a Devouril. The most human of all her friends, the one who gave her humour, kindness and devotion was not human at all. His eyes, bright with intelligence, allowed her to access his purpose of implacable malice so insanely diffused with appreciation of her kind.

"I believe we have visitors at last," he spoke in his singsong accent.

"Together we will witness the final act that will bring the Perfidium to its original form."

Kier watched as figures appeared on top of the scar, unaware of the silent audience beneath. The sky was grey with small dots of light flittering from the torches of those who had reached the top of the scar. She recognised Beeston's grating tone, his breath coming in harsh grunts.

"Why have you brought me here Brassock?" He looked around.

"Where's Jackson? Surely you can't hope to see anything in this light. We'll end up breaking our legs."

Kier heard the sound of a kick and bone snapping and Beeston screamed in agony.

"Just yours you fool," answered the harsh angry voice of the brutish ex wrestler, "Mr Jackson will be up shortly."

Beeston screamed in pain and Kier watched the old man trying hopelessly to pull his weight along the treacherous stones crying out as he became stuck between them. The sound of rock scree falling down the hill outside

echoed strangely in their underground prison and signalled
the arrival of Jackson accompanied by one of the
mercenaries that had attacked the bookshop. The other man,
who had been part of the invading group, his name was
Cross she remembered, came up on to the ridge nudging a
youth of about sixteen.

"Jackson," moaned Beeston, "I've done everything you
asked, you're my heir now."

Jackson merely stared, looking around and struggling to
take in his surroundings.

"So, he is," said Brassock. "Get over here boy," he called to
the youth who reluctantly came forward.

The bullish figure bent down and opened his rucksack,
from it he took a small case and placed it on to the limestone.
The knife he retrieved from the case seemed to produce a
recognition in his employer who started walking towards it.
The man who accompanied him however pulled him back at
which point it seemed that Jackson forgot what it was that
had interested him.

Brassock handed the knife to the youth whose pale
face and wide eyes gave him a ghostly appearance and
offered no resistance. Even as he took it the blade seemed to
grow, its dark sharpness slicing through space, a black hole
in the landscape.

"Get on with it," barked Brassock. Another voice sounded
and Kier realised that Adam was speaking directly into
Brassock's mind, not for the first time today she thought. He
had to use a roughly cut instrument in place of the finely-
honed weapon that Jackson had become.

"No force. Cajole- use his name."

Brassock stepped back and touched his ear, then he
softened his tone.

"Come on Luke, Mr Jackson's got your money ready as soon as we get back. You'll be doing the old man a favour, look at the state of him."

Beeston was in tears, rolling his body in pain, trying to release himself from where he had become lodged. He opened his mouth to speak but found no words.

Luke edged sideward so that he was further away from them both. He was, as Jackson had previously instructed, free of any drugs or alcohol and the horror of all that he had done was a drumbeat that had dogged every step of the climb up Whistmorden.

Brassock softened his voice further.

"It's not like you haven't done it before Luke."

The youth's face looked suddenly lost and hopeless, "I didn't mean…." he whispered.

"But you did," continued Brassock, "no problem. Your own friend, but because you're one of us it'll be ok. Mr Jackson'll make sure no one will ever know who stabbed the girl. The old man, he's done business with Mr Jackson, he's sick, he just wants to go."

Beeston keened louder as the dagger tip appeared to reach towards him and slowly Luke stepped forward.

The Perfidium lifted into the sky as Luke prepared to plunge the blade into Beeston's chest, a look of total despair on his young face.

"Luke," the voice was rich with youth and vibrant with determination

"Luke, no.!"

It was Gabbie's voice and Luke turned towards the sound, hope and disbelief somehow framed in his expression at the same time. Brassock lurched forwards.

"Do it!" The sound from his mouth had a Scottish tinge, as Luke looked desperately around for Gabbie unable to see as thick fog descended over the limestone pavement. The

unnatural mist choked the atmosphere and all that was
visible was the blade, a streak of darkness that plunged
downwards, it's edge curving and elongating until it bit into
the flesh beneath it.

Chapter Thirty-Three

Brassock screamed in agony at the same time as the fog
dispersed. Luke jumped back in horror seeing the obsidian
blade buried in the abdomen of the ex-wrestler whose body
dropped to the ground like a felled tree. Every vein of the
brutish figure swelled with a black oil like substance and
then his whole body was suffused in darkness as final as
obsidian itself.

Whistmorden trembled, white shards of rock scattered
across the pavement and the hollow grikes widened
unbalancing those that were still standing. Luke tripped
backwards over Beeston and his leg caught in a grike
between the stones. Cross and Hardy leapt towards the edge
of the scar. Beneath the surface the three tortured faces saw
the flesh fall away from the man Kier had known as Adam
Kirkbride, a man she had cherished.

Nephragm manifested before their suspended gaze, filling
the domed space and giving off a smell that she associated
with volcanic ash. The blue-rimmed hollow pits that were his
eyes confirmed that there was nothing human remaining. The
coal black figure reached upwards, his animal limb a
contorted suggestion of writhing snake and muscled feline
power. The domed ceiling bowed like viscous liquid as he
thrust the limb above the surface.

Kier could see that the spear was still not fully formed and
guessed that Brassock had been stabbed trying to force
Luke's hand. Siskin grabbed Cross's gun as he tried to save
himself from toppling over and then used it to render the

mercenary unconscious. Hardy, furious, lifted his gun towards Siskin's back only to have it kicked out of his hand by Klim who leaped to his friend's defence and delivered a clean kick that broke Hardy's wrist. Siskin's punch then left him lying beside his violent companion. Gabbie came from behind Klim, her slim legs deftly jumping across the gaps in the half-light to get to Luke's side.

Then Klim saw his uncle standing vacantly holding the spear and moved towards him. He stared at the pathetic creature his uncle had become and Jackson held out the spear towards him. Klim took it, and as he did so the blade shimmered and grew. It's jewel encrusted hilt glimmered with blood red rubies and yellow adamite.

"This is the man who murdered you father," the hiss of words seemed to come from the pavement itself as Nephragm bent his will towards Klim. Kier saw the youth's eyes turn black, his handsome face distorted with pain.

"He poisoned him, knowing your Father would not take the digitalis until he was out of the country. He put it in his nightcap. The drug caused his heart to stop." The dark words reverberated inside Klim's head. He saw once more his father pouring the one drink he had every night before bed and knew in his heart that the mystery of how his uncle had been involved in his dad's death was finally resolved. Bile constricted his throat as he remembered his mother's resulting illness, the evil his uncle had generated in so many ways. Now Klim could finally punish the man who had ruined his life and that of so many others.

Kier screamed, a motionless, soundless invisible scream that came from the depth of her being and echoed in the crystal tomb. A crack split the crystal and Nephragm suddenly turned the full force of his attention towards Kier as the crystal substance shattered around her and her lungs opened to receive breath as if for the first time. The shock dropped her to the floor and her limbs, unmoving for so long, would not yet obey her.

Echin had quietly arrived behind Klim and the youth, his eyes full of sadness, shook his head and turned away from his uncle to the Mourangil and his friends. He held out the Perfidium just as Nephragm lifted his entire body above the surface springing on to the pavement, his paw-like appendage pushing Klim aside and sending the spear into the air. A silver light flew between Echin and Nephragm and the blade disappeared within it as it tore across Whistmorden to land on Ravensmount. Then the silver form revealed itself to be Faer who stood luminescent and equally as massive as Nephragm. The spear in Faer's right hand had reverted to the form of a round black stone.

On Overidgetor a green flame shot from the summit and, visible within the emerald blaze was Tormaigh, a huge and forbidding sentinel. Only Echinod Deem remained entirely in his human form and his eyes were sad as he looked at the enraged figure of Nephragm. The sounds that emerged from the repulsive figure were harsh and guttural.

"She will not be found in this generation of man, lover of humans, betrayer of your own kind."

Echin said nothing and Nephragm glanced back towards the open surface of the domed cave he had created, waiting to spawn the new earth that would bear the Devourils. Kier, unmoving, trying to force some strength back into her limbs, was a small bundle amongst the broken shards of crystal, her face tilted upwards.

Nephragm's writhing left limb reached downwards suddenly towards her and Echin was instantly by her side to fend off the blow. It was all the time Nephragm needed to spring forth from Whistmorden, a shooting black arrow that headed northwards. Immediately Faer and Tormaigh followed after him, relentless missiles in the dawn sky, soon invisible in their continued pursuit.

Echin turned to Kier reaching out his hand. As she took it she felt the strength return to her limbs and tears, blessed tears, pricked her eyes. She turned towards the figures of her brother and Marianne. Echin felt around the crystalline substance that contained Gally and signalled to Kier to stand in front of the encased figure.

"Put your right hand on his forehead and your left over his heart," he instructed placing his own hands in opposition behind her brother.

Kier looked into her brother's frozen features and as she did so felt a vibration course through her as the cruel prison fell away and Gally 's lungs heaved in that first breath. Gally fell forward into his sister's arms and Kier would have collapsed backwards, still weak as she was, were it not for Echin holding them both. Gently he guided them away from the broken shards to a space just beneath the tear in the domed ceiling that Nephragm had created. Echin walked across to Marianne and his fingers traced her face underneath the crystal

"Marianne," he told her, "it is over seven days since you last wore the Chalycion and all that keeps you alive is the dreadful case he has wrapped around you. Courage still, I must take you to Tinobar or you will certainly not survive once it is broken."

Those waiting above had taken themselves to the edge of the deep chasm that had appeared on the pavement and Echin shouted to Siskin. First, he lifted Kier upwards. "It was not Adam," he whispered against her ear as his arms enfolded her and then gave her up to the safe hands of the musician. Kier blinked, trying to understand what he meant but then Siskin moved them both aside as Klim came to assist and Gally was lifted towards them without seeming effort on Echin's part. Once he too had reached the surface Echin told them to clear the area.

Cross, now awake was enlisted to help carry Beeston on a makeshift stretcher that Siskin fashioned from their coats. He had splinted the old man's leg using a tree branch and rope from his pack and he walked behind them, Cross's gun in his hand. Hardy, holding his injured hand, stumbled alongside. Luke limped between Klim and Gabbie, whilst Kier and Gally, hand in hand, awkwardly moved limbs stiff from inactivity.

Just as they reached the first part of the descent, where the land levelled, the ground began to shake and Siskin's voice rang out.

"Get down," he cried just as a massive explosion ripped through the pavement they had just left and sent a giant plume of fire into the atmosphere. Instead of falling over the mountain however it flew upwards and did not discharge its debris until it reached the other side of the valley where an abandoned quarry became the repository for the abnormal products from underneath the surface of Whistmorden. Part of the plume continued onwards across the sky and Kier was sure she could see inside the flame the lapis blue she associated with Echin wrapped around the crystal case that held Marianne.

Chapter Thirty-Four

The August sun bathed her skin and Kier felt herself luxuriate in the sensation of her lashes tickling underneath the orbit of her eye. Then she opened them and drank in the beauty of the rare wildflowers in Marianne's private garden, each flower momentarily surrounded by an aura of light as her eyes accustomed themselves to change. A fountain cyclically pumped tinkling water and she watched for long minutes, absorbed by the interplay between the falling droplets and the still pond. Words had not yet returned to her in the week that had passed, neither she nor Gally had tried to speak during the journey from the scar as their limbs reasserted themselves in the amazing sensation of movement and touch.

Gally had found his voice when Matthew and Josh appeared on the lower slopes alarmed by the noise of the explosion that was clearly going to provide years of study for volcanologists all over the world. Siskin gave them the news that Marianne had been found but was gravely ill.

"I want to see her," Matthew cried, "take me to this Tinobar."

"I don't think they can dad," said Josh gently, his own eyes filled with tears.

"You must," the big man demanded of Siskin.

Gabbie went across and took the landlord's hands and she looked like a child soothing a giant.

"Echin would not have taken her if it was hopeless. He'll bring her back to you."

Two days previously Matthew would have reacted with anger to this statement but he merely put his hand over Gabbie's and kissed her forehead. He continued to hold her hand as they made their way down to the old Land Rover that Matthew had kept on the road even since Gally had been a student. It was Siskin who linked with the authorities to explain that they had been on the surface at the time of the volcano and that two of their party had been lost.

Cross and Hardy had taken their opportunity to escape as the group took cover during the eruption. Beeston was taken by ambulance to the hospital, shocked and broken, and Kier wondered what impact this would make on his future. Siskin spoke to Luke and arrangements were made for him to be taken back to his home. The boy clung on to Gabbie, tears running down his cheek as he said goodbye.

The walled garden was attached to the back door of the kitchen and on one side grew the fresh salad and vegetables for use in the restaurant. In Marianne's absence, it was clear that Matthew had continued to tend the produce, for the two greenhouses flourished and baskets of tomatoes and fruit had been harvested. The other half of the garden was, to Kier, a place of refuge, and it was mostly here that she had spent the last few days following the events on Whistmorden.

Matthew went about his care of the garden with great tenderness and chatted to Kier easily as she sat in the beautifully carved chair he had brought out for her and that undoubtedly belonged to Marianne. With immense sensitivity, the big landlord had talked about the rare flowers that grew in Marianne's care including a type of orchid that could only be found in this part of the world. On the other side of Overidgetor special wildflower walks were arranged for tourists he explained patiently, unconcerned that she did not reply, her voice still buried deeply inside. It was the most she had ever heard him speak.

Marianne's husband and son had listened to Gally's words with growing horror as he told the story of his capture.

"I was standing with Evan on the prom and looked up at the Seven Rivers," he explained, "and Adam's face appeared at the window. I wondered what he was still doing there as he told us he was leaving the evening before. I was going to suggest to Evan that we went over to see him but then everything was a blur and I found myself in the flat with Adam. But it wasn't Adam anymore," his eyes found Kier's and she could see that he acknowledged her sense of loss. "It was the same voice and body," he continued, "but there was nothing of the Adam we knew."

Again, he looked up and his sister had no doubt that in the flat Gally had suffered more at Nephragm's hands than he would ever let her know. She was racked with guilt that she had thought Adam had betrayed her, that she could have ever thought her quirky, talented assistant had housed such evil. Now she had no doubt that the despair that she had felt as a result was part of what the malign being had intended her to feel. In some way, she understood that this had made her more vulnerable to him.

"He took me to Whistmorden and then he brought Marianne."

He turned his eyes away as they filled with tears,

"Tell me," demanded Matthew, and Josh nodded beside him.

Gally turned back and took a deep breath before continuing.

"At first I thought he had framed her dead body in glass like some despicable trophy."

Kier was glad that he had not described to father and son the frozen moment of agony of Marianne's incarceration.

"Then I realised she was still alive for he brought some baryte towards me. It's a common mineral in this part of the world but I think this one was the stone that was smuggled into Kier's café."

She sighed and her head bent until she realised that Gally was talking again.

"The baryte touched my forehead and a residue of the mineral lodged between my eyes, it made me feel numb.

Then it was like liquid pouring slowly all over my body and each part that it touched became immobile. I thought I was going to die as the substance slowly crept over my face prising my eyes open. But I did not die- instead we were held captive, unable to move the smallest muscle or blink. Then he brought my sister to stand where I could watch her suffer." His voice broke, "he kept us there until Echin freed us," he finished firmly.

Gally's tortured expression was a plea to let him stop telling of those endless hours and Matthew nodded, asking no more questions. Kier, still wordless, had allowed tears to fall down her face and Gabbie and Swift had come and sat either side of her. Each of them held a hand, comforting her as she had comforted them that morning in the bookshop a few days and a millennium ago.

Evan and Swift had been prevented from going with the others to Whistmorden for Echin would not allow either Stozcist near the toxic Perfidium. Matthew and Josh, with great resignation, had done as Echin had instructed and remained behind. All four were now in constant attendance of the others as if to make up for their absence.

Kier's reverie ended with Josh's call from the back door.

"Lunch," he shouted to them and Matthew smiled at Kier as he buried a pitchfork in the ground and waited for her to lead the way inside.

One by one, all of the group gathered in the main room and as Matthew went to wash his hands Josh and Swift began serving salad and bread. Evan planted a jug of juice in the centre of the table. They had hardly touched the meal when the huge brass knocker of the front door banged against its solid surface. The big oak door had remained closed, a clearly marked notice of closure firmly fixed on its surface. Kier looked over at Matthew as the sound insistently demanded entry. Josh stood and went over towards the window leaning towards the porch.

"No one there" he told them, his voice tense.

Klim made his way behind the bar and into the kitchen that had a view onto the side of the building.

'There's a truck in the car park," he said returning, looking at Gabbie.

Gabbie ran past him and out the side door into the car park where her Father was climbing back into the truck, having circuited the building.

"Dad," she cried and her father turned and swept her up in his arms as she ran towards him. After a short while Klim went out to join them to receive a hearty handshake from the middle-aged man who had driven relentlessly, between waiting in long queues of traffic, to get home to his daughter. His exhaustion left him the moment he saw her.

"How did you know I was here?" Gabbie asked.

"I didn't," he told her wondrously, nodding towards the cab, "when I couldn't find you a woman came to me and asked for a lift, I was so restless I said yes. I was just coming to tell her no one's at home."

A light foot dropped onto the gravel as the passenger door opened and Gabbie recognised the sandals she had seen a few days previously. Marianne closed the door and her arms encircled Gabbie.

"Thank you," the young woman whispered 'thank you so much."

The rest of the group had gathered around the table wanting to give Gabbie and her father some privacy and Matthew and Josh busied themselves behind the bar.

"A drink is definitely in order," said Matthew as Gabbie brought her father in to meet her friends. Gabbie's dad, dressed in polo shirt and trousers, both travel stained, tried to adjust his appearance as Gabbie dragged him to the table, her eyes the brightest Kier had ever seen them. Matthew poured a pint for the visitor and Josh brought drinks for Gabbie and Klim. Matthew lifted his glass.

"To you all" he said.

"To us all," said a gentle voice from the doorway in a Canadian accent, "may we never be parted again in this life," continued Marianne.

Matthew automatically placed his drink on the table and looked in astonishment towards the doorway. The big man's eyes were a mixture of joy, apology and infinite tenderness at the appearance of his wife. Josh was by his mother's side in an instant hugging her, his face full of smiling tears. Then he made way for his father who reached out to touch the face that was so dear to him, unable to speak as his wife put her small hand over his.

It was Kier who found the words for him.

"Welcome home Marianne," she said.

The End

ACKNOWLEDGEMENTS

My immense gratitude to Matthew Duncan who helped shape the amorphous mounds of paper I have written over the years. His humour, insightful direction and unfailing patience, teased out the story I intended to write. Thanks also to Alan for proofing this new edition and Jenny for her inspiration. To my first readers: Bridget Hume, Claire Lawton and Veronica Watson- I am very grateful for your unfailing support.

To Carol Williams, among all the words we have shared, thank you for reading so many of mine. Your critical expertise and abiding friendship is so highly valued. And of course to you the reader, I am very grateful that you have chosen to read my novel and for the encouraging messages that have enabled me to produce this latest edition.

About the Author

Frion Farrell is a contemporary fantasy writer living in North West England. The unique landscapes of this diverse area have provided much of the inspiration for the Myriar series.
After many years working in the NHS, she now spends most of her time writing and travelling.

Printed in Great Britain
by Amazon

12989786R00185